THE LAST DEFECTOR

KININ CHRONICLES #1

R.T. RYE

This is a work of fiction. All of the characters, organizations, and events portrayed are either products of the author's imagination or are used in a fictitious manner.

THE LAST DEFECTOR

Cover design by Miblart

If you enjoyed this book, please take a moment to review it on Amazon.

Every review helps.

OTHER KININ CHRONICLES BOOKS

The Last Recourse, Kinin Chronicles #2

Available at Amazon

The Last Nuke Mission, Kinin Chronicles #3

Available at Amazon

The Last Hope, Kinin Chronicles #4

Available at Amazon

Often used term-'Your better half' does not come close to defining my wife Phyllis.
She is not my half;
Phyllis is my everything.

I love her dearly!

GLOSSARY OF TERMS

AIRCRAFT

130- C130 cargo aircraft.

Four engine turbo prop. Used by military throughout the world.

F16- Fighting Falcon

Multi-roll fighter used by military throughout the world.

AWACS

Airborne Early Warning and Control aircraft. Boeing 707 airframe.

COD- Carrier Onboard Delivery.

Twin engine. Used by Navy to ferry people and equipment to carriers at sea.

G4- Gulfstream G450.

Twin engine executive aircraft.

HAWKEYE

Navy version of AWACS. Smaller airframe, able to operate from carrier at sea.

HORNET-F18

Twin engine fighter. U.S. Navy

MIG
Term applied to continuous line of Russian fighter jets.
TOMCAT-F14
Twin engine, two seat jet fighter. U. S. Navy

LOCATIONS

ANKARA
U. S. Air Force base in central Turkey
HO CHI MINH TRAIL
Road system used by North Vietnamese Army to move troops and supplies to the South.
INCERLIK
U.S. Air Force base in Southern Turkey
SIG- Sigonella.
U. S. Naval Air Station on the island of Sicily.

MILITARY COMMAND UNITS U. S.

CINCLANTFLT
Commander in Chief Atlantic Fleet Vice Admiral, Norfolk, Virginia
COMEUR
Commander of Forces in Europe, U. S. Air Force General. NATO Headquarters. Brussels, Belgium.
COMSIX
Commander Sixth Fleet (Mediterranean) Vice Admiral. Naples, Italy
COMSUBSEVEN
Commander Submarine Forces of Seventh Fleet, Japan
COMSURFLANT-
Commander Surfaces Forces Atlantic Fleet, Norfolk, Virginia.
NATO

Treaty of Military Cooperation of joint forces of most western European countries and the U.S.

MILITARY TERMS

BROWN SHOE
Navy slang for Navy aviators. When wearing khaki uniform aviators wear brown shoes rather than black shoes.
CIC
Combat Information Center. Designated room (space) on ship. Usually next to bridge.
C.O.
Commanding Officer of any Military unit.
CON
Term used for person having control.
RESCUE JUMPERS
U. S. Air Force unit of highly trained personnel.
X.O.
Executive Officer. Second in Command of any Military unit.

SHIPS

USS *EISENHOWER*- American Aircraft Carrier
USS *FORRESTAL*-American Aircraft Carrier
USS *CARL KING*-American Destroyer
ADMIRAL STENKOV- Russian Destroyer
MARSHAL TACANISH-Russian Destroyer

WEAPONS AND EQUIPMENT

AK-47
Russian made automatic/semi-automatic assault rifle.
BERETTA
Italian made 9mm semiautomatic pistol.

CZECH SKORPION

Old model of Czech made submachine gun.

GLOCK

Austrian made 9mm (most popular) semiautomatic.

GPS

Global Position System. Receiver that plots position from specially positioned satellites.

RPG

Rocket Propelled Grenade. Shoulder fired rifle.

SCOOTER

Small propelled unit used to pull diver underwater.

ZODIAC

Many sizes of utility watercraft with inflatable sides and outboard engine.

PROLOGUE

SUMMER, 1960

During this era, most all 10-year-olds would become immersed in whatever sport was in season. Summer was baseball. These two, as best of friends, however, were consumed by baseball year around. Living a few houses apart on the same street, they were constantly together. Luis, a Cuban national and Brady, a mostly Cajun transplanted from South Louisiana.

Luis had moved to Houston two years earlier with his family. His father represented Cuban cigar wholesalers. His area was the Central United States; living in Houston gave him ready access to his territory. Luis quickly learned English, thanks mostly to his friend Brady. At school and when around Brady's home, they spoke English, when at Luis' home they spoke Spanish, as both sets of parents were willing participants in helping Brady learn Spanish and Luis learn English. The many hours evenly split between the two households allowed the boys to quickly learn their new language. Brady a near fluency in Spanish and Luis acquired his English with very little accent.

When Brady's Grandparents came to visit, they forced the

two boys to learn some French. His Grandmother spoke fluent French. Her Cajun family had kept the speaking of French going. Along with his mother, all six of his mother's siblings spoke French. Brady's father, being part Cajun, understood some French. However, he must have understood enough of the true language of love. Brady had one older sister, two younger sisters, and a younger brother. And it didn't seem as though the stork was unwelcome at the Kinin home.

As was normal at Christmas, Luis and his family returned to Cuba for the Holidays. However, during these times, there was political turmoil in Cuba. This year Luis and his family did not return to Houston after the holidays. Nothing was heard from them until one day in March when Luis' father came to Brady's home to explain the situation. He was allowed to continue representing the cigar industry; however, his family was not allowed to leave Cuba. The U.S. was threatening a trade embargo. If implemented, it would stop the import of Cuban cigars into the U.S. He would continue to go to Canada, but there would be no business for him in the U.S.

Over the next few years, Brady received a few postcards from Luis' father, postmarked from Canada. He learned Luis was still playing baseball and doing very well.

Houston had a large Spanish-speaking population. Brady's command of the language let him easily converse with people in many situations, thereby he could not only keep his fluency of a child, but he expanded it to the fluency of an adult. Many times he wondered if his friend Luis was able to use his English.

~

Madrid, Spain, Summer 1967

International Juniors Baseball Tournament

"NEED to get your ankle out of the way Gringo; I could have sliced it open with a good slide."

"Wasn't a play here, you didn't need to slide." Brady answered, somewhat surprised by the Cuban's use of perfect English.

As the Cuban got to his feet and dusted himself off he stood behind the American second baseman. "Don't turn around or act like we are in real conversation, Brady I am Luis."

It was all Brady could do to not spin around as the smile engulfed his face.

Luis continued, "We are watched closely, we are not to make friends with the other teams. The girl in the blue flowered dress is my cousin. See her after the game. Don't look at me or acknowledge me any different than you would my teammates."

For the remaining 4 innings Brady had trouble keeping his mind on the game. Fortunately his next at bat he drew a walk. He wasn't sure he could have hit the ball if he had taken a swing. And since the game was not close, Brady was replaced at second base by one of the younger players on the team. After the game Brady found the blue flowered dress waiting near the stands.

Brady greeted her in his best Spanish, which was still very good. "Buenos Notches, senorita."

He was again surprised to be greeted in perfect English. "Hi Brady, I am Theresa, Luis' cousin."

"Wow, the whole family speaks it."

"I am from Jacksonville. I am an architecture student at Georgia Tech, doing summer study in Spain. My parents were living in Florida since 1950 and never returned to Cuba. I was born in Tampa. So as Luis calls me, his gringo cousin."

"Well that explains why y'all speak better English than I do, my Cajun gets in the way."

"I love hearing the Cajun idioms and inflections. I could listen to you talk all day. Luis really wants to see you."

"He said they were watched pretty close all the time."

"Luis has a plan. They go out for their evening meal then they are allowed the run of the hotel. The coach watching the lobby is usually in the bar. If one of them happens to leave with a girl nothing is said as long as they are back by 11. Luis and I have met casually at the ball field; they do not know we are cousins. I will go to his hotel tonight about 8; I will be the girl he leaves with. Can you be at your hotel tonight?"

"What if you get caught?"

"They can do nothing to me, Luis said they get seen leaving like that all the time, nothing happens. Can you be there tonight?"

"Of course, I wouldn't miss it for the world."

"Great. We should not be seen talking any more so I won't see you again Brady. Luis is very excited to see you."

"Thanks Theresa, I'll be there."

It was an evening of great reunion. It was as if the two had never been apart.

Brussels, Belgium,
NATO Headquarters, 1973

"Commander Phillips. First Lt. Brady Kinin reporting for duty." Brady snapped his best salute as the Navy Commander stood up from behind his desk.

"At ease Lt. Shut the door and have seat."

"Yes sir." Brady was somewhat unsure of the proper

demeanor he should pose. This was his first assignment to a formal command since entering the Army some months ago. The formalities in Vietnam were close to nonexistent.

Brady had graduated from the University of Texas last spring. Although he had been a four year scholarship baseball player at Texas, he knew he was not Major League Baseball quality. Having a lower number in the Selective Service lottery he had a high probability of being drafted. Since he had no compelling aspirations or job prospects, he volunteered for the draft and was able to opt for Officer Candidate School. As with all new officers he got orders to Vietnam. After his time in Vietnam his fluency in Spanish and near fluent use of French, thanks to his Cajun Grandmother, had landed him orders to NATO Headquarters in Belgium.

As Brady seated himself across the desk from Commander Phillips, "Relax Lt. Kinin. That will probably be the last time I call you that outside a formal setting. In this setting you should continue to refer to me as Commander Phillips. However outside this setting please call me Andy."

"Yes Sir, I understand"

"OK, Brady it is. Now Brady, I am not really your Commanding Officer, the command structure is somewhat different here at NATO. If you do your job and stay out of trouble you will seldom ever actually deal with your Commanding Officer. I am a Department Head. For practical purposes I am your Commanding Officer. You will report to me or the Assistant Department Head, Major Castillo of the Spanish Air Force. He is away on assignment this week. I will be writing your Annual Evaluations, although they will be signed by a two star. Fortunate for you that happens to be a U. S. Army two star. It will look very good in your record. Being he is your branch of service that will pretty much guarantee you normal promotion all the way to Lt. Colonel if you stay out of trouble. He also signs my fitness report, being a US two star is good, but if he was Navy would be better. Don't know what happens to the poor guys that get theirs signed by a non US officer. But you hit a homerun, if you stay out of trouble for the next few years, it will be with bases loaded. Any questions?"

"Just, what do you want me to do?"

"Take a few days to get settled in, the Sergeant will get you pointed to the right people. With your speaking French you will easily settle in to living off base. You will not be involved in high security stuff so you are not classified as a security concern. Therefore you are authorized to live out on the economy. Because of Vietnam we are not held in the highest regard by the local citizenry. You should not have any problems if you don't cause a scene. Although we maintain our best military bearing and formality here we have relaxed the length of hair. When off base it helps to not be so readily identified as a GI. Just keep it off your collar and not too far on your ears. We also allow you to wear civilian clothes to and from work. When on base strict uniform requirements are upheld. As a personal hint, buy some civilian clothes on the local economy. Don't wear Levis, they scream American. Report back to me Friday afternoon, that is a slow day. Most of our European officers head home for the weekend. We will have time to go over your job and what I expect of you."

"Also, Brady, I am a baseball fan."

"Play or just a fan?"

"Mostly fan now, was mostly a fan from the end of the bench at the Academy. Not much use for a slow outfielder except pinch hit. I could do some damage to a curve ball from time to time. However Major Castillo is a huge fan and player. He had a chance to play for a junior college in Florida."

"Must be pretty good for them to pull him from Spain. Where did he play?"

"Never did, got accepted to the Spanish Military Academy. He always dreamed of being a fighter jockey. Knew his only chance of that was to graduate from their academy. Couldn't pass it up. He still plays. The command has softball league, I attempt it myself. However, there is a baseball team for you hardcore that are young enough. All of the US installations in Europe have a base team. They get around and play each other a lot, bragging rights for the base CO. Due to our schedules here our team goes to about three tournaments each year."

"Not much of a season. Are they competitive?"

"Not very, pitchers don't get enough work. But they have a good time. Mostly single guys, most wives won't let their husbands travel with that bunch."

"Same problem at Texas, but they had to go."

"You will like Major Castillo. Anything else?"

"Nothing I can think of, thank you Sir." Brady stood, offered a somewhat less ridged salute and left the Commander's office.

The next couple of years proved very formative for Brady. He learned his Cuban friend Luis was in Paris studying International Economics. Many weekends were spent in Paris with his friend. Living in Paris, Luis had met many young ladies.

Brady had also formed a strong relationship with his boss, Commander Phillips. He learned Commander Phillips as a submariner was not able to return to the fleet due to a training accident which had caused him a ruptured eardrum. After Brady had been at NATO for about 10 months it was finally deemed the Commander would never be medically cleared for submarine duty. Commander Phillips was order back stateside for training in Navy intelligence. After one year Phillips was assigned again to NATO as the Intelligence Officer at the NATO Southern Command in Lisbon. Within one week of arriving in Lisbon, Commander Phillips had secured orders for now Captain Brady Kinin to be assigned to his intelligence staff in Lisbon. In that assignment, Brady became enthralled with the intelligence business. He quickly assimilated to the job and remained in Lisbon an extra two years until he was recruited by the DSA to become a field agent.

The Defense Security Agency was a civilian agency of the Department of Defense. They conducted intelligence gathering around the world. Their primary focus was to go out on the local economy around U.S. military bases worldwide. They were looking for direct threats against base or personnel. The DSA conducted very few operations, usually only if something fell in their lap.

However, they did offer support to the CIA if there was an operation that may need military support. Brady was assigned these types of missions more and more, as he was good at thinking on the run and quick improvisation. He would not be involved in the mission but he would be as close as possible, usually teamed with the CIA agent in charge of the operation. Brady knew all of the military units and their capabilities within the area of the mission. And as usual, operations seldom went as planned and the needs often changed rapidly. Being with the DOD gave Brady more rapid access to military assets. The CIA was very reluctant to share any more information about an operation than was necessary. However, usually the agent he teamed with was very sharing of information. This field agent knew that if things went wrong there would not be much time to explain the whole picture well enough for Brady to make the best decision.

In his intelligence gathering roll he would return to DSA Headquarters and discuss his findings with an analyst to determine the potential threat and appropriate measures to thwart the threat. A few years after joining DSA he was reunited with his former mentor. Now retired, Navy Captain Andy Phillips had joined DSA as an Area Supervisor and Assistant Director. Brady's area was part of Andy's group. Although there were numerous retired military at DSA, Brady was most comfortable with Andy Phillips. He knew the information and opinion he brought would not be wasted with Andy.

PART I

CHAPTER #1

MONTREAL, FEBRUARY 1987

The Spaniard turned away from the coffee bar with one hand carrying his hot coffee cup and a bagel balanced on top as his other hand carried his satchel, then a newspaper clutched against his body by his elbow. The coffee shop at the Montreal airport was small and very crowded this time of the morning. He spotted an empty chair at a small table in the far corner. A past middle-aged man with longish graying hair occupied the other chair, the gentleman seemed completely occupied with his Paris newspaper. As the Spaniard approached the table, he caught the seated man's eye over the Paris newspaper. He gestured with his head toward the empty chair and was rewarded with an answering nod of permission. He gently eased his cup on to the table as he sat and placed his satchel on the floor next to his chair. After rearranging his bagel to the table and taking a sip of the hot coffee, he opened his European edition of the New York Times and scanned the front page as he hoisted his coffee to take another sip. Within a minute, both men were engrossed in their reading and coffee, seemingly oblivious to the other's presence.

The Spaniard broke the silence, speaking in French to the stranger across the table and pointing to an article in his paper. The other man, seemingly annoyed, gave a curt answer, then pulled his paper closer to his face. After a moment of silence, the Spaniard spoke again and gestured to his paper. The other gentleman, seeing he was destined for a conversation, answered, and now changed the conversation to Spanish. He then held out his paper and pointed to an article. This back and forth continued in subdued voices for a few minutes in a courteous manner, although the one gentleman never seemed to get over his annoyance. The Frenchman then excused himself when his flight to Paris was called. An art history professor, he was returning to his home in Paris. The Spaniard, a fresh fruit distribution representative, would finish his coffee, then head down the concourse for his flight to Vancouver.

Before reaching the gate for the Paris flight, the art history professor went into the restroom, never to be seen again. When in the restroom, he quickly removed his sport coat, goatee, wig and glasses, stuffing them silently into the trash. From his shoulder bag, he pulled out and donned a neatly pressed windbreaker and a Toronto Bluejays ball cap. He exited the restroom and went to the gate of his now boarding flight to Philadelphia. From there, Brady would take the train back to his office in the Washington area. This would give him time to mull over the most interesting information his longtime friend Luis had just given him, as they used the charade of discussing newspaper articles in Spanish. Brady needed to fashion a scheme to make the most of this information.

The Spaniard, however, was not so fortunate as to be able to directly board his flight home. He would continue to Toronto and Vancouver to complete his planned sales schedule. It would be four days before he would fly back to Toronto and then take a flight to his home in Havana.

This clandestine meeting of two old friends must remain the utmost secret. While gesturing and pointing at their newspapers was only a distraction to anyone noticing, they were discussing very sensitive information. DSA agent Brady Kinin had only told his immediate boss, Andy Phillips, he needed to go to Montreal to meet an informant. Luis, Head of the Cuban Intelligence Service, was truly on a routine intelligence gathering trip to the various Cuban consulates in Canada. He used the role of cigar sales as his cover to travel through Canada, South and Central America, and Western Europe.

During the flight to Philadelphia, Brady had time to formulate just how he would present his information to his boss and develop a way to use this information.

CHAPTER # 2

NEAR HAVANA, NOVEMBER 1986

Yuri Metroff laughed heartily as he downed his third rum laced coke. The Russian was now mixing his own fourth such drink; Luis noticed it was more like rum laced with coke. The warm Cuban sun was a welcome relief from the miserable Russian winter, which had already begun when Metroff left Moscow ten days earlier. He and his wife were enjoying the hospitality of General Arturo Espinosa, the military commander of all Cuban forces. Metroff was commander of the Russian Air Force. The two men were very friendly and gracious to each other, although both considered the other to be inferior in status.

Also in attendance at the luncheon on the veranda of the Cuban General's Villa, a supposed social event, were two others. One was the Russian military attaché to Cuba, the other was the head of the Cuban Secret Intelligence Service, Luis Quiroz. Although Luis ran his Intelligent Service pretty much independently, his organizational chain of command was to the Cuban General of Forces.

"Yes, my friend Arturo, anyone can buy an Apple computer or even an IBM mainframe. But it would be worth millions to get our hands on the latest American technology. Their military computers are probably two to three years ahead of what is on the open market."

"Well, Comrade General, I thought money could buy anything."

"Not these. They are strictly controlled and securely guarded. None leave the country. Not even NATO commands outside the US have them."

"Surely your KGB could manage to acquire such secret machines."

"HA! Even if they did, it would do us no good. By the time they ever shared them, and that is, if they ever shared them, you would be able to buy them used on the open market."

"Too bad your Mother Russia has banned Christmas or you could ask Papa Noel for one."

"Yes Arturo, and have him also maybe bring some of those new high tech deep hole oil drill bits."

The Russian attaché and the Cuban Intelligence Officer exchanged glances, both displaying displeasure at having to be in attendance.

Havana, December 1986

"WELL LUIS, thank you for coming on such short notice." He stood near the General's desk. Knowing if he remained standing, it would encourage the General to make this short and to the point.

"Always a pleasure, General Espinosa." The Intelligence officer still knew who his overall superior was.

"Do you remember last week at my Villa, the conversation with our dear friend Comrade General Fat Pig?"

"Much was said that afternoon. What, in particular, are you referring to?"

"His desire to get his hands on an American computer."

"Yes sir, your jab about Christmas even brought a smile to the attaché."

"Is it true what he said? Those computers are untouchable?"

"I pretty much believe that is true."

"Find out. If we, the lowly Cubans, could secure one, it might be worth literally millions in cash, as well as unprecedented stature to the Mighty Mother Russia. How many of such computers are there?"

"I cannot answer that with any accuracy." Luis knew this was not an acceptable answer for the General; he always wanted something more solid. "My best estimate would be in the range of anywhere from fifteen to twenty." This type of answer would satisfy the General. It gave the Commander a general range for his lie when he passed the information on. Depending on what suited his purpose, his latest 'intelligence' may say there are only a few, less than ten. Or if the situation warranted, as many as fifty.

"Do we know where these computers are located?"

"Would be easy to identify the obvious locations of ten or twelve. The rest may be difficult to know."

"What would be the obvious locations?"

"Standing here unprepared......." Luis had been in this business long enough to know always cover your answer, especially in the harsh confines of a totalitarian system; he hated it. ".......after the Pentagon in Virginia, the CIA in Langley, the NSA in Maryland, and probably the FBI in Washington. I would say NASA has a few. One in Houston, Goddard in Maryland, Canaveral in Florida, their think tank in Los Angeles at the Jet Propulsion Lab, and probably in Huntsville, Alabama and Stennis in Mississippi. Each branch of the military may have one outside of the Pentagon. After that, it would be much more of a guess."

"Look into these locations. Find a location that might be breachable. This is a priority; Russia is in turmoil. That offer may be short-lived. As well as those making the offer."

"That is not a small thing you are thinking, General, but I shall pursue it immediately." No matter how eccentric, Luis knew not to immediately voice too much doubt.

"And also,those drill bits he wanted on his Christmas list. I will give you great latitude for this operation." Luis saw immediately that this operation was not an exercise, it was going to happen.

"If your plan involves an air component, you are to use my personal pilot. He is an excellent pilot with broad experience and a true patriot. It is Lt. Col. Ibarra. Have you ever met him?"

"Yes sir, he has helped us before." To Luis that was the only good news he had heard since entering the General's office. Lt. Col. Ibarra was the best, as a pilot and as someone to work with.

"Also, director Quiroz, the funding for this operation need not be from your normal budget, nor from the Air Force budget. I want this to be known to as few people as possible. The funding will come directly from my office. Give me a cost estimate so the funds can be transferred to your agency account. Your comptroller need only know it is for special development."

Luis had one touchy question he had to ask, "The other people in my agency, am I to involve..."

The General raised his hand to stop the question. "You are referring specifically to your assistant director. Of all people, do not let that incompetent stooge know anything; he will go directly to his uncle. He shouldn't be allowed to be a bank teller. Use anyone you need on the mission, but keep the knowledge of the specifics to a minimum."

This was the second piece of good news he had heard. The rampant nepotism had forced his assistant director on him in this utilitarian regime. The man's uncle, the Minister of State, had succumbed to his sister's pleading. Her son wanted to be a spy and thought he could. They had even forced the Russians to put him through some training by the KGB. He had made a fool of himself and of Cuba. On his return, they assigned him to the more active intelligence arm of State Security. Word was he had been little more than a clerk there. For nepotism to remain active, they decided he could do little damage as the assistant director for Luis. It pleased Luis to know his boss understood his staffing dilemma.

"General, you understand we are best suited to gather the intelligence for this type of undertaking. But we are really not an agency structured to plan and implement a mission. Would not the security agency or the Rangers be better suited for this?"

"For most things, you are right. However, this has some very different elements to it. If the security group had this, everyone in Cuba would know about it and then the Russians would become involved. It would no longer be a Cuban operation. I can rely on only you to keep this off everyone's radar. As for the Rangers, you were one once. You know they couldn't do this without making it an armed invasion. I want no casualties; don't want the Americans to know we are involved. You may use some military people, but do not involve anyone from the security group. No matter their orders, they would keep their agency informed of everything."

"I can use some Rangers on the mission?"

"Yes, but I would suggest you not involve them in the

planning. Won't need their input. You know what they are capable of."

"There are some excellent soldiers there."

"I am glad you feel that way. Thankfully, we have been able to keep a lot of nepotism out of the military. Are there any other questions at this time, Director Quiroz?"

"No General." Thankfully for Luis, the General ended the brief visit with a laugh and wave of the hand.

As Luis left the building, the enormity of the task General Espinosa had just demanded of him consumed his mind. He knew he would need to involve his best agent, Rudy Perez, in this from the beginning. Rudy had done a six-year stint in the Air Force before resigning and coming to his agency five years ago. In fact, it had been on the recommendation of Lt. Col. Ibarra that Luis became aware of Rudy Perez.

Cuban Air Force Base, January 1987

"INTELLIGENCE DIRECTOR QUIROZ. To what do I owe this pleasure? Someone as important and busy as yourself to call upon a humble servant of the state like myself." Lt. Col. Ibarra stood to shake hands as Luis entered what was used by the pilots as a ready room.

"Cut the crap Barra...." the name the pilot was called by his friends. "....you know why I am here and you knew I was coming. How else would it be that I might find a lazy bureaucrat here on a Sunday morning? Your Lola won't let you escape Mass. You are not even allowed tardiness."

"Yes, Luis, you know my life well. I gained my weekly absolution last night. But only by the intervention of General Espinosa."

"How are your lovely wife and her kids? They can't be

your kids. She is too pretty and smart to have done anything in bed with you besides sleep."

"Ouch, you cut so deep. Your vile qualifies you to be the director of the security division. Not running the library division. And we best not get into your Alicia's lack of taste in men."

"Sorry, you are still jealous they never could find a meaningful job you could handle. Maybe we finally have something for you, tame that flaming ego of yours." If there was ever a person without an ego problem, it was Barra. He was very unassertive until it came to airplanes and his piloting skills. Not in a boastful sort of way, but with absolute confidence he would tell you he could do it and what equipment would be best for the mission. When he talked, he instilled that same confidence in you.

"Espinosa called to tell me to meet you today, but he did not give any specifics. Said I should make myself completely available to you. Your mission had priority over my being his chauffeur."

"The General has tasked me, now us, with a very unusual undertaking. You, Rudy and I are the only ones privy to this. I have some ideas, but we have not even put together a plan. It is going to sound wild, but I can assure you General Espinosa is serious about this."

"As his pilot for the past two years, I have spent a lot of time with him. Nothing he came up with would surprise me."

Luis explained the commission given to them.

CHAPTER # 3

VIENNA, MARCH 1987

Brady sat in his rented car and waited. The man had left his apartment building and was now at the trolley stop. Unsure as to which trolley he would board, Brady would wait until Hans boarded, then drive to the next stop, park his car and board the same trolley car.

Brady needed to talk to this deal broker.

Hans Freling was a Russian by ancestry and an Austrian by birth. He had lived in Austria for most of his 42 years. He moved to the South of France for a couple of years, but the hot weather was not for him.

Hans' father had been a mid-level officer in the Russian Army. After the war, they had garrisoned him with the Russian troops in Hungary, monitoring the border with Austria. His mother was the daughter of a Russian General that had been killed during the war. Because of her 'hero' father, she was allowed the privilege to visit her husband at his garrison every few months. Most of the focus was on the German border that split that country into East and West. This area of the Hungarian border his father had charge of was very loose. His counterpart of the Hungarian Border

Police became a good friend. This Hungarian had married an Austrian. Her parents had agreed to take-in Hans' mother for the birth of their child.

During her ninth month of pregnancy with Hans, his mother came for a scheduled visit. One night, when his father was the duty officer in charge, he smuggled his pregnant wife across the border into Austria. His fellow Officers swallowed the explanation that she had returned to her home in Samara, one thousand kilometers east of Moscow. With all the confusion in the post-war Russian Bureaucracy, her whereabouts slipped thru the cracks. Therefore, Hans had been born in Austria.

A few months later, his father applied for release from the Army. The Russian Army Headquarters in East Germany was where he received his discharge. He forfeited his return trip to Moscow, telling the Army he was taking a position as a police lieutenant in Estonia. He too then slipped into Austria to join his wife and new baby son.

A few years later, when the Russians had figured out what his parents had done, especially the daughter of a hero, they were officially recorded as permitted to immigrate. This saved perceived embarrassment to the glorious leaders. No one would have ever noticed or cared.

The Austrian government was still in disarray from the German occupation of the war. The family that had taken his wife in had lost a son in the resistance movement against the Nazis. They suggested Hans' father take their son's name, thereby instantly becoming an Austrian. That is the name they had used for the birth certificate of his son. The baby was Hans Freling; the father was now Jacob Freling.

Hans' parents hated the Communists and what they had done to their homeland. All Hans ever heard during his youth was his parents berating the Russian Communists, so Hans had an almost inbred dislike for the Communists. But because of the happy, good natured disposition of his parents, he harbored no harsh feelings to the Russian people. With his parents' continued love for their home country, they spoke Russian around the home, giving Hans a complete command of the language.

However, Hans knew to keep his political feelings mostly to himself in the business world. In fact, it had helped his business and broadened his contacts to let it be known of his displeasure that his parents had stolen him from the glorious cradle of the Russian empire. None of his business contacts in the West cared one way or the other, but voicing these feelings endeared him to the eastern bloc governments. His fluency in the Russian language also benefited him. The bloc governments had a profound effect on his clients. Some of the governments even used him from time to time.

Hans was now well known in certain circles. If not admired, he was respected and known to be a straight dealer, and his word was as good as it could be in his line of work. And his words were many. Not only fluent in German and Russian, he had become very articulate in French and English. Hans could also speak Spanish, Portuguese, and Italian to conduct business in those languages. He had minimal conversive skills in Greek, Turkish, and Egyptian. He was not really a dealer. Hans was a broker of deals and sometimes an agent. His trade was bringing deals and people together. None of what he did was illegal. He never owned any merchandise nor moved anything. His only function was bringing people needing a service or having something to sell together with people they might do business with. He knew most of the things he brokered were very shady, a lot of black market deals. He avoided murder, assassination, drugs and arms deals, all of which could get someone killed for knowing too much. There was still a lot of business for a middleman. He didn't work on commission when brokering;

that would involve him knowing too much. He charged a flat fee of twelve thousand Swiss Francs per arrangement, cash only. Everyone was comfortable dealing in Swiss currency. He charged a commission if he negotiated the price.

Someone needing to move something or someone into a country without the cumbersome paperwork of Custom officials, Hans probably knew a ship captain or air cargo outfit also adverse to such paperwork. The Russians were very fond of his services, as was the CIA. He cut his fee in half for the CIA if the deal involved poking the Russians in the eye. The CIA understood this, so after a mission was closed, they would explain to Hans how they had stuck it to the Commies. Although he had learned to be somewhat skeptical of what he was told.

The approaching trolley caused Hans to move toward the boarding area. Brady started the car and slowly pulled away from the curb. As he drove past the partially fogged windows, he saw Hans taking a seat. By the time the trolley got to the next stop, Brady was waiting to board. Engrossed in a newspaper, Hans did not notice Brady take the seat directly behind him. Being late morning, there were few passengers, however there was a lady sitting across the aisle from Hans. It was two more stops before the lady headed for the exit.

In a somewhat hushed tone, Brady began speaking French. "Good morning Herr Freling. A late start today?"

"Yes, my friend Brady, I thought that was you. I miss our time together." Hans replied.

"Do you have a new place for lunch you would like to show me?"

"Is this a discount deal?" Hans asks.

"You must decide that."

"It is not new, but we've not been there in a few years. In case it is a discount, I will let you pay. And since you are paying, it is expensive." Hans replied with a slight chuckle.

"Isn't every place we go as expensive as you can find?"

"Only for the discount deals. That little inn about four kilometers out on the old Salzburg road."

"Tomorrow at eleven thirty." Brady replied as he left his seat and headed for the exit.

The next morning, Brady was seated at a booth in the back corner as Hans entered, being his usual 20 minutes late. Brady expected this, so he did not get concerned that the tardiness was a sign that Hans may not show up.

After the usual pleasantries and small talk waiting for their meal to be served, Hans inquired.

"To what do I owe this unexpected visit?" Hans spoke somewhat broken English, but he used and understood American idioms and nuances.

"We need you to make contact with the Chinese."

"A Chinese dealer of what nature?"

"No, the Chinese government."

"Never dealt with them. They are difficult to approach. Even though they are Commies, they are not on the discount list." Hans replied with a questioning twinkle in his eye.

"This will be just the initial contact; it will trickle down to your favored gang."

Hans had been dealing with Brady for many years and had learned to trust what Brady told him. There had been a number of times Brady had used him on what appeared to qualify for a discount. Brady had told him otherwise and paid the full twelve thousand Francs.

"You will need to make initial contact through the Chinese embassy in Paris." Hans listened intently as Brady explained what was required of Hans.

After his second meeting with Luis, he had a general outline for the Cuban plan. With this information, Brady and Andy had developed a plan to use the Cuban escapade to their advantage.

"That will be an extra expense. I cannot go to Paris without taking my wife. We will take a sleeping compartment on the train to Paris but will return by air. The return train is a very poor schedule. We will have to stay at least two days."

"No less than we expected. Here is an advance for expenses." Brady handed an envelope to Hans.

CHAPTER #4

PARIS, MARCH 1987

The Austrian businessman, Hans Freling, entered the Chinese embassy in Paris. He had an appointment with the head of the Commerce section of the Chinese delegation. After showing his papers and satisfying security, they showed him to a small, stark waiting room. He remained standing, as the chairs were not very inviting. A door opened, and they ushered him into the Commerce office. It was necessary to use the embassy in Paris rather than the embassy in Vienna, because Brady told him the Paris embassy had an intelligence officer.

When the door was shut, he removed a sealed envelope from his pocket and laid it on the desk across from the seated Chinese diplomat. "Sir, I really have nothing to discuss with you directly. You were the only way I could get an appointment in this building. Please give this envelope to your intelligence officer here."

Hans had an idea what was in the envelope. Brady had given it to him sealed, and he had left it sealed. Knowing too much was dangerous to his personal safety. Brady had explained what was being offered for sale. But he had not gotten a hint of how the Russians would be involved.

The diplomat rose from his chair and with a slight lean over the desk, “Sir, you are mistaken; this is a diplomatic and trade facility. With an intelligence officer, you would be accusing us of spying. I must ask you to leave immediately. I cannot help you.” However, the diplomat did not look at nor gesture toward the envelope. It remained on the desk as they escorted Hans out of the office.

“I’m leaving contact information on the envelope. Good day.” Hans responded as they jostled him through the door.

The Austrian left the building and hailed a cab to meet his wife for lunch. The meeting had gone exactly as Brady had told him it would.

VIENNA, Austria

HANS SAT in his apartment drinking his morning coffee and reading the newspaper; there was a slight scraping in the hallway outside his door and he looked up to see an envelope slid under his front door. He smiled as he walked over to retrieve the envelope. Thinking, ‘Pretty fast for them, only two weeks.’

He opened the envelope and unfolded the note ‘1300, 2 April, Assistant Director for Manufacturing‘. Again he thought, ‘Very fast for them, only two days from now.’

PARIS, France

Hans was rapidly and somewhat ungraciously ushered to a small, bare walled office in the Chinese embassy. One man was behind the desk and another was seated in the corner. They showed him to a chair in front of the desk.

"I am Mr. Wong and this is Mr. Chu. Mr. Freling. Your proposal is very aggressive, if not impossible. Why would we believe you could fulfill this proposal? These things are strictly controlled." The Chinese had obviously done some investigation into the proposal.

"I am merely asking. Would you be interested if I had them?"

"We are not interested in 'what if' child games, Mr. Freling."

"Nor am I Mr. Wong. My client wants a legitimate buyer before he undertakes the procurement of these."

"Who exactly are we dealing with here, Mr. Freling? Who is your client?"

"My client does not wish to be known at this point, nor would I reveal such information anyway. That is how I lose commissions."

"We are not concerned with your commission, Mr. Freling?"

"I am and you need not be. That, the seller pays."

"We would not only need to know the seller, but we will deal only with the seller for such a commitment."

"Yes, we assumed that."

"Why do you come to us? We know your allegiance to Russia." Again Hans could see they had done some homework.

"My allegiance is to money. And that is exactly why I come to you first, because of my Russian heritage. As a faithful expatriate, they would expect me to deeply discount or even waive my fee. There are other reasons which will become apparent to you as negotiations unfold."

"Yet you are not the principal here?"

"As I am sure you have investigated me, you know I am never the principal. But that would not keep the Russians from thinking they should get my services for free. You are their buddy. You know how they work."

"If you are inferring we are a puppet of 'The Bear', you are very wrong. The People's Republic of China is completely independent, dealing with the USSR only when it suits our purposes." Hans expected this standard line.

"Yes, I understand. Please do not take offense. I wish to remain neutral in all my dealings." Not quite true, he had an affinity for the US, especially Brady Kinin and a couple of the CIA agents he had come in contact with.

"We would need to inspect and test the units. And verify the data as true. Also, the source of the data."

"Inspect, yes. Test, no. A sample of the data would be forwarded to you for confirmation. That is all the information I can share with you. Anything more will need to be negotiated directly with my client."

"Is your client ready to meet?"

"Yes, time and place of your convenience. But my client will ask it to be in Canada."

"You shall hear from us in the next few days, Mr. Freling. Good day."

Hans Freling left the embassy as unceremoniously as he had entered, knowing they would follow him for the next few weeks, if not for the next few months, until the deal was done. Just as they had followed him since his first visit to the embassy two weeks ago. It was easy for them to track him because he made it easy. The Chinese could not wait to get their hands on the data and merchandise. In this instance, Brady had discussed the pricing of the deal. He told Brady the offered price was somewhat on the cheap side. He was not sure of the DSA interest in the deal, but he knew it wasn't money. Didn't really matter to him, he didn't do their deals for commission. But they took care of him. This deal would probably be good for the usual commission and many times Brady threw in a bonus. This could easily be $20,000.

Hans Freling boarded his flight back to Vienna knowing his job was pretty much done, and that the Chinese Commies were going to get, as the Americans would say, 'a sharp stick in the eye'. All that remained for him to do was pass on the contact information to the Brady. Hans also knew there was a lot more to this than he was privy to at this point. The DSA had asked for this to be a cash deal. Transactions with the Chinese were usually done by bank transfer, not cash. In his business, it was known that for cash, the Chinese went to their friends, the North Koreans, masters of counterfeit currency. So the DSA wanted some counterfeit currency to 'stick someone else in the eye'. He maybe saw the hint of Russian involvement. Hans loved this; he couldn't wait to hear the story when it was over.

Three days later, Hans found another note slipped under the door of his apartment in Vienna.

April 20
Victoria BC, Victoria Grand Hotel, High Tea

THE GAME WAS STILL ON; it was now time to pass this information on to Brady. Brady had laid out the general plan; Hans' client was the Cuban government. However, the Cubans knew nothing of these dealings. He would need to make it look like he was passing this information to the Cubans. They had an embassy in Vienna, so it would be simple to make it appear he was meeting a Cuban official.

Getting the information to Brady was also fairly simple;

Hans mailed a postcard to his 'cousin' in Baltimore. A few days later, Hans made a phone call from a public pay phone to unravel the coded message on the card.

Although the Chinese were watching him, they could not do a very good job of keeping tabs on him. The rather small Chinese population in Vienna made it easy for him to spot whoever was tailing him, even though they kept their distance. And keeping such distance, they could never get on the same bus or tram with him. Merely going to a bus stop and boarding a bus near the Cuban embassy would give the appearance of having contacted someone at the embassy.

It also made it easy to pass information to the DSA. Although. Here, there was really no need for direct contact. Things had played out just as Brady had said. Although they enjoyed each other's company, he and Brady needed not to be seen together. These Commies were so regimented and predictable.

CHAPTER #5

EARLY APRIL, 1987

As Brady sat in his office one Tuesday morning, the phone rang. He answered to hear the receptionist tell him this was a call that came in on the Global Evaluations line from an Otto Kaisler. Brady knew immediately it was something important and of great urgency. Otto Kaisler was the name Hans Freling was to use if he ever needed to contact him immediately. Hans had never used it nor called him direct at this number.

"Hello Herr Kaisler, this is Kinin. What can I do for you?"

"Mr. Kinin, thank you for taking my call. I know you scout for baseball and futbol, I believe you call it soccer. We have met a few times at matches. Do you remember me?"

"Yes, that is true. I do scout baseball and futbol." Brady was used to the term futbol as used in the rest of the world. "And I do remember meeting you."

"I have recently seen a young futbol player I believe you should see. He is a genuine talent, but not yet discovered. He plays in club league in Northern Italy."

This was a message in code for Brady. It told Brady that Hans needed to see him. Hans had probably gotten wind of something vitally important to Brady's security job. The term Northern Italy told Brady they should meet in Oslo, the northern city they had previously selected.

"I am certainly interested. It so happens I will be in Spain next week. I can certainly arrange to come to Italy. When does he have a match?"

"He plays Saturday in Milan. 1400 hours. I will wait for you at the gate."

"I look forward to seeing you again, Herr Kaisler, and watching this young prospect." Brady hung up the phone with a feeling that Hans had some very bad news. They would meet two days before the day mentioned, and the 1400 was U.S. east Coast time. It was now Tuesday and Hans wanted to meet on Thursday, very short notice. They had prearranged the meeting place. Neither he nor Hans worked the Northern Europe region; therefore, the chance of either of them being recognized in Oslo was slim.

Oslo, Norway, Thursday evening

When Brady entered the restaurant, he knew there was trouble as Hans was seated and waiting, not his customary 20 minutes late.

"Very nice of you to come so quickly, Brady." Hans said nervously.

"I figured it was very important. You had never called me before. And especially with such short notice."

"There is a situation within my family has developed." Hans' nervousness had made his English more choppy and difficult to understand. "But it is such a situation I believe the U.S. may be interested in."

Brady's interest waned somewhat with the mention of

'family situation'. But Hans had helped him in the past and Brady genuinely liked Hans, so the least he could do was listen. "Please explain for me."

"The evening before I called you, my sister called me. She lives in Moscow, is married to a midlevel diplomat that is currently posted at the Austrian embassy in Moscow. Her visit back to Austria had been previously scheduled. She said that last week our cousin, my mother's sister's son, contacted her. He is a manager with the state railway in Russia, working near Moscow. He does the routing and scheduling of shipments. His sole focus is shipments for the Red Army. His office is at a large arms and equipment center that supplies the troops. He has been doing it for years." Hans finished his beer and ordered another.

"Was this unusual for him to contact your sister?"

"Yes, it is not known by anyone outside the family that we have relatives in Russia. So he sought her out specifically to see if her husband could help."

"Is her husband able to help?" Brady thought he was seeing a way out if this family situation.

"She didn't even tell her husband about this. When she heard the story, she thought that with my connections, I might know of someone that was better suited to help. She knows I deal with a lot of international trade people. She knows nothing of my ever working with you or the CIA."

"Why didn't she feel her husband could help? That is his line of work?" Brady was trying to keep himself out of the solution.

"When you hear the story, you will understand the level of help needed and why I am sure your government will be interested." Hans pulled a small notebook from his coat pocket and flipped thru some pages as he spoke. "I had to take notes from our conversation. Her memory of the spoken word is excellent. Some people have a photographic memory of a written document; she is like that with the spoken word. Terrible as children, she told everything I said."

Hans got to the page he was searching for and continued. "As I was saying. My cousin does the routing for arms shipments. Over the last few months, he had noticed some things in the paperwork didn't match up. When he sends a shipment, he will get back paperwork confirming the arrival of the shipment, usually a week or two later. No one ever pays much attention to matching the numbers. He would send ten cars of arms and equipment, but only eight would show as received. He caught this purely by accident. There was a week when all three shipments happened to be twenty cars, very unusual for all the same number in one week. The number itself wasn't odd, just the coincidence of being the same. That made it somewhat memorable. A couple of weeks later, when the paperwork from the receiving end was being put together, one of his clerks mentioned the odd incidence of the week with the same number. This paperwork showed a different number for one shipment, it registered eighteen and the other two were twenty. If all three of those numbers had been the same, no one would have caught it. He went back and looked at some of the previous weeks and found they didn't all match up. He looked up the car numbers that were unaccounted for and found them all to be of shipments of arms and munitions. This involved everything from small arms and ammunition to hand held rocket launchers and rocket-propelled grenades. Nothing heavy like artillery shells. Only things that a single individual could carry and use."

"Was he sure of this?" Brady had regained a keen interest in the story.

"Yes, he did all the routing. He had to know what was in each car to route it to the correct destination. A single train may drop cars at different locations, so the cars had to be aligned properly." As Hans got into the story and downed his second beer, he began to relax.

"Does he know where they went?" Brady inquired.

"He thinks he does. The cars that were missing were always on the trains carrying arms to the troops in Afghanistan. The train's final destinations may have been different, but they took the same route through Russia."

"There were no stops along the route?"

"No, these military shipments had clearance. When he checked the logs, he found that the same crew manned all the trains that had missing cars. It was only this crew that ever had any missing cars."

"But you said he thinks he knows where the missing arms are located."

"Yes, he followed the switching logs along the route. He found a length that normally took about 50 to 60 minutes. These suspect trains took about 90 minutes to travel the distance. Enough time to stop and drop off cars. He also noticed that on the routing manifests, the missing cars were the last ones on the train. They were scheduled to be delivered at the first listed destination point in Afghanistan. These always had the smaller type arms." Hans was well into his story and hadn't touched his third beer.

So, do we have any specific information? '

"Wait, my friend, there is more, and it gets worse."

"Doesn't sound so good now."

"Yes, but one day they had a shipment leaving first thing that morning. His chief clerk was out for a few days, so they were a little behind. He went in early, about 4 a.m., to make sure the paperwork was ready for the departure. From his office, he saw some lights on at the far end of the loading area. He walked across the terminal to see if there was possibly a mix up on loading the cars. When close enough to see what was going on, he saw some crates being loaded from a truck. The markings on the crates identified them as tactical nuclear weapons." At this, Hans stopped and downed a half liter of beer.

Brady would have downed his beer at this revelation, but he was too shocked to move. It overloaded his mind, the possible implications of this. The Soviet Union was on the road to collapse and some nuclear weapons being stolen.

"What else did he see?"

"He was in the shadows and felt they had not seen him. He went back to his office and tried to complete a normal day. Although he didn't think they had seen him, he feels he was being followed. For the next few weeks he followed my sister, trying to get to her in some casual way. She always took the bus to go shopping about mid-morning on Wednesdays. For a couple of weeks, he went to the same area to establish this as normal activity. During this time, the paperwork from the destination points of the rail shipments were received at his office. The rail car he saw being loaded that night was missing, and it was the same crew."

"Can he get this information out?"

Hans had become more nervous and finished his beer in one long guzzle. "Yes, he will gladly give the information. But to get it out, he wants to come out with his family."

"He wants to defect?"

"Yes. Is that the term we still use?" Hans tore the sheets out of his notebook and proceeded to set them on fire in his empty beer stein. "I am so happy to be rid of that."

"This type of thing is very much out of my league, Hans. I will pass this on, but that is all I can do."

"I understand, Brady, but you are the only one I know that could be of any help."

"You have done work with the CIA. Can't you go to them? This is more their type of thing."

"I agree, but I don't have a contact there. They always

contact me when they need me and it is someone different each time."

"You mentioned him and his family. How many?"

"His wife and their daughter and her two teenage children live with them. Her husband was killed in Afghanistan a few years ago."

"So a total of five. Are they all mobile?"

"Yes, the wife's mother is in a home, bedridden. Her mind is about gone. She will probably never know they are missing."

Brady got some more specifics about Hans' Russian cousin before parting ways. Brady returned to his hotel and got on the phone. He reserved a seat on the first flight out of Oslo to D.C. the next morning. A connection through London got him back to Washington the soonest. He called Andy to tell him to stay at the office until he got there, cancel his Friday afternoon tee time, and cancel any dinner plans for Friday night. Andy asked if there was anyone else he needed to keep around. Brady thought maybe Katie (the DSA Director of Mission planning, which also involved her in a lot of intel analysis) but Andy and only Andy needed to hear this first. However, Brady knew that before he got halfway through the story, they would both agree to get Katie on board. Her unconventional thinking always brought great insight into any problem.

By three o'clock Friday afternoon, the three of them were in the conference room at DSA headquarters. The director of DSA was out of the country until Wednesday, which left the decision for Andy. Should they pass the information along through the department of defense or to another federal security agency, NSA or CIA. There was a semblance of protocol that must be followed.

DSA was not under the control of the military; therefore, passing such information to the military was not an acceptable option. They knew if they passed the information up the channel through the department of defense, it would be to career bureaucrats and political appointees. Both of which were always looking to curry favor with the press or politicians. Before they could evaluate the information, much less confirm it, there would be a Congressional hearing. This would be behind closed doors, of course, with only three hundred of the most trusted aides in attendance. Of which, maybe eight or ten would have security clearance.

By four thirty, the obvious consensus of the three had Andy on the phone to the CIA. Because he couldn't declare it an imminent threat, they were scheduled to meet at 10 a.m. Monday. Andy requested it be at CIA Headquarters, which was grudgingly agreed to. The CIA really did not want to be bothered by information from a group that fixed the fences at military bases. However, the CIA sure liked the DSA when they were liaison with the military to back up an operation.

About 3:30 Monday, Brady and Andy were leaving CIA Headquarters. This was after Brady had to relate the story no less than three times, each time to someone more senior. He was pressed very hard about the reliability of Hans Freling. What upset Brady the most was that they knew all about Hans, having used him themselves. Since they both knew the way the CIA worked, today might be the last they ever heard of it unless something was on the news.

CHAPTER # 6

VICTORIA, BRITISH COLUMBIA, CANADA, APRIL 20

Brady knew the Chinese would be comfortable with Canada as the place for the meeting. The great Asian population of British Columbia would allow them to move freely without attracting notice. For visiting tourists, there was no itinerary required. Once in the country past immigration control, the Western Governments had no interest in the activity of visitors. One could travel randomly with no government intrusion.

This would also be the Cuban choice for such a meeting, as there was easy business entry to Canada from Cuba. Luis came often using his cover as a cigar wholesaler.

Brady, with his Cajun heritage, could easily pass himself off as Hispanic. This time, he would pose as a representative of the Cuban government acting as a tourist. He entered the room at the Victoria Grand precisely at 4 p.m. for the ceremony of High Tea. This was the beginning of the tourist season, so it was somewhat crowded. Although there were several Asian tourists in the room, Brady's years of training and experience allowed him to pick out his Chinese contacts immediately.

While seeming to enjoy mingling with the crowd, Brady and the Chins innocently met.

"Did I hear you say you are Mr. and Mrs. Chin?" Brady put out his hand as any westerner would. The Chins gave a slight bow, then Mr. Chin took Brady's outstretched hand.

"I am sorry sir, we are the Yongs."

Brady offered an apology and then continued a casual conversation with the couple. When it was appropriate to move on, he again shook hands with the gentleman. There was a small piece of paper exchanged to Brady's hand during the hand clasp. They had used the proper phrases during the innocent conversation. Brady then offered a slight bow in return of the couples and discretely slipped the paper into his coat pocket. Brady visited randomly for another 20 minutes, then casually left the gathering and returned to his room.

Once in the privacy of his room, he removed the paper Mr. Yong had given him. He unfolded the note. '9pm #324'.

At the appointed time Brady stepped off the elevator on the 3rd floor. He casually walked to 324 and gently knocked. The door immediately opened. He stepped into the room and was ushered to a seat. "Please sit Senor Ramon." They knew the name he was traveling under; he had introduced himself to the Yongs at the reception earlier. They made no introductions of the three others in the room, none of which were Mr. or Mrs. Yong.

One of the Chinese facing him began. "You are the principal for what is being offered?"

"Yes."

"You are authorized to negotiate and make decisions?"

"I am and I will." Brady knew this was very bewildering to people from such a controlled government. Such authority would never be bestowed on a single individual, especially someone of the status of field representative. "If I am assured that you also have such authority."

He knew the answer. They were authorized to negotiate within very narrow limits, but he needed to press issues from the start. Easy negotiations would make the naturally suspicious Chinese become very leery of the deal. The numbers Hans Freling had given the Chinese in Paris were high, but with that information, he knew this delegation would have an amount they were authorized to agree upon.

"Yes, we have eminent authority." Brady could not help himself as he cracked the smallest hint of a grin. "This is a very interesting proposal the Cuban Government offers. We will not waste time discussing any proposed arrangements with the Russians, and we are only interested in what you are offering us."

"We...", Brady knew he must stay in plural. In their society, they would do individually nothing of this magnitude. "... make this offer to anyone interested."

"Of course, Senor Ramon, many may be interested. But we both know very well there are very few entities able to deal with these amounts of money and even fewer able to make use of what you offer. The prices you are asking would leave no room for someone to resell this for a profit." This was exactly the line he knew would be used. The Chinese were so regimented in their thinking. They were very predictable. But again he had to play the total game to waylay suspicion.

"Other proposals are out there and the Russians are always an option. However, let us only concern ourselves with the negotiations between our two countries. A satisfactory arrangement between our two countries would, hopefully, open a greater friendship."

"Something beneficial to all concerned." Brady withheld a smile, knowing the Chinese had every intention of bilking the 'dumb Cubans'.

Brady agreed, "Yes, very beneficial."

"Very well Senor Ramon. There are some parts of your offer we are not comfortable with."

"I am sure I can answer those concerns."

The gentleman on the left spoke for the first time. He obviously had an expertise. "The depth soundings in the Florida Straits. Our information says only two ships were involved in that venture, one a US oceanographic vessel and the other a research vessel owned by an American University. That data will be archived and available to the public by this summer. By this fall it will be published and charted. We can buy the new charts for $20."

"Of course, those are recent depth soundings and chartings the US oceanographic service did last Fall in the straights between Florida and Cuba. Do you know there was a third ship involved? Do you really think they had three ships there just to measure depths? That ship was there to do very precise seismographic readings for oil and gas. Russia has plenty of oil, our two countries do not."

"The records show only two ships, Senor Ramon."

"Of course, there were officially only two ships. The third ship was a privately owned French ocean exploration vessel. It was leased to an Australian ocean exploration company for three months. They contracted with an engineering company in Scotland, which monitors the drilling activity in the North Sea. This Company then contracted with a Canadian oil and gas exploration company to supply the scientists and engineers aboard the vessel. At the beginning of the lease period, this vessel went into a private shipyard in Pascagoula, Mississippi; Haskin Marine. It was in dry-dock for ten days, getting special sounding monitors fitted. At the end of the lease period, it returned to the same shipyard for six days to get the fittings removed. Do you really think they were coincidentally in the Florida Straits at the same time just counting fish?"

"This shipyard is in the US?"

"Yes. Mississippi. The north coast of the Gulf of Mexico."

"We will verify that with the Harbor Master's log."

"Please do."

"When would we see the data?" The first negotiator interjected. Brady saw now that all negotiations would be with this man. The other two were experts in their fields. The one was an oceanographer and the other would be an oil and gas expert.

"The data within the next couple of months. Check the Houston police reports for burglary of a data processing company over the next few weeks. It would then take our engineers a couple of weeks to extract sample data for you. Mr. Freling will be the contact with your delegation in Paris."

The third gentleman of the delegation now began. "These drill bits; they also are not on the open market. How do we know they will be what you promise? We would need to inspect them."

"They can be inspected at time of delivery, although there will be a tiny window of time."

"We will uncrate one and inspect the bearings."

"You are welcome to do what you need in the span of less than an hour."

"That is very small time. We would need at least two hours."

"Two hours is impossible, an hour or possibly a little more."

"That is possible. How many of the bits can you deliver?"

"How many do you want?"

"No less than 10 and no more than 25."

The negotiator intervened. "We would need to know the exact number at least 30 days prior to the exchange."

Again, no surprise, he knew they needed time to 'prepare' the money. "Of course, that will be no problem. Again, Mr.

Freling will call your Commercial Office at the Paris embassy. He will confirm a meeting; the hour given will be the number of units. Read the police report in the Morgan City, Louisiana newspaper in late November for confirmation that the items have been acquired." Brady knew they would set the exchange before it appeared in the newspaper.

"If all you have told us is true, we are prepared to pay $75,000 per drill bit and $3.5 million for the information." This negotiation was just where he thought it would be. About a third of what the original asking had been and probably about half of what they were authorized to pay.

"That is substantially less than what we are asking. I believe we will need to consider other offers. How long is this offer good?"

"Our offers are only good for as long as you are in this room. Do you have another price that may be more reasonable?"

"I believe we could deliver for $150,000 per bit and $6,000,000 for the data." Brady did not want to hit the number they could go to this soon. In fact, he did not want to settle on those expected numbers at all. Let the Chinese negotiator feel he had outdone the unworldly Cuban.

"That is in the right direction, Senor Ramon. I can make one more offer, but that is all. Let us do more checking. If you can deliver, we will pay $100,000 per drill bit and $4 million for the data."

"That would be acceptable if the delivery point is of our choosing, a Central American port."

"We will expect the sample data from Mr. Freling after we see the police report. No other personal meetings will be used. We will pass messages to Mr. Freling. Good evening Senor Ramon."

"I will deliver the data. It will pass directly from me to your people. Let Mr. Freling know if we are to proceed. You have ten days, and then we will need to reopen negotiations with other buyers."

"Yes, I am sure you have many buyers."

"You might be surprised. The Norwegians and Brazilians are very much into both exploration and production."

"Very well Senor Ramon. When we notify Mr. Freling, you may deliver the data in Toronto. Call our embassy in Ottawa and leave a message for Mr. Wou. The next day go to 1:00 p.m. lunch at a restaurant in Toronto, the Lotus Café. Leave the data envelope on the table under your napkin when you leave."

"One last thing. Your only contact shall be with me or Mr. Freling. Not everyone in my government is involved in this adventure. There are some that would demand we involve the Russians and give it to them in the spirit of friendship. The ones in control of this feel we need no more friendship with the Russians. Cuba needs cash. Myself, I am only a messenger."

"We understand. We too would not want to involve 'The Bear'."

The three men facing Brady stood and offered a slight bow; he returned the gesture then exited the room. Probably a little more legwork for Hans, but of course, there would be his bonus.

Brady knew the Chinese would follow him. He took the red eye that night from Vancouver to Montreal, arriving about sunrise. The more sparse Asian population in Montreal would make it that much easier for him to spot a Chinese agent following him.

He had a couple of hours to kill, so he went to a restaurant at the airport and had a leisurely breakfast. From the airport, he took a taxi to a large shopping mall. Entering one side of the mall, then quickly exiting the other side, he could easily lose anyone following him. He had left his rental car at the mall yesterday before he flew to Vancouver. As there was no car rental at the mall and no taxi stand, they would not be able to follow him. He would drive to Ottawa, return the rental car, and fly home.

The four-hour drive to the Ottawa airport would allow him time to process the rest of his plan and get things in order.

The next few weeks would be very busy for Brady. Acquiring the drill bits and arraigning for the bogus data would require a lot of legwork. He would need to go to Houston to secure an office space for a ghost company to be broken into and arrange for a bogus police report in the Houston paper. In Morgan City, he needed to lease a place to store the drill bits until Luis could steal them. He would also organize an inspection tour of security at some NASA facilities, especially Stennis in Mississippi.

However, his most immediate action would be to get the bogus sample seismologic data built.

CHAPTER #7

DSA OFFICE, JUNE

The Defense Security Agency had access to their parent agencies, the department of defense branch that did computer programing type of work. As everything was being converted from printed manuals to computer, the DOD had established an office available to all their branches and departments. As projects unfolded for this group, everything became more complex. The clients were asking for the manuals to be more interactive with practice scenarios. They also wanted assessments and exams on the computer. It had become too much for the office to handle, so they had evolved into a clearinghouse type of organization. They knew the companies and consultants with expertise in every area to get the work completed. All the groups they used had varying levels of security clearances therefor they knew where to send projects depending on the level of security required.

Brady could take his request to them and get to the right consultant for what he needed. This project, having a low need for security, there would most likely be an extensive list to choose from. The only actual security needed was for whom the work was being done. A larger list would be necessary because of the short time available.

By the end of June Brady had contracted with Geological Engineering Data in Denver to get known soundings of the Florida Straits and meld into it some seismological data that would hint at hydrocarbon deposits. They had decided that three separate locations of about ten miles each would be a large enough sample set to satisfy Brady's client. He had spent two days at their office in Denver to make sure they knew what he wanted. They were not told why or how this was to be used. They knew not to be concerned about that, this having a level of government classification.

Right after the Fourth of July, Brady found himself in Houston having lunch with a former teammate from his baseball days at the University of Texas. Mic 'Skinny Red 'Camey was now an FBI agent in the Houston office. This was a very different Houston from where he had spent his childhood.

Brady gave Mic the sketchiest outline of his needs.

Through official channels, the FBI would have wanted to know the complete plan. Because it was on U.S. soil, they would have claimed jurisdiction, which was technically correct. The DSA had no jurisdiction, as there was no threat to any DOD facility or personnel. Then, if they would have allowed it to precede, the FBI would have taken complete control.

The FBI controlling the mission would have been a failure, as some elements of the plan would push the envelope of their comfort zone. They were too PR conscious. But worst of all, they would have demanded to know his source for this information. If he ever mentioned his association with Luis, it would ruin everything. There were no secrets when information got to the upper level of any civilians in any organization. Passing on good information was always felt to be a career builder. That he had a direct connection to the head of the Cuban Intelligence Agency was too important not to be passed along the chain of command. It would probably be put in a memo for an unknown number of eyes to see. Luis would be in prison or executed within six months. Only his confidant, Andy Phillips, knew of this friendship. Andy knew the absolute nature of not disclosing this to anyone. With Andy knowing, the two could develop the mission. Andy could cover Brady's time and expenses through other missions, investigations, and Brady's normal travel seeking information.

"So Skinny, they find anything for you to do here besides paperwork?"

"I see you know what FBI agents do. And let's drop Skinny. I am not so skinny now and as you can see, the red is going into exile on the shower floor. Some of the guys I see around have at least gone to calling me SR. But I am really Mic now. I must admit, it was more fun when I was called that."

"Yeah, it was for me too."

"You don't have much of the Cajun accent anymore, too much time on the continent."

"Change with the needs. I can do Cajun, but most of the people in my own country don't understand me."

"OK Brady, so what do you need from me?"

"Just information, nothing classified. And point me to some leads."

"Unclassified is easy. Now I am leery."

"I need an address, a location to set a ghost company. Then I need a break in at that location to appear in the paper in the police report."

"This is out of your normal operating sphere. How long do you need the location? Getting it in the police report is easy. We have a great relationship with the Houston Police."

"I need the location for just two or three months. My contact may call or visit to validate the existence of the company."

"We have a location we keep for just such instances. We're not using it now, as we have nothing going on now. You know the routine if you try to get approval to use the place, would be after Christmas before it got approved. And we would become part of the package. I'll give you the address. Just hire someone to change the name on the door. When not in use, we never go there. No one ever goes there unless they are sent and if they did, they would not know the last name we put on the door. How about an answering service?"

"We have our usual source for an answering service, one in Pittsburg and one in Tucson. But I think it is best to use one here. My contact is very suspicious; I would prefer to have a Texas accent on our end of the phone."

"We have a very good one we use here for such times as this."

The agent gave Brady the name of the answering service and the address of the unused office. While they finished their lunch, Brady gave his friend a vague outline of the plan. No hint of direct contact with the Cubans or Luis was given. His relationship with Luis was too delicate to drop any trace.

They parted outside the restaurant, with Brady offering a sincere thanks to his friend for making things so easy.

"We are on the same team here, even if the Bureau makes others feel like we aren't sometimes."

Brady spent the rest of that day and the next getting things arranged. Locating and working with a sign painter to change the name on the office door. He also went by the answering service to visit with the manager. The service needed to give the impression that they were not a service, but actually employees of the data analysis firm. He would fax them information they could use with callers, they would not be expected to talk technical information. Brady knew there would be only one call, if that. He contracted the service to answer only during normal business hours on Monday thru Friday.

The next day, he drove east into Louisiana. It felt very much like coming home as he neared Lafayette, since this is where he had gone to high school. However, he could not stop even to visit his folks. He didn't want it to be known that he was in the area. But he had to see the location he would lease to store the drill bits. He passed thru Lafayette on his way to Morgan City. From Morgan City he would continue on thru Houma to the New Orleans airport. His flight back to D.C. was later that night.

During his recent travels, he had been reading all he could about oil drilling and the types of bits used. He had picked the brain of one engineer in Denver that had experience in the exploration business and knew a lot about the equipment. Brady was going to have to call and buy several bits. He could plead he was just a new buyer, but he had to know something about the equipment.

It took a couple of calls to get to the right person to work with him on the order. They referred him to the specialty desk to Karla. These bits were restricted as to where they could go. There was some paperwork and approvals required before the shipment could be filled. Fortunately, Karla was extremely helpful and understanding. She had the order processed and completed in just a couple of days. There was usually a five to six-month delivery on this type of bits. Karla was able to accommodate him with a delivery in mid-November.

While Brady was in Denver, Houston, and Morgan City, Andy had been arraigning an informational inspection trip to some NASA facilities in the southeast, Kennedy Center in Florida, Stennis Center in Mississippi, and the Center in

Huntsville, Alabama. The supposed purpose of the trip was to see the security at these facilities; looking for security measures NASA used that might be helpful for base security at military installations around the world. The real purpose was to learn and see the security at Stennis. This was the facility that Luis had targeted to take the super computers. Brady wanted to see how the guards were armed and their protocol for the use of lethal force.

His inspection tour was scheduled for late September. On that trip, he would then take a few days off to visit friends and family in Lafayette and Baton Rouge.

PART II

CHAPTER # 8

AUGUST, 1987

Brady was sitting in his office after lunch, finishing the report on his recent inspection tour of various facilities in the Southeast including the NASA facilities. Andy poked his head in the door. "Boss wants to see us."

Brady smiled. "What did you do now that is getting me in trouble?"

"Don't think you need my help to get in trouble, let's go."

As they got to the end of the hall where the office area for the Director of the Defense Security Agency, his secretary told them to go right in. Mr. Buford was expecting them.

Gilbert Buford was a Retired Air Force General that had been around Washington since his retirement 20 years ago. He was very efficient and comfortable in this position in the bureaucracy. He aspired for no other job. Knowing he wouldn't go any higher, he didn't play the game of politics. He was not a regular at every social function available, playing golf and sailing on the weekends. He would retire from this job in a few years. The staff at the DSA joked that their director was too soft-spoken and nice to have ever made General.

As Buford stood to shake hands and offered them a seat. "Please sit gentlemen."

Andy replied. "Thank you Sir." They were always formal at initial greetings.

The Director Buford took his seat. "Well, Brady, it looks like your little sojourn to Oslo has panned into what the CIA feels is gold. They are going to do an extraction of the guy and his family next week."

Brady and Andy were both somewhat speechless. This was the first they had heard anything since they had left CIA Headquarters some four months ago. Brady finally asked. "Is that all you know of it?"

"First, I must tell you both that you were right in taking this to the CIA immediately." Always the 'atta boy' talk after things had turned out good. "No, I don't know a lot more about it, which is normal. Except they want someone from here to liaison for military backup. I thought since you helped hatch this, you might want to go."

"I most certainly would, Sir." Brady replied. He relished anything to get him out of the office and into the field.

"OK, I already told them I would assign you this operation. You are to be at their big house tomorrow morning at 10. Security guard at the door will direct you to your meeting."

"Who is their person I will work with there?"

"You know they wouldn't share that with a 'red haired step child' like the DSA." The director said with a smile as he stood to usher them out. "I assume Andy will be able to function without you for a few days."

"Yeah, that is the only time I can get anything done, when I don't have to keep him straight." Andy joked as they left the office.

The next morning at CIA headquarters, they escorted Brady to a conference room. There were three people there to greet him. He had met none of them before. This type of meeting was normal to brief him on the mission plan. With this information, especially the location, he could then get back to his office and get himself current on all the military assets in the area. He had never met the CIA operative controlling the mission on location. He would not meet the agent until he arrived at the control location.

They showed him a map of the location and the general details.

"Mr. Kinin, you have worked with us before in this capacity and the feedback from our people on you has been very good. We are pleased they have assigned you to this."

"I too am happy to help with this operation." Brady replied. He knew this compliment and his reply were not empty bureaucratic chatter. That type of talk didn't happen in this building.

They dimmed the lights and turned on a projector. "We do little of this type of operation any more. So we need you to have the widest array of capabilities available. When dealing with Ivan, there are many surprises waiting. This is a nighttime extraction with no force involved. We don't want to start a shooting war. One person is to make the pickup, as a civilian." Brady would not be told who the active agent would be and he knew there was no sense in asking.

"If they catch him, he will be treated as a spy. They will probably never exchange him, and most likely they would deny anything happened. They would not want word as to why they have someone. As you know, the type of information the asset has, it is very volatile. We assume our man would go to the gulag and the asset and his family would be executed. Questions?"

"Will your man be armed?" Brady asked

"He will have a small side arm. We don't want a firefight. The old guard in Russia that sees things crumbling and

Afghanistan turning to shit would like nothing more than to have a real adversary."

"So any military backup would be pretty much logistical support. Correct?"

"Exactly. We both have Navy in the area. Which gets us to the plan. It will be from the beach on the northern coast of the Black Sea at night. Your control location will be Istanbul."

"A new location for me." Brady replied.

"Not a problem. We will have a house with all the secure communication gear needed. The asset and his family take their holiday every summer about this time. They have had this planned for months, so the timing worked out for us. They always go to the beach near Yalta. Our man is to embark on a medium-sized Turkish freighter from Istanbul to Yalta the night before. This freighter works this area regularly."

"How trustworthy is this freighter and the captain?" Brady inquired.

"Let's just say we have experience with this captain."

In fact, this particular captain had been to some special schooling by both the CIA and British. He was a second generation ally. His father had helped the allies in World War II. The family had lived in Albania, operating a small coastal freighter. He helped smuggle people and arms in and out of Albania when it was occupied by the Germans. After the war, when the Communists took power, they left Albania for Turkey. For his service, the British gave him a medium-sized freighter they had seized. With that, he built a fleet of three freighters working out of Istanbul. Both his brothers captained freighters. A nephew was now a first mate and his youngest son had picked up the notion to help the West against Communism.

The British had sent the son to communication and small arms training. As the British lost interest in the area, they offered him to the CIA. The CIA accepted and continued to use them all. They had installed some very sophisticated communication equipment on his ship. It looked like any ship's normal radio. By entering a special code, it would then send and receive on special frequencies, send a directional signal or to a satellite link. So the CIA highly trusted this captain.

"Will he run or roll over if confronted?" Brady asked.

The CIA maintained their secrecy. "Only such an encounter will tell us."

"Where were we? OK, yes. On the evening of the extraction, our man will leave the freighter about here some ten miles off the coast. He will be in a fourteen foot Zodiac with a forty horse outboard. It is soft sided but specially made with more separate air chambers in the hull. The radar signature should be minimal, as the engine cowling is the only thing to reflect an image. Being right at the water level will also help reduce the signature."

"How many are you bringing out?" Brady knew what the request was.

"All that he asked for. He, his wife, his daughter and his two teenage grandchildren will be extracted."

"So you really like the information he has." Brady made as a statement, not a question.

"We are only doing as we are told. The freighter will continue another hour and a half to the small port at Yalta. It will take about two hours to offload. Then it will return back along the coast to the west. Our man will have five hours to get to the beach, get his passengers, and return to the rendezvous point. Re-boarding will be the dangerous part, especially getting the passengers on the freighter. He can't stop the ship as this would be very unusual and alert the Russians. They will have to get off the Zodiac and on to the boarding platform at night while moving. Once aboard the freighter, the Zodiac will be hoisted to the deck. The freighter will continue on a southwesterly course. They will be about eight miles offshore and it should take them another forty-five minutes to get outside the Russians claimed 12-mile zone. The Russians, although claiming 200 miles, won't stop them then on the high seas."

The speaker changed the screen image to an expanded area of the Black Sea. "One of our destroyers, The USS *Carl King* will be about sixty miles south. Don't want them too close so as to raise any suspicion by the Russians. A few more hours will put the freighter some fifty miles out. At that time, on an open marine frequency, the captain of the freighter will hail the Turkish Navy for assistance with a medical emergency. Information will indicate two crewmen sustained severe back and head injuries. The Turkish Navy will have no ships in the area. *Carl King* will offer help, being less than two hours away. The freighter will accept the offer and turn south to close the distance between the two ships."

"Won't the Russians offer help?" Brady interjected.

"Very unlikely. They are not interested in having civilians aboard their glorious instruments of peace. Especially foreign civilians."

"My understanding of the standard procedure is if we have a vessel within 200 miles of their coast they will have a destroyer shadowing within five to twenty miles." Brady offered his thought.

"True, and having them around will be an obstacle. They usually back off at night; don't play tag in the dark. They will steam their destroyer in closer to the area and observe. They won't interfere, but they may get within a half mile."

"It will make transferring five individuals a problem." Brady again offering his thoughts.

"Definitely, that is why the captain will report two crewmen injured. After the transfer, the *Carl King* will turn south at flank speed to get the injured back to Turkey. They should be back in Istanbul that evening."

"Well, doesn't seem like there is much I can do if there is a problem."

"As always, we are hoping we're sending you on a three-day vacation to Istanbul."

Brady left the CIA headquarters by mid-afternoon. Timing was good; he had a sailing date with Cindi at four on the Chesapeake. He needed to remember to stop and get a bucket of chicken, extra crispy for her, and a bottle of white wine for the dinner outing. His preference was a six-pack of cold brew for the sailing experience.

CHAPTER #9

ISTANBUL, TURKEY, AUGUST 23, 1987

The noise was deafening, and the blast was blinding. Thankfully, both effects were over in a moment. However, the lasting effects were both physical and mental, but they too dwindled over time, but never disappeared.

Brady last remembered seeing was the flash and the two Vietnamese Army Regulars being thrown across the grassy field, or parts of them. The concussion slammed Brady back against a tree. The force of hitting the tree knocked him unconscious and broke his left collarbone. He never knew if it was a mine, a grenade, or a mortar round.

Brady had been in Vietnam about four months. They assigned him to infiltrate villages along the western end of the Demilitarized Zone (DMZ) adjacent to the border with Laos. The Ho Chi Minh Trail was very near there. They had chosen Brady for this because of his ability to speak French. Before the Americans, the French had occupied Vietnam. A lot of the villagers spoke some semblance of French. The villagers in the area were not very cooperative with the South Vietnam Army, and it seemed to the translators that the villagers were not great supporters of either side. The thought was that if an American came to the village and could speak French, the locals might be more open to talk.

They were working out of a forward base called Khe Sanh. He was on his fifth such mission; the first four had not been very fruitful. A squad of South Vietnam Regular Army accompanied him, Lt. Vy and four enlisted. The Lt. spoke very good English. During their time together Brady had come to like the young Lt.

This was the afternoon of their third day. Because of the threat of mines and North Vietnamese Army units, the going through the countryside was very slow. The best they could figure, they were about four miles north of the DMZ and about 2 miles from the border with Laos. The village they were headed to was approximately five miles north.

When Brady regained consciousness, he was in a small hut made of twigs and branches. His back was to the wall, and they tied his arms to a pole running horizontal that was part of the framework for the hut. His wrists were bound to hold his arms straight out from his body. There was a tremendous pain in his left shoulder. It was not yet dark, so he could see a number of rents in his uniform. He assumed these were from shrapnel. The blood around some of them pretty much confirmed to him the cause. He didn't feel he had lost too much blood as he was not particularly weak, just a dandy headache and the shoulder pain. Any attempted movement of his left arm sent a shooting pain through his shoulder. His right arm ached, but not in the same way as his left. He could relieve the right arm by pushing up with his feet and resting his butt on another horizontal pole. That, too, was part of the hut. As long as he stayed like this, the ache in his right side was completely relieved and he could notice a lessening of the pain in the left shoulder.

From outside there were voices and movement, but no

one poked their head in to check on him. By feeling, he knew his boots were gone and his ankles tied together and tethered to the wall.

About the time it got dark, there was a lot of yelling and chattering outside as a truck pulled to a stop. Two men entered the hut with a flashlight. They came right to Brady with the light in his face. The man, seemingly in charge, said something to the other man, who then hurried out the door of the hut.

Speaking to Brady in a language he didn't understand, the man with the flashlight became very irritated. The other man then came back into the hut, carrying what appeared to be a small stool. He placed it by the door and sat down. The man with the flashlight turned to talk to the guard by the door and then began to leave. Just as he got to the door, he turned around, came back to Brady, reached to Brady's neck and yanked his dog tags off, then left. The guard remained seated on the stool by the door.

As the night wore on, Brady became drowsy. But every time he dosed off, his legs and ankles relaxed, which caused his butt to slide off the pole he was balanced against. When he slid off, his arms took all of his body weight, which caused a tremendous shooting pain in his left shoulder.

After a sleepless and painful night, someone brought him a small bowl of food, rice, and something. His right wrist was untied so he could hold the bowl to his mouth to eat. They also gave him a small bowl of water. This routine continued for three more days. There was one guard for the day and one for the night. When he needed to relieve himself, the guard would release his right arm.

The moon gave enough light in thru the opening that served as a door to see shapes and movement. The night guard seemed to get great amusement by using a very sharp bayonet to make small stab wounds in Brady's ankles. This would cause him to flex his ankles and drop off the pole, causing him to wrench in pain. The guard seemed to enjoy this immensely.

Early evening of the third day, an unfamiliar truck pulled into the village. There was a lot of commotion and yelling. What appeared to be a North Vietnam officer came into the hut and looked at Brady for a moment, then turned and left.

Late that night, Brady felt some movement at his right hand. A rock was slipped into his hand and his wrist was cut loose from the pole. Not knowing if the guard was awake, Brady did not move. He then felt his ankles were no longer restrained to the wall, although still secured together. He felt something slide on to the pole behind his butt. A voice in very good English said, 'knife behind you'. It was the voice of Lt. Vy.

Brady waited a few minutes, then made some noise to arouse the guard. He indicated to the guard that he needed to relieve himself. The guard went through his usual routine. He came to Brady with the blade of the bayonet shining before Brady's face. He would then go to one knee to begin his tormenting ritual. This time, however, when the guard began to kneel, Brady dealt a crushing blow to the side of the man's head with the rock in his right hand. The man did not fall but sank to his knees and weakly tried to shuffle away. Brady was able to bring his legs up and get his ankles around the man's neck. The cord holding his ankles together gave him enough grip to pull the man toward him. While doing this, he reached behind him to grab the knife from the pole. As the guard came forward he started to yell, very little sound come out before Brady plunged the knife into the man's throat. As he fell, Brady untangled his legs from the body. He used the knife to cut the cord holding his ankles, then turned to cut the cord holding his left wrist. The action of the last thirty seconds had caused terrible pain in his shoulder. His arm fell to his side to just hang there.

Brady moved to the door but saw no one. There were huts on either side of his, he went left. After a couple of steps, a man with a rifle came from between the huts and yelled something. As the man began to raise his rifle, Brady, leaving his feet, lunged at him with his right shoulder leading. The man turned to deflect the charge. As they were chest to chest, Brady drove the knife in just below his breastbone. With this as a lever, Brady was able to pull the guard sideways as they both continued to the ground.

Two explosions shattered the hut they were next, about a second apart. The guard's body shielded Brady from the shrapnel, but the concussion rolled the two of them ten feet away. Before Brady could regain his senses from the blast, Lt. Vy was there, pulling him to his feet.

Pulling Brady along, they ran up the road at least two hundred yards before Lt. Vy disappeared into the heavy foliage at the roadside, Brady immediately behind him. When in the brush a few yards, they stopped to rest. Vy put his finger to his lips to indicate no noise. They waited about 10 minutes. When they heard nothing, they made their way back to the road and began a slow jog for another 30 minutes. There was a trail leading to the left that Vy turned down.

After another 30 minutes, they stopped to rest. This was the first they spoke. After inquiring about Brady's injuries, he explained what had happened.

Lt. Vy wasn't sure if their point man had tripped a delayed fuse on a mine or a grenade was thrown. Sporadic gunfire erupted, which drove him and the other two soldiers back into the trees. There appeared to be twenty to twenty-five heavily armed North Vietnam regulars. They did not engage the squad but remained to see what your injuries were. When Vy saw them pick you up and carry you off, he knew you were not seriously injured. He sent the two men back to their base camp at Khe Sanh to report the location and that they had taken you prisoner. The camp was at least a day and a half away. He remained to follow so they would know where you had been taken.

The day the truck arrived, he knew you would be taken the next day, so he had to make the move to free you that night. Most of the soldiers were sleeping in the hut that exploded. The guard yelling had done just what needed to be done. The yell had brought the sleeping soldiers to their feet. With a few seconds for them to be standing, the two grenades he threw in had maximum effect. It must have taken them all, as no one was chasing them.

The two continued along the trail at a brisk walk for another couple of hours until they could see the sky beginning to lighten. Vy directed him off the trail some 30 yards, being careful not to leave any signs of where they left the trail. He adjusted some leaves and branches for Brady to lie on. They would only travel at night. Vy would keep watch for now. After three days of little sleep, Brady was asleep before he was done arguing with Vy about taking turns. Even the pain in his shoulder did not disturb his sleep.

When he awoke, the sky was turning dark. Vy was sitting nearby, leaning against a tree. He handed Brady a can of GI field rations. Brady was able to keep watch while he slept. He explained to Brady he had disassembled his rifle and buried it in the forest. It would do them no good now. If confronted, they would be easily overrun and killed. Not being seen was their only option. They did not want to travel too early in the evening.

Brady figured it was about 10 that night when they moved back to the trail, again being careful to not leave signs of their passing. They walked thru the night, probably 8 hours before the night sky began to give way. They moved off the trail just as the morning before. Water was not a problem, as there were numerous streams. Their progress was very slow, maybe 8 to 10 miles a night. If they heard any unusual sound, they would move off the trail and sit quietly for 20 to 30 minutes. If they came to a village, they would have to retreat and find another trail around the village.

During their rest periods, Vy had explained his plan to Brady. They had gone north, then turned west. Brady's captors would look for them to the south, plus there were too many enemy units along the DMZ. They had turned west into Laos, which they were in now.

The next night, they would probably cross the Ho Chi Min trail. Would need to be very careful and do it at the darkest time of night. After getting a few hours across the trail, they would split up. Vy, dressed as he now was in traditional mountain peasant clothes, would work his way back to their base camp. As a Vietnamese he would not be welcome in Laos, even by the peasants. Dressed as he was, he could move through the forests and fields of Vietnam. He spoke the dialect of that area of the country.

Brady was to continue northwest, staying along the mountains for cover. He was to continue in the northerly direction until he came to a river that ran east to west. Then stay in the forest south of the river. The mountains would run in a somewhat west direction. Stay south of the river for about eight to ten days, traveling only at night. When this river curved to the south, he was to cross it, then continue due west in the forest. Another three or four days would bring him to a large river running south, the Mekong River. This was the border between Laos and Thailand. Once across into Thailand he would be safer, but not much. He must still travel at night and avoid contact. There was an American Air Base along there to his west. Watch and listen for the planes, then follow to where they go.

They could hear the aerial attacks and bombs all night. The North Vietnamese moved their war supplies down the Ho Chi Minh Trail mostly at night. The Americans attacked them all night. It was not hard to know they were close. When they got to the trail, it was down the middle of a wide open area. The Americans had defoliated the jungle along the trail. They waited at the edge of the open area for an hour or so to make sure no convoys were coming. Then they crossed the Ho Chi Min Trail without incident. They slept that day about two miles from their crossing point, then parted company just after dark. Vy had given him all the remaining GI rations, which were about eight days' supply. He had also shown Brady which roots and plants were edible. After this ordeal, Brady was never again much of a salad eater.

After a couple more days, Brady got into a routine. His shoulder hurt, but they had fashioned a sling that kept the weight of his arm off the shoulder. It was on the fifth night he came to the west flowing river. He then went west for ten days until he was certain the river had turned south. Using only one arm, he had more difficulty swimming across than he thought. The fourth night on a westerly course brought him to the Mekong River. This was much larger and had more current than the last river. He had to rummage around in the forest to find a piece of tree large enough to help him stay afloat. By the time he felt mud under his feet, he figured the current had taken him two miles downstream. He had passed two small riverside villages. This reminded him to stay away from these small villages, which seemed more numerous here in Thailand.

He began to hear the sounds distinctly of the air traffic all day and night. The roar of jet planes, the buzz of props and the distinctive thump of helicopters. Staying deep in the trees during daylight hours, he was not able to see any aircraft.

After a couple more days, he began to get a bearing on the direction the noise ended. The next night brought him close enough he could hear the difference in intensity used for takeoff. One more night should bring him to the base.

The next day, as he settled down, it was cloudy and rainy. No traffic today to lead him. About mid-afternoon, the blast of jets taking off jolted him awake. Sounded like he was next to the runway. No alarm clock had ever sounded so sweet. The weather had cleared enough for air operations. He did not want to approach the base at night. So he needed to move some now while it was light to know his precise location. He got about a mile from the base before he could access his position. There was a wide cleared area outside the perimeter fence with three rows of razor wire before the fence. He was across the runways from the base buildings.

Waiting until dark, he then skirted the perimeter, staying at least a half mile away from the fence. He guessed there would be a minefield surrounding the base. The eastern sky was just hinting at day light when Brady came to what appeared to be a well-maintained road. He backed away into the brush to wait for full daylight.

CHAPTER # 10

VIETNAM, 1973

The noise was deafening and the blast was blinding, thankfully both effects were over in a moment. However the lasting effects were both physical and mental, but they too dwindled over time, but never disappeared.

The last Brady remembered seeing was the flash and the two Vietnamese Army Regulars being thrown across the grassy field, or parts of them. The concussion threw Brady back against a tree. The force of hitting the tree knocked him unconscious and broke his left collar bone. He never knew if it was a mine, a grenade or a mortar round.

Brady had been in Vietnam about four months. For all of January and February he was assigned to infiltrate villages along the western end of the Demilitarized Zone (DMZ) adjacent to the border with Laos. The Ho Chi Minh Trail was very near there. Brady had been chosen for this because of his ability to speak French. Before the Americans, Vietnam had been occupied by the French. A lot of the villagers spoke some semblance of French. The villagers in the area were not very cooperative with the South Vietnam Army, and it seemed to the translators that the villagers were not great supporters of either side. The thought was that if an American came to the village and was able to speak French the locals might be more open to talk.

They were working out of a forward base called Khe Sanh. He was on his third such mission; the first two had not been very fruitful. He was accompanied by a squad of South Vietnam Regular Army. A Lt. Vy and four enlisted. The Lt. spoke very good English. During their time together Brady had come to like the young Lt. This was the afternoon of their third day. Because of the threat of mines and North Vietnamese Army units the going through the countryside was very slow. The best they could figure, they were about four miles north of the DMZ and about 2 miles from the border with Laos. The village they were headed to was approximately five miles north.

When Brady regained consciousness he was in a small hut made of twigs and branches. His back was to the wall and his arms were tied to a pole running horizontal that was part of the framework for the hut. His wrists were bound to hold his arms straight out from his body. There was a tremendous pain in his left shoulder. It was not yet dark so he could see a number of rents in his uniform. He assumed these were from shrapnel. The blood around some of them pretty much confirmed to him the cause. He didn't feel he had lost too much blood as he was not particularly weak, just a dandy headache and the shoulder pain. Any attempted movement of his left arm sent a shooting pain through his shoulder. His right arm ached but not in the same way as his left. He was able to relieve the right arm by pushing up with his feet and resting his butt on another horizontal pole that too was part of the hut. As long as he stayed like this the ache in his right side was completely relieved and he could notice a lessening of the pain in the left shoulder.

From outside there were voices and movement but no one poked their head in to check on him. By feel he knew his boots were gone and his ankles were tied together and tethered to the wall.

About the time it got dark there was a lot of yelling and chattering outside as a truck pulled to a stop. Two men entered the hut with a flashlight. They came right to Brady with the light in his face. The man seemingly in charge said something to the other man who then hurried out the door of the hut. The man with the flashlight spoke to Brady, none of which he understood. The other man then came back in the hut carrying what appeared to be a small stool. He placed it by the door and sat down. The man with the flashlight turned to talk to the guard by the door, and then began to leave. Just as he got to the door he turned around, came back to Brady, reached to Brady's neck and yanked his dog tags off, then left. The guard remained seated on the stool by the door.

As the night wore on Brady became drowsy. But every time he dosed off his legs and ankles relaxed which caused his butt to slide off the pole he was balanced against. When he slid off all of his body weight was taken by his arms which caused a tremendous shooting pain in his left shoulder.

After a sleepless and painful night someone brought him a small bowl of food, rice and something. His right wrist was untied so he could hold the bowl to his mouth to eat. He was also given a small bowl of water. This routine continued for three more days. There was one guard for the day and one for night. When he needed to relieve himself the guard would release his right arm.

The moon gave enough light in thru the opening that served as a door to see shapes and movement. The night guard seemed to get great amusement by using a very sharp bayonet to make small stab wounds in Brady's ankles. This would cause him to flex his ankles and drop off the pole causing him to wrench in pain. The guard seemed to enjoy this immensely.

Early evening of the third day a truck pulled into the village. There was a lot of commotion and yelling. What appeared to be a North Vietnam officer came in the hut and looked at Brady for a moment then turned and left.

Late that night Brady felt some movement at his right hand. A rock was slipped into his hand and his wrist was cut loose from the pole. Not knowing if the guard was awake, Brady did not move. He then felt his ankles were no longer restrained to the wall although still secured together. He felt something slide on to the pole behind his butt. A voice in very good English said, 'knife behind you'. It was the voice of Lt. Vy.

Brady waited a few minutes then made some noise to arouse the guard. He indicated to the guard that he needed to relieve himself. The guard went through his usual routine. He came to Brady with the blade of the bayonet shining before Brady's face. He would then go to one knee to begin his tormenting ritual. This time, however, when the guard began to kneel down Brady dealt a crushing blow to the side of the man's head with the rock in his right hand. The man did not fall but sank to his knees and weakly tried to shuffle away. Brady was able to bring his legs up and get his ankles around the man's neck. The cord holding his ankles together gave him enough grip to pull the man toward him. While doing this he reached behind him to grab the knife on the pole. As the guard came forward he started to yell, very little sound come out before Brady plunged the knife into the man's throat. As he fell Brady untangled his legs from the body. He used the knife to cut the cord holding his ankles then turned to cut the cord holding his left wrist. The action of the last thirty seconds had cause terrible pain in his shoulder. His arm fell to his side to just hang there.

Brady moved to the door but saw no one. There were huts on either side of his, he went left. After a couple of steps a man with a rifle came from between the huts and yelled something. As the man began to raise his rifle, Brady leaving his feet, lunged at him with his right shoulder leading. The man turned to deflect the charge. As they were chest to chest Brady drove the knife in just below his breast bone. With this as a lever Brady was able to pull the guard sideways as they both continued to the ground.

The hut they were next to was shattered by two explosions about a second apart. The guard's body shielded Brady from the shrapnel but the concussion rolled the two of them ten feet away. Before Brady could regain his senses from the blast Lt. Vy was there pulling him to his feet. Pulling Brady along, they ran up the road at least two hundred yards before Lt. Vy disappeared into the heavy foliage at the roadside, Brady immediately behind him. When in the brush a few yards they stopped to rest. Vy put his finger to his lips to indicate no noise. They waited about 10 minutes. When they heard nothing they made their way back to the road and began a slow jog for another 30 minutes. There was a trail leading to the left that Vy turned down. After another 30 minutes they stopped to rest. This was the first they spoke. After inquiring of Brady's injuries he explained what had happened.

Lt. Vy wasn't sure if their point man had tripped a delayed fuse on a mine or a grenade was thrown. Sporadic gunfire erupted which drove him and the other two soldiers back into the trees. There appeared to be twenty to twenty five heavily armed North Vietnam regulars. They did not engage the squad but remained to see what your injuries were. When Vy saw them pick you up and carry you off he knew you were not seriously injured. He sent the two men back to their base camp at Khe Sanh to report the location and that you had been taken prisoner. The camp was at least a day and a half away. He remained to follow so they would know where you had been taken.

The day the truck arrived he knew you would be taken the next day so he had to make the move to free you that night. Most of the soldiers were sleeping in the hut that exploded. The guard yelling had done just what needed to be done. The yell had brought the sleeping soldiers to their feet. With a few seconds for them to be standing the two grenades he threw in had maximum effect. It must have taken them all as no one was chasing them.

The two continued along the trail at a brisk walk for another couple of hours until they could see the sky beginning to lighten. Vy directed him off the trail some 30 yards being careful not to leave any signs of where they left the trail. He adjusted some leaves and branches for Brady to lie on. They would only travel at night. Vy would keep watch for now. After three days of little sleep, Brady was asleep before he was done arguing with Vy about taking turns. Even the pain in his shoulder did not disturb his sleep.

When he awoke the sky was turning dark. Vy was sitting nearby leaning against a tree. He handed Brady a can of GI field rations. He said Brady could keep watch while he slept. He explained to Brady he had disassembled his rifle and buried it in the forest. It would do them no good now, if confronted they would be easily overrun and killed. Not being seen was their only option. They did not want to travel too early in the evening.

Brady figured it was about 10 that night when they moved back to the trail, again being careful to not leave signs of their passing. They walked thru the night, probably 8 hours before the night sky began to give way. They moved off the trail just as the morning before. Water was not a problem as there were numerous streams. Their progress was very slow, maybe 8 to 10 miles a night. If they heard any unusual sound they would move off the trail and sit quietly for 20 to 30 minutes. If they came to a village they would have to retreat and find another trail around the village.

During their rest periods Vy had explained his plan to Brady. They had gone north then turned west. Brady's captors would be looking for them to the south, plus there were too many enemy units along the DMZ. They had turned west into Laos, which they were in now. The next night they would probably cross the Ho Chi Min trail. Would need to be very careful and do it at the darkest time of night. After getting a few hours across the trail they would split up. Vy, dressed as he now was in traditional mountain peasant clothes would work his way back to their base camp. As a Vietnamese he would not be welcome in Laos, even by the peasants. Dressed as he was he could move through the forests and fields of Vietnam, he spoke the dialect of that area of the country.

Brady was to continue northwest staying along the mountains for cover. He was to continue in the northerly direction until he came to a river that ran east to West. Then stay in the forest south of the river. The mountains would run in a somewhat west direction. Stay south of the river for about eight to ten days, traveling only at night. When this river curved to the south he was to cross it then continue due West in the forest. Another three or four days would bring him to a large river running south, the Mekong River. This was the border between Laos and Thailand. Once across into Thailand he would be safer, but not much. He must still travel at night and avoid contact. There was an American Air Base along there to his west. Watch and listen for the planes then follow to where they go.

They could hear the aerial attacks and bombs all night. The North Vietnamese moved their war supplies down the Ho Chi Minh Trail mostly at night. The Americans attacked them all night. It was not hard to know they were close. When they got to the trail it was down the middle of a wide open area. The Americans had defoliated the jungle along the trail. They waited at the edge of the open area for an hour or so to make sure no convoys were coming. Then they crossed the Ho Chi Min Trail without incident. They slept that day about two miles from their crossing point, then parted company just after dark. Vy had given him all of the remaining GI rations which were about eight days' supply. He had also shown Brady which roots and plants were edible. After this ordeal Brady was never again much of a salad eater.

After a couple more days Brady got in a routine. His shoulder hurt but they had fashioned a sling that kept the weight of his arm off the shoulder. It was on the fifth night he came to the west flowing river. He then went west for ten days until he was certain the river had turned south. Using only one arm he had more difficulty swimming across than he thought. The fourth night on a westerly course brought him to the Mekong River. This was much larger and had more current than the last river. He had to rummage around in the forest to find a piece of tree large enough to help him stay afloat. By the time he felt mud under his feet he figured the current had taken him two miles downstream. He had passed two small riverside villages. He would need to remember to stay away from these small villages, which seemed more numerous here in Thailand. He began to hear the sounds distinctly of the air traffic all day and night. The roar of jet planes, the buzz of props and the distinctive thump of helicopters. Staying deep in the trees during daylight hours he was not able to see any aircraft. After a couple more days he began to get a bearing on the direction the noise ended. The next night brought him close enough he could hear the difference in intensity used for takeoff. One more night should bring him to the base.

The next day as he settled down it was cloudy and rainy, no traffic today to lead him. About mid-afternoon he was jolted awake by the blast of jets taking off, sounded like he was next to the runway. No alarm clock had ever sounded so sweet. The weather had cleared enough for air operations. He did not want to approach the base at night. So he needed to move some now while it was light to know his precise location. He got about a mile from the base before he could access his position. There was wide cleared area outside the perimeter fence with three rows of razor wire before the fence. He was across the runways from the base buildings.

Waiting until dark he then skirted the perimeter, staying at least a half mile away from the fence. He guessed there would be a mine field surrounding the base. The eastern sky was just hinting at day light when Brady came to what appeared to be a well maintained road. He backed away into the brush to wait for full daylight.

CHAPTER #11

The sun was well above the horizon when one of the guard dogs at the security gate announced the lone figure approaching. The high power optics in the two nearest guard towers focused on the scruffy figure. From two hundred yards Brady could tell all the men and two dogs came to high alert. Brady kept moving at a slow study pace. At fifty yards, Brady stopped and yelled. 'US Army, get your duty officer.' One man got on the radio, while another took a few steps toward Brady. 'Stay where you are, no closer.'

In less than a minute, a jeep came to a screeching halt just inside the gate and four armed security men jumped out. Two of the new arrivals and two of the handlers with dogs spread out along the fence with rifles ready. The other two new arrivals began walking slowly down the road toward Brady.

"Are you the duty officer?" Brady yelled. He had not talked in such a long time, he was not sure of the volume of his voice.

The one leading the group was about twenty yards away. "Who are you, and what do you want?"

"I am Lt. Brady Kinin, United States Army."

"Yeah and I am Daisy Duck. Put your arms up and get on your knees."

Brady went to his knees and put his right arm in the air. "I can't lift my left arm. My collar bone is broken." The second man circled around behind Brady. The first man was now about five yards away and Brady could see his arm patch. "Sgt. I have been walking thru the jungle for eighteen days to get here."

"Are you armed?" The Sgt's tone of voice was still menacing.

"I have a knife in my belt. I will remove it."

"Very slowly, Mudbug has a gun five feet from the back of your head."

As soon as the knife hit the ground, the Sgt's foot was on it and Brady's right arm was grabbed from behind. "OK, son, tell me what is going on here."

"Did you say Mudbug? You got you a Cajun here?" Brady inquired with enthusiasm.

From behind Brady. "Yeaa, ya don lik Ka-jons?"

"Yo soun be Houma-T-ba-doo. I be Beau Brid." Brady replied in his deepest Cajun drawl.

"Yo soun mo city guy."

"I be some La-fy-ette." Replied Brady as he felt the tension diminish. The Sgt. in front him was relaxing his posture.

"Me ontee, Miss. Pel-t-a teach dare."

"Ho skul mat, I do hur class."

"Damn Mudbug, he sounds just like you." From the Sgt. with the hint of a smile.

"He be wit us Sarg. He know I be Houma and know ma ontee, he be fra dow baa-u."

The Sgt. kicked the knife away as he reached to take

Brady's elbow and help him up. "Get up son, let's figure this out."

In less than a minute, the Sgt. was a complete believer. By the time he had walked Brady back to the guardhouse, a base ambulance was pulling to a stop. The entire base there had a great time referring to the Sgt. as Daisy Duck.

They spent the next three days establishing who he was and what to do with him. Without dog tags to help, it took some doing. After a good medical exam, they deemed him in very good shape considering his ordeal. He had lost 26 pounds, and it really showed. He didn't recognize himself in the mirror. His cheeks were sunken and the bones under his eyes protruded, as did his ribs and pelvic bones. X-rays showed his collarbone was a clean fracture, but all the movement had caused some displacement. It would have to be surgically reset, probably stateside. But that decision would be made elsewhere.

Four days later, he was on a transport to Clark Air Force Base in the Philippines. Then, the next day, he was on a medevac flight to California. He had a sling fashioned to relieve all the pressure on his left shoulder, so he could walk to and sit on the flights. They landed in Travis Air Force Base northeast of San Francisco. The patients were then to be separated to their own service hospitals. Air Force to the hospital at Travis, Army to Letterman in San Francisco and Navy/Marine to Oaknoll in Oakland.

While waiting for transportation, a change of routing came. The mobile ones like Brady were being sent on east. He was on another medevac heading for Texas. The Air Force and some Army were going to San Antonio, the Navy and some Army would continue to Washington, DC. Brady was routed to DC.

When they stopped in San Antonio Brady got off with

those deplaning there, with the amount of confusion he didn't think he would be missed anytime soon. He wanted to be treated here, as it was closer to his home. He got on the bus to the Army hospital there. It didn't get figured out until the medevac flight was long gone. Since he was there, they kept him.

His surgery was two days later. They had to put a small plate in his shoulder to stabilize the fracture. His folks came over from Lafayette and he was released three days later on medical leave to go back to Louisiana with them. He didn't explain the full story of his ordeal to them. Six weeks later, he was fit for duty and received new orders to NATO in Europe.

It was almost three years before everything got officially corrected in his service record. Lt. Vy never made it back to Khe Sanh; he had been detained and put in a labor camp by the North Vietnamese for two years. After being released, he worked his way to a US contingent in Thailand, and was brought to the U.S. as a refugee. They finally coupled his recount of his experience with Brady's. Brady's dog tags were found with the material that was turned over after the POW exchange in Hanoi. Brady was officially listed as a former Prisoner of War-Escaped.

By this time, he was posted in Lisbon. He was called to Washington, DC, for an official awarding of medals. His friend and boss, Andy Phillips, accompanied him. The ceremony was at the White House Rose Garden. Included in the small group in attendance were his parents, just then learning about his ordeal.

The President awarded Brady a Silver Star, POW Medal, and his Purple Heart. Along with Brady, Lt. Vy was awarded a Defense Superior Service Medal for his part in Brady's escape.

Brady had later gone to see Vy at a refugee placement

camp in Wisconsin. After that, he lost contact with him. He heard a Federal agency had recruited Vy, either the CIA or Drug Enforcement Administration, then posted him back to Southeast Asia.

CHAPTER #12

ISTANBUL, TURKEY, AUGUST 24, 1987

Brady and Sofi were sitting at the kitchen table over a cup of coffee when one of the communication techs came in and handed Sofi a piece of paper. She quickly read the note, then exclaimed, "Aw shit." Then handed the paper to Brady.

It read, 'Mission scrubbed. Point man in a hospital in Rome. Broken hip. Hit by a taxi.'

Brady looked at the stunned agent across the table. "No back-up plan, no replacement?" He asked.

"Too late. The ship needs to depart between one and three. It is already scheduled with the harbormaster."

Brady knew the emotional cost to Hans' family of a canceled movement. There would also be the loss of vital information to the U.S. It would probably cost that family their lives.

"You can't cancel this. Do you know the importance of this extraction?" Brady was almost pleading.

"I have no idea what this is about, only the logistics of the extraction. I don't even know who the point man is. We are big on the need to know thing."

"What about the ship?"

"I have to go there and let the captain know."

"Can I go in his place, be the point man?"

"You don't know the plan."

"I know the basics; you can give me the rest."

"I don't know that much, especially the contact for the beach at Yalta." She couldn't believe Brady was serious about doing this.

"That can be made to work. These people will be desperate. I know the feeling. They will respond to any appearance of help. They know it is their only chance." Brady was not so much pleading any more. He was commanding.

"I am sorry; I do not have the authority to allow this change."Sofi responded.

"You don't have to authorize it. But do you have the authority to prevent it?"

Sofi's eyes lit up. "You are dead serious, aren't you? Let's hope you are not just dead." Then, in a much softer tone, she continued. "I do understand the stakes must be very high to do an extraction, especially of five people."

"OK, give me all the information you have on the mission."

"I guess that would qualify you pretty much as need to know." Sofi said with a sly smile. "If this works, I will be in for a severe slap on the wrists. If it doesn't work out, I might wish I could go to the Gulag."

Sofi went to the communication techs and told them to hold tight, don't breakdown any equipment yet. Brady made a fresh pot of coffee.

The two talked for the next few hours, until it was time for him to head for the port to board the freighter. She would need to go with Brady to explain things to the captain. She knew the man, as she had worked with him before.

After the ship had sailed, she would let Washington know

what was happening and reactivate the system. There would be some pretty nasty messages, but there was nothing they could do to stop it. The ship could not be stopped. The captain was one with a contrary streak and would probably ignore messages to abort the mission.

CHAPTER #13

DSA OFFICES

Andy Phillips was in his office finishing his second cup of coffee. He had just gotten his day organized. Andy felt he could get a lot of paperwork done today. Of the three field agents he supervised, one was on leave for a week, another was on a routine security tour of Northern Europe, and Brady was out of his hair for a few days. Since Brady was on the assignment with the CIA, anything Brady came up with would be theirs for a few more days.

Andy was just pulling the least interesting forms from the stack on his desk when the communications supervisor barged into his office. No need to knock, as Andy rarely shut his door.

"Andy, this just came in. What you submariners would call a flash message. Says it is for the director's eyes only. Since he is on a plane somewhere between Seoul and Anchorage, I figure you're the guy." He shut the door and handed the piece of paper to Andy.

"Oh crap, you shutting the door is not a good sign." Andy said as he took the paper and opened it. He read the message, shook his head, then read it again. "Aw shit, I can't believe he did this. Damn it to hell." Andy exclaimed as he slammed the paper on his desk.

"Is this a joke Brady had you pull on me when everyone is gone." He knew better,the communications guy was too straight and nervous to step out of protocol.

"Oh, no, sir. I would never do something like that. Dealing with Mr. Kinin would only get me in trouble." The man quickly retorted.

"Yes, he has a way of doing that to us all. I hope this is a misinterpretation. Let me call the CIA now."

"No reply to send now? Should I message the director?"

"Better wait until I sort this out. Shut the door on your way out and tell the gals I am not taking any routine calls." Andy said as he dismissed the man and reached for his Rolodex.

After being transferred a couple of times and waiting for the line to be signaled as secure. The CIA agent in charge of the Black Sea operation came on the line. "This is Deputy Director Andy Phillips of the DSA. I just got a very disturbing message from you about your mission today."

"You are damn right it is disturbing. This has gone all the way up to our director. What in the hell kind of stunt is your man pulling there?"

"First of all, he is your man this week. All I know is what is in the message I received. I guess from your tone, I didn't misread it. Can you please enlighten me?"

"You know the general plan of the mission, I am told. Correct?"

"Yes, a solo operator making a night time extraction. The control point is Istanbul. No other details."

"Our operative was to embark on a freighter a few hours ago. He was flying in that morning. Apparently, on his way to the airport in Rome he was hit by a taxi. He sustained a broken hip and leg, he is in the hospital for a few days. Your man did not want the mission to be scrubbed, so he hopped aboard the freighter. "

"Why didn't your control agent stop him?"

"That is something the agent is going to have to thoroughly explain. Everyone here is furious with both of them."

"Can't say I am any too happy with him myself right now." In truth, Andy was more concerned for Brady than unhappy. Why would he have expected anything less from their agent that was at his best when making rapid decisions under stress, although this decision was way over the top and extremely dangerous? As Andy knew from a submarine patrol into unfriendly waters, the Russians were ones to shoot first and ask questions later. A few bullet holes in the sail of their submarine had been proof of that. Andy's best friend was putting himself in severe danger.

"Just how good is Kinin?"

"You know everything about him. I have never been around anyone that could think on the move like he can. Isn't there any way you can stop the ship?"

"It is in international waters. We have sent a message to the captain. We've not gotten any response in return. The captain, too, is a bit of a maverick."

"Great, sounds like we have two peas in a pod."

"But I am afraid they are heading for a boiling stew pot."

"Can you give me any more details? Maybe I can at least pick up his part of the mission."

As the agent told him the plan and the timing, Andy was trying to formulate a strategy. After another ten minutes, they explained everything. "Please, if you hear anything from the ship or your control agent, let me know. I will be here until about five. Let me give you my home phone. I will be around all evening."

"I wish I could do the same. All the screaming around this

place will pretty much keep us here most of the night. Mr. Phillips, would you like to come here to our control room tomorrow during the operation? We know you have the right clearances."

"I would very much like that."

"He should go on the water at five thirty our time tomorrow afternoon. Be here at five. The security guard will expect you. Meet Agent Mike Jenkins."

"See you at five, thanks." Andy replied as he replaced the phone.

Andy grabbed his coffee cup and headed for the break room.

Back in his office with a full cup of coffee and a much needed stop at the men's room, he reached for his Rolodex.

Going thru the proper numbers and commands to get a secure line, he heard a friendly voice. "Sixth Fleet Headquarters, Petty Officer Ryan, how may I help you?"

"Mr. Ryan, this is Andrew Phillips with the Defense Security Agency. I would like to speak with your Sixth Fleet Deputy Commander, Admiral McGrew. Find him wherever he is. This is top priority. As in a flash message, do you understand?"

Rear Admiral Dan McGrew had done his first tour out of nuke school on a submarine with Andy. Andy was a Lt. Commander and the navigation officer. As such, the Navigator spent a lot of time with junior officers, helping them to qualify. The two had kept in touch ever since. Andy was sure McGrew would get his third star any time now.

"Yes sir, I am submarine service. The Deputy Commander is in his office with someone. Are you sure I need to disturb him?"

"Yes, tell him who it is, and it is a flash."

In less than a minute, Andy heard a voice he recognized.

"Phillips, you don't have to flash. I'll take your call. How is my favorite double dipper?"

"Just wait, your time will come. But I shudder to think when it comes, you will probably be my boss. You've got to pick up a couple more stars before then."

"The department of alarm and fence repair. Hopefully, I can do better than that. So how is everybody?"

"Personally, everything is great Dan. But that is not what this is about. We have a problem."

"You taught me not to take on someone else's problem."

"You still shouldn't. But this is OUR problem. You know about the event tomorrow night in the Black Sea?"

"The general plan, one of our ships, the USS *CARL KING* is involved. The Forrestal is finishing a port call in Istanbul. Will be less traffic out there, theirs and ours."

"Yeah, well, it is becoming a bigger problem."

Andy explained the situation. They did not properly verse the operative going in on the details of the plan. Most everything he will know will come to him secondhand.

"What type of help is *Carl King* able to give?" Andy asked the Admiral.

"Very little, besides what is already planned. We were told this was definitely not to be a hot mission. No rough stuff."

"Does *Carl King* carry any small boats?"

"Just the usual tender."

"Can you get a Zodiac out to her?"

"Give me a few minutes. We have a Seal Chief on staff here, just came from an active unit a few months ago. He will be current on the capabilities. Don't know if he is still in the building. I will get back to you within the half hour." Andy heard the line disconnect. Dan was nothing if not efficient. He had taken the bull by the horns, no time for a goodbye.

By the time Andy had sent a message to his director, called his wife about no plans for tonight, and gotten his fourth cup of coffee, and hit the men's room again, his phone was ringing.

"This is Phillips."

"Andy, my Seal was a wealth of information. We have things moving here. COMSIX is out with the fleet. One last ride before he retires. What we are doing now is not operational orders, just moving people and things, so we don't need his approval. The Seal unit at Sig has some Zodiacs without ridged hulls and the engine cowlings are a special composite material. That makes them give virtually no radar signal. He is getting two of them on a 130 with a team of two men per boat and a unit commander. We will get them to the air station at Ankara tonight. I will reroute *Carl King* south. The fleet sends a chopper out a couple times a week on a mail run. It stops at Ankara for fuel. It will go out tomorrow with the boats and the Seals, will look like a normal run, mid-day, nothing unusual for Ivan to see. Any type of air cover would really rattle Ivan. The best that could be done is the choppers on *Carl King*. I can get our carrier group to the eastern Med, but Ankara will be closer. The F-16s at Incirlik could be put on runway alert, but as soon as they head north, Ivan will put up a flight of MIGS. Might see if the Air Force has a team of Rescue Jumpers there, they could have a 130 on alert. I would send some more Seals and leave our 130 in Ankara, but that would really be a slap in the face if they have jumpers there. I can fix the mail run, but you will have to work your magic to get their F-16s and the jumpers. If need be, I can still get a larger Seal team to Ankara by tomorrow night. And by the way, Andy, the skipper on *Carl King* is a good man. You might remember him. Your last duty, Intel at CINCLANTFLT, he was a junior Lt. on your staff, Bill Kaar. He will do the right thing. He won't tolerate any interference from Ivan."

"Yes, I remember him. He has a ship already?"

"He was deep selected for Lt. Commander and Commander. He deserved it. When I was COMSUBSEVEN, he was XO of the flagship. I took a few rides on it, got to know Kaar. Glad to have him here."

"Rising like that, he will be your boss before you have time to retire."

"I agree. So I don't think he will take any shit from Ivan."

"Thanks Dan, getting late there. You going to charge me overtime?"

"Just the usual, steak and lobster at the place of my choosing. As soon as everything is moving here, I will let COMSIX know. He still has the CON. I can't make any operational moves. He and his boss will do that. But if one of our guys is hanging out, he will do everything he can, even if the guy was a grunt."

"Some grunt, you should read this guy's record, Dan. Remember the story of the guy that escaped and walked out of Vietnam barefooted?"

"You are shitting me. This guy? Sounds like the Air Force can stay in bed tomorrow night. And the Seals won't have their poker game disturbed. How the hell did the Army let him get away? How did we miss him? Should be a Seal."

"Wouldn't have worked for him. He is like a Grant or Patton, great when the heat is on but a waste of talent when it is calm, a quick thinker and doer under fire. Don't know about his thinking on this move though. Let's hope that their poker game doesn't get disturbed, CIA is still trying to get the ship to abort."

"Can we send *Carl King* to go stop him?"

"The CIA says no. Turkish flagged ship in international waters. Will cause a diplomatic incident, blow the freighter's cover. Guess they use it regularly. And not an area of the world where you want to put a shot across the bow."

"You are right about that, no loud noises. I will talk to you later Andy."

Andy had one more call to take. The director of DSA should be in Anchorage by now and would call him at any moment. He needed for his director to get through the proper channels to have the Air Force involved with their F-16s and Rescue Jumpers in Turkey.

The call from the director went as Andy had expected no yelling and cursing. Cool and calm, assessing the situation and deciding what needed to be done to get the best outcome. The director, being at the end of his career, didn't need to play the CYA game. As Andy put down the phone, he knew there was no way he was going to get any paperwork done today. He had done all he could to help Brady, which wasn't much.

It weighed heavily on his mind to call Brady's wife Cindi. He knew she had the clearances, but she still wasn't authorized for this mission.

The CIA would crucify him if he talked to her. Nothing she could do anyway but worry. Andy would do enough of that for the both of them during the next day and a half.

It was getting close to noon; Andy called his wife to meet him for lunch. Getting away from the shop and an enjoyable meal would help him clear his mind, he hoped. They could also swing by their church and say a prayer for Brady. It was completely out of his hands now. Other people were more in a position to help Brady, other good people like Dan McGrew and Commander Kaar on the USS *Carl King*.

As he was leaving the office to meet his wife for lunch, he stopped at his secretary's desk. "Please call Agent Sanak at the CIA. He is our liaison for this. Tell him I am bringing Katie with me tomorrow. She has the same clearances as I have. Don't ask, just tell him."

CHAPTER #14

ISTANBUL HARBOR

The freighter, *DENIZ ESEN*, passed the outer channel marker into the Black Sea at four thirty. Brady had been allowed to be on the bridge after the harbor pilot left the ship. The captain, Savas Dushku, was a quiet, efficient man. Not saying much, although he was most gracious and friendly to Brady. He stayed busy working with the helm, guiding the *Deniz Esen* through the channel traffic and out to the open water.

When well past the outer channel marker, he gave some instructions to his first mate, then turned to Brady. "Mr. Kinin, will you please join me for some coffee? I know our coffee differs greatly from what you would be accustomed to in the USA. I will not be offended if you make it how should I say, less strong." With this, he left the bridge, with Brady close behind.

The two were settled in comfortable chairs in the captain's cabin. "As you can see, Mr. Kinin, this is for living. I have a separate space for the office. I spend so much time aboard, I want to have a place to relax and get away. Sometimes my wife or children join me. I can't bring her very often, though. She is part Greek and part Italian, goes to the galley and cooks for the crew. The cook gets lazy, and the crew gets spoiled."

Even though Brady had been briefed that this captain had been to school in England and the US, it surprised him at the quality of English he spoke. His English had a British accent with just a hint of a Middle-eastern undertone. It also surprised Brady at the depth of usage he was hearing.

After an hour of small talk, Brady was very impressed with his host. He was an intelligent man with a deep-seated commitment to fight Communism. Calling on Russian ports along the Black Sea for many years had only hardened his resolve to drive Communism down. The Ukraine people were a good friendly people. He saw what the hand of Communism did to them and their lives.

Savas told Brady he did not know many specifics of the mission other than what his ship was about to do. He went over the few coded call messages and their meanings. He would show Brady the equipment tomorrow. During the evening, they were served a meal in the captain's cabin and a crewman brought the captain a few messages. Some were routine ship's information. But some were more involved. As Sofi had explained, they would get some pretty definitive messages.

After the third message, he looked at Brady and smiled. "They are getting very excited about what we are doing. You are being very naughty and I, by association. Your boss has denied you permission for this assignment. Appears you will be needing to look for a new job next week. Not sure I read this one correct. Said 'I was to throw you overboard, and I was released from service for the rest of the week'. Get some sleep Mr. Kinin; you have a busy night tomorrow."

The slight vibration and motion of the ship made for a long, restful sleep for Brady.

The next morning, after showering and stopping by the galley, he stepped onto the bridge a little after nine.

"Good morning to our guest." Came a cheerful greeting from the Captain. "You rested well, I think."

"Very well, thank you."

"Did you get something to eat? We have a busy day. I have arranged for some small arms practice for you. Follow me, please."

Brady followed the Captain down the ladders to the main deck, then aft to the fantail of the ship. A small table was covered with a 9mm automatic and an AK 47 with spare clips and ammunition. On another table was a shoulder fired grenade launcher.

"I know the mission plan did not involve so much. But I believe the situation demands more. I happen to have found a few little things around. My wife must have forgotten them the last time she was aboard." The Captain said with a big laugh.

"Are you familiar with any of these?"

"I remain qualified with a pistol, little different from this one. Had other small arms training in the Army, but has been over ten years."

"Just toys, like riding a bicycle. Never forget how." Again with a laugh.

Pointing to the pistol and the AK 47. "These two are Russian and the RPG is Chinese. If they find them, it will lead them nowhere. If you must use any of these, when you are done, throw them over the side. And do not get caught with any. Practice now. Use all the ammunition you care to in the two. But don't fire the RPG. They are harder to come by and they are very expensive. These are out of my private stock."

"Don't we supply you?"

"Only what is needed for a mission. These aren't needed."

"That is because the person deciding what we need is

sitting behind a desk in Washington." Brady understood this problem. He faced it every time he worked as a liaison on a mission. The local agents he worked with always complained about this very thing.

"Yes, so be it. Here are some boxes you can throw overboard as targets. First, let me show you how the RPG operates."

After a few minutes of instruction about the RPG. "If you have no more questions, I will return to the bridge. We will have lunch about noon, and then we have some final plans and signals to go over. I also need to show you the operation of the GPS and satellite radio. You will need to eat early and try to get four or five hours of sleep. We will have you on deck in plenty of time. Along with the various toys, we will have sandwiches, apples, and water." The Captain then turned and headed forward along the rail.

The weight and action of the pistol was different from the S&W Brady was used to handling. After going through a few clips, he felt pretty comfortable. The AK 47 was a new experience. It took about a dozen clips before he was confident he could think ahead of the gun and make it do what he wanted. He put the clips and remaining ammo in one of the remaining boxes, along with the two smaller weapons. The shoulder strap of the RPG was slung over his right shoulder. He remembered seeing gun cleaning paraphernalia on a shelf by the table where he sat to eat breakfast. He wanted to clean the guns and clips before reloading them. The RPG didn't really concern him. He figured if it got to a point that he needed to use it, then it wouldn't really matter whether or not it worked.

About the time he was finished cleaning his arsenal, a crewman came in and indicated the Captain wanted him. By hand gesture, he was told to leave the guns on the table.

He stepped onto the bridge but didn't see the Captain.

One of the bridge crew pointed aft toward the Captain's cabin. Brady walked the few steps down the passage and knocked on the door. He heard the voice from the next door, the Captain's office.

"Go in, my friend, sit down. I shall be right there in two minutes."

Brady entered the cabin and saw the table was set for two, but there was no food on the table. As the Captain entered through the door from the office, the door Brady had entered from the passage opened. A crewman carrying a tray of food entered.

During lunch, only friendly conversation going from topic to topic filled their time.

The conversation eventually led to the ship, so Brady asked. "Savas, you tread in very dangerous territory. You must have great faith and trust in your crew to not sell you out."

"Yes, I do, to both parts of the question. It is true the crew would always be of concern. But I have what you would call trump cards. First, for each event they receive an extra day's pay, this trip is two events. One event when we drop you and one when we retrieve you. The second and more powerful trump card is that every crew member has a relative on the crew; brother, father, son, cousin, uncle. I select my crew from the other two ships of our company. All of these men have sailed with my family for at least two years and we have learned about their family closeness. If they were to inform, the entire crew would have the same fate as me. If by the slim chance the informant was released as a reward by the Russians, one of his relatives will be in custody of the Russians. The informant would never be able to return to his family."

"I have heard family ties are very strong among the Turks."

"Very true. The third is really, as you say, my 'Ace up my

sleeve'. And the KGB provided it. The KGB would most likely treat the informer nearly as harshly as the rest of us, for not exposing us sooner. He would undergo extreme interrogation, the same as all of us. If not satisfied with his answers, and they would not be satisfied, he would suffer the same fate as us all. They all know this without me having to tell them. My crew, just as the Russian people, fear and mistrust the Soviets."

The conversation continued over many topics of general interest. However, once lunch was over and the table was cleared, the Captain put a handheld GPS unit and a handheld field radio on the table. He carefully went over the use of both units.

"The GPS will give you your long and lat constantly and mark where you are. It will also show the local time. There are seventeen waypoints programmed in and marked, both land and water. You are to only be concerned with three of them. The others are for confusion. #3 is where you will leave the ship. Not of real interest once gone. #7 is your target point on the beach. And #12 is our rendezvous for pick up. Be as close as possible. We will need to get you all onboard as quick as possible. Dawn will just be breaking. We will need the morning light to help find you, as we would probably never spot you in the dark."

The session went on for another three hours. The handheld satellite radio was the most difficult. It only sends the signal in a narrow beam so it would not give away the location. However, it must be aimed at the proper satellite. It needed to be just west of due south-205 degrees and at about forty degrees above the horizon. There was a margin of error of about ten degrees for both angles. It could send voice or beeps for Morse code. It would receive nothing other than two pre-programed signals from the ship. One signal would cause the red light to come on, telling him danger/problem.

Another signal would cause the red light to flash. This was an absolute abort signal.

Brady then heeded the Captain Dushku's advice from earlier in the day. He went to the galley and retrieved the beer he had earlier placed in the fridge. He sat and ate a couple of hard rolls with butter and a banana. Thinking, as he finished the beer, he should have cooled two beers to help him sleep. Some last dinner, convicted murders get steak or lobster or whatever. But they don't get cold beer, he didn't think.

Sleep came easier than he would have thought until a knock on his cabin door roused him. He looked at his watch, now 11:30 p.m.; it was near time to leave the ship. Before he fell asleep, he had written a letter to his wife. The letter was wrapped around his watch. He would give it to Savas; he knew the man would get it to Cindi.

Now it was time to leave the ship. He changed into the wet suit to help protect him from the harshness of five hours on the open ocean.

When he reached the main deck, the Captain was there along with three crewmen. Cables from the overhead cargo crane were attached to the Zodiac. There was a separate small hoist with a harness to lower Brady on to the Zodiac.

Captain Dushku had some last instructions for Brady. "We can only slow to about six knots for a few minutes without raising suspicion. Once the Zodiac is on the water, we can release the aft harness with a pull line. We will then be dragging the boat as we lower you to it. When you are in the boat and out of your harness, you will have to release the bow hook. You must pull the cable to achieve some slack to unhook the boat. Start the engine before you release. They strapped all of your equipment into the boat. Good luck my friend. See you in a few hours."

As they shook hands, "Savas, in my cabin is my watch and a letter...."

The Captain held up his hand to stop him, and with a deep look of compassion. "Yes, I understand." Then with a smile, "I will hold them for you until morning. You will need the watch to catch your flight home."

A crewman had finished securing the harness around Brady. The Zodiac was over the side and halfway to the water.

In less than five minutes, Brady was free from the freighter and moving at idle. He could hear and feel the engines of the freighter powering up to regain speed. It was a very dark night. He slowly turned the tiller throttle and headed north. No hurry, as he had three hours to go thirty miles.

CHAPTER #15

CIA HEADQUARTERS

Andy and Katie were quickly and efficiently escorted through the security checkpoints as they progressed deeper into this closed world of America's most secret building. They were escorted into a large octagonal shaped room. Six of the walls had large illuminated monitors with a workstation facing the wall. The workstation module was a bank of electronic devices. All the workstations were occupied and somewhat busy, the large wall screens all had different images. Most of the images were maps of different locations around the world. The remaining two walls had doors, one of which they had entered through.

Agent Sanak that had been Andy's contact, met them at the door. "Mr. Phillips, glad you could join us and this must be Katie." He extended his hand to both guests for a welcoming handshake. "Please come this way. Not much is happening yet. We will work from this module." He led them to a workstation occupied by three people wearing headsets. "We refer the three here to as CommOps. These two will monitor all communications for us. Jessica is in contact with our ops director in Istanbul, where your man should be right now and she handles internal communications. Do not talk to the CommOps, they won't answer you. They will only talk to the supervisor in this chair." He pointed to a slightly raised chair behind the row of three communicators. A real time illustration of the area is on the wall monitor in front of them. He pointed to one of the large screens, which had an image of the Black Sea.

There were some icons illuminated with markers. With a quick glance, even those new to the system could identify what was happening. There were two points marked south of Yalta, 'A' and 'B'. These would be the points of disembark and pickup for the Brady. There was an icon showing the Turkish freighter-*Deniz Esen*. Another pair of Icons was far to the south. One marked as the USS *Carl King* and the other the Russian destroyer shadowing *Carl King*. They identified the Russian as Sov. #1. The Turkish freighter was very near marker 'A'. In the upper corner of the screen a digital 24-hour clock showed local (Black Sea) time. The line below it read 'Sunrise 5:51'. Below that was a listing of planned times. Point A 0:30, Beach 3:45, Point B 5:30, etc.

As they stood there studying the monitor, they could see the icons of the ships moving. Katie leaned over to Andy and commented, "The only thing missing is a countdown clock to doomsday."

"I am afraid that for your man, that may be a little too true. You realize there is very little chance of him making it out of this. Hopefully, he won't take the *Deniz Esen* with him." Agent Sanak replied in a matter-of-fact tone. Then he added, "I am sorry. But that is how we see it. He must be a good man and we do realize he is on our side and trying to do the right thing."

"You will know what a good man he is when you meet him." Andy answered in a somewhat defiant tone. Mostly because he truly believed he would be able to bring Brady here to meet them in a couple of weeks. He became even more resolved as he saw a tear running down Katie's cheek.

"Once the operation begins, you cannot leave the center. Through the blue door is a hall leading to the restrooms and a break room with comfortable chairs and drinks." He pointed to the wall opposite where they had entered. "Feel free to use that area any time. That area can only be accessed through this room. I am not sure who all will be coming in to observe. We will not bother with introductions."

Andy and Katie stood observing the only action, which was the slow movement of the ship icons on the big screen. When the clock displayed 0:25, the time listing on the screen of 'Point A' turned yellow. At this time, an older gentleman left a group from across the room and moved to the supervisor chair behind the module. When the clock display read 0:30, the numbers became red and began to flash.

Katie asked the agent next to her, "How do we know if he has left the ship?"

"We won't. There is the standard GPS tracking of all commercial shipping, so we know where e *Deniz Esen* is. We don't know if the Russians have gotten wind of this operation, so don't know how close they are watching the area. No signal of any kind from the operative, and nothing but standard or critical communication from *Deniz Esen*. At this point we have to live by 'No news is good news' until something shows us different."

"The icon for *Deniz Esen* is past point A. So, would the good news be that Brady left the ship or remained aboard?" Katie replied with a coy grin.

Andy leaned to her and with a little chuckle said, "Easy Katie, we're guests here. Don't start with the riddles."

The next time point was not for three hours, but both Andy and Katie remained glued to their spot next to the supervisor's chair. Katie had gone to the restroom and returned with a cup of coffee for her and Andy.

The Black Sea

An hour and a half later Brady could see a faint glow to the north, but he could not see any shore lights. The only thing he was using was the gps. He had not needed the radio, so he had not yet taken the radio out of the bag. He would never see the red light telling him about danger and abort. Or maybe he did not want to see it.

Brady regularly checked his GPS to keep him due south of the beach where he was to meet Hans' cousin and his family. He also wanted to stay far enough away from the beach to not get caught in the wave action that would take him onto the sand before he was ready. Neither did he want any swells to splash against the boat and make a white spray.

At exactly 3:45 Brady had the small Zodiac 300 yards offshore. He saw the three small flashes from shore. Thirty seconds later there were three more flashes, with the third remaining aglow for five seconds.

As Brady turned toward the light and slowly increased the throttle, he quickly stuffed the GPS into his bag. Keeping his speed down to prevent making a wake, he approached the shore. Even a few yards from the beach the waves were small. He reduced the engine to idle and put it in neutral to let the waves and his momentum carry him in. He was using the small oar to gauge the depth as he slid toward the beach. The Zodiac needed to remain in about two feet of water to keep the prop from bottoming out.

When the oar told him his desired depth, he slid over the side into hip deep water. Just as he hit the water, he saw some figures move from the rocks above the beach and begin to run toward him. Brady turned the boat around, then slowly pulled it toward the shore until he felt the prop skeg bounce against the bottom.

The five figures running toward him were about eight yards from the water when a voice to his right yelled something in Russian. In the darkness, Brady could see the person yelling as he ran toward them. Another command was yelled, then there was a burst of automatic rifle fire from the man. By instinct Brady grabbed the AK 47 from the boat and returned fire toward the man. The man's weapon went silent, and he fell to the sand. Brady turned to the group coming to him. They had stopped a few feet away and were huddled around two of their group lying on the sand.

Brady let go of the boat and ran to them. He pushed someone aside to see the victims. One of those on the sand was a teenager. Brady could not tell for sure who the other victim was except that it was an adult woman. The teenager was moaning and moving; the woman was quiet and still. An older man, Dmitry, was kneeling next to the woman. As Brady knelt next to him, the man looked at Brady and shook his head. This was his wife, and she was dead. Brady turned his attention to the wounded teen; he could now see it was the boy. His mother was holding him in a sitting position. She pointed to his chest. There was a vehicle approaching on the road above the beach. Brady dropped the AK 47 and picked the boy up.

The skeg bouncing on the bottom had kept the boat from drifting far. As he placed the boy in the boat, he saw Dmitry helping the other two into the boat.

The vehicle had stopped and he could hear yelling and then a burst of automatic weapons fire from at least two places near the vehicle. Again, by instinct, Brady grabbed the RPG from the floor of the Zodiac. He stepped a few feet away from the boat, aimed the weapon, and pulled the trigger. The propellant carried the grenade directly into the vehicle on shore. From the light of the explosion, he could see it was a small truck type troop carrier. The grenade had no sooner hit the car when Brady dropped the spent weapon into the water and with a push of the boat, he jumped over the back.

Brady was just sitting up when there was more yelling and automatic weapon fire from the other direction down the beach. Just as he grabbed the tiller to open the throttle, he felt a tremendous pain in his left shoulder. The woman in the boat let out a scream. Ignoring all else, Brady turned the throttle wide open. By the time the shooter had changed clips, the Zodiac was about out of range.

After he was sure they were out of range, Brady rolled the throttle closed, then back open, then closed. He wanted it to sound as if the engine was missing and sputtering. They were now a good fifty yards out. He turned the engine to idle, then pulled the pistol from his holster. The gun was held next to the engine cowling on the side away from the shooter on the beach. He fired once into the water. The noise and flash might make the man believe the engine had blown out on them. Brady then eased the throttle open slightly. If the man thought the engine had blown, Brady did not want to offer engine noise or a wake to spoil the ruse. He maintained the speed for another ten minutes.

During this time, the woman had padded and bandaged her injured son. She had found the small kit of medical supplies. Her attention was then turned to Brady's shoulder. The daughter was holding pressure on the boy's chest would. Brady could not see his own wound, but he knew a bone was involved by the way it hurt whenever she put pressure against it. By packing gauze in it, she had stopped the bleeding. Rummaging around the boat, she came up with some small cord. She wrapped this around Brady's chest and the injured arm to keep it from moving. He would not have been able to use it anyway, and being unable to move it reduced the pain. It was obvious she was a physician or nurse. All of this time, she seemed oblivious to the bleeding wound in her thigh.

This whole time, Dmitry sat near the front of the boat staring at nothing. The man was in shock from having just seen his wife murdered. Brady could not relate to such a jolt to the psyche.

At full throttle now, Brady retrieved the GPS from the bag. His next objective was the rendezvous point for *Deniz Esen*. He had thirty miles to cover in just over an hour. When he had his course corrected directly to point 'B' he pulled the food and water Savas had supplied him from the bag. When doing this, the radio fell out of the bag. Brady saw the flashing red light.

CHAPTER # 16

CIA OPS

The coffee was urging Andy to use the head. Just as he started to move, one of the module communicators turned to the supervisor.

"SatCom from *Deniz Esen* at time stamp zero one five three. Armed boarding party at the dock in Yalta." The supervisor acknowledged, then picked up a telephone handset from the arm of his chair and punched two buttons. After a brief conversation, he returned the handset to its cradle.

Andy and Katie looked at the clock at the same time: 2:01. Andy turned to Katie. "Not normal for an armed boarding party. Captain sees it as a problem."

"Will Brady know?" Katie replied.

"Not sure. Would it change anything for him if he did?" Andy asked, mostly to himself.

As nothing else happened for the next ten minutes, the anxiety of the message wore off and Andy had to make a head call. He wasn't drinking any more coffee tonight.

Time began to drag when a different CommOp announced, "From Site director. Standard communication to shipping company from *Deniz Esen*. Harbor closed until 6 am."

The supervisor stood up and turned to Andy. "Will that damn cowboy of yours listen to an abort command now?" Not expecting a reply, and Andy not offering one, the man sat down and picked up the handset and slammed his finger into the buttons again.

Andy approached Agent Sanak. "Surely there is an abort signal?"

"The Captain can send an abort signal."

"What would Brady be expected to do?"

"That is something he and the Captain will have worked out depending on the weather and sea conditions in the area at the time. If it were me, I would see if a Zodiac could fly and get the hell out of Dodge. It will be daylight before *Deniz Esen* leaves harbor, so it will be difficult for your guy to hide from a search. Our man would have known all the shipping lanes and scheduled traffic, as well as the proposed route of *Deniz Esen*. Stay away from the traffic and try to catch the freighter when she gets back out to sea. They can probably reduce cruise speed to 10 to 12 knots. While the Zodiac can do maybe forty-five. The Captain can also make his diesels put out some black smoke to give some visibility over the horizon. If he sees the freighter, he can catch her. I hope your man is smart enough not to send a signal. Ivan will really have his ears on."

Katie could not contain herself any longer. "Sir, you have no idea of what smart is until you know this man."

Andy rolled his eyes, looked at the floor, and shook his head. But he was glad she said it.

USS *Carl King*, The Black Sea

Carl King HAD RESUMED a routine cruise after coming south to meet the mail run from the fleet. As was normal when they were this far south, the Russian destroyer shadowing them would drop back a few miles during this routine helicopter landing. Being that far away allowed *Carl King* to off load the Seals and their equipment without raising concern. They had made a long slow arch and were now heading on a north by northwest course about 120 miles south of Yalta. This would put them in the northwest part of the Black Sea at midday, when the freighter would send the request for help with a medical emergency.

The Commanding Officer of the USS *Carl King*, Commander William Kaar, was in his cabin fully awake and dressed when the messenger knocked. "From fleet, Sir."

The Captain opened the door immediately. He took the message from the sailor. "Reply, Sir?" the sailor asked.

After a few seconds to read the message, the Captain replied. "Get the XO to the bridge."

As the seaman turned, the Captain followed him into the passageway to the bridge.

A few minutes later, the Executive Officer (XO), John Akers, stepped onto the bridge. "John, we just got a message from fleet. There was an armed boarding party waiting at the dock in Yalta."

"They know something is up."

"Yes, and I don't like it. Let's get the Seals in the water. Get their commander up here. Also, the deck officer and his chief."

After five minutes, the XO ushered the Seal leader, Lt. Phil Nelson, onto the bridge.

"Lt., are your men ready to go?" Kaar asked.

"They are getting their gear at the boats now. They will be ready to go over the side in less than ten minutes."

The skipper turned to the two deck officers that had

entered the bridge. "With the seas at three feet, what speed can you launch those boats?"

The Chief Boatswain's Mate answered. "Anything over five knots will be really dangerous. Could lose a boat."

The captain turned to his XO. "Too slow for anything normal. How far is Ivan now?" Referring to the Russian destroyer following them.

The XO answered immediately, "Seven miles aft, one mile port. He hasn't wavered all evening."

"We don't know which side he will come up on. He will be on us before we can get the boats away. We need to give him something to look at to control which side he approaches. Chief, what could draw his attention to the deck, either side?"

"Tear something apart for repair, but that wouldn't require slowing."

"How about if we were putting the tender in the water?"

"We would slow for that, and then the winch could hang up before it got in the water. Would take 20 to 30 minutes to hang new gear and get the tender down to the water. Could take most of an hour to tear the housing off the winch and replace something. Could take another fifteen minutes to get the tender back aboard. I could give you a max of two hours."

"Very good, Chief. We will launch the Seals on the opposite side from the tender. They will need to launch without lights. I want all the light to be for the Chief on the tender side. XO in five minutes we are going to do a man overboard drill. That will bring us to a full stop and put the tender in the water. Any questions Chief? Lt.?" The Captain said as a dismissal.

Then turning to the Seal leader, "Nelson, have your men get some distance as soon as they are free from us." He was interrupted.

"Skipper, from fleet. Yalta harbor closed until six am. Recovery vessel still in port."

"OK, Nelson, now your guys have their plate full. Head due north for eight miles at minimal speed, do not show Ivan a wake. Then go to Point B at a safe speed. The point man will not know they are coming. He may have an itchy trigger finger. Further orders following." Then mostly to himself, "If I could just get Ivan off my ass."

As the Seal leader left the bridge, Kaar said to the XO. "Message fleet- man overboard drill and put out the standard warning to ships in the area. Drill, say clear, and no assistance needed."

The XO had just disappeared through the hatch when the ship's intercom came alive with the horn and 'Man Overboard. Man Overboard. All personnel to their stations. Man Overboard. This is a drill. This is a drill.'

The Captain ordered. "Helm. 180 degrees to port then dead slow when on new course."

As was routine, the order was repeated to the Captain as the ship began to turn. Before the ship was no more than halfway to the new course, the helicopter was in the air to begin a standard search pattern for the crewman in the water drill.

When on the new course, Cmdr. Kaar felt the ship begin to slow. He stepped to the starboard wing of the bridge and raised his binoculars. He could see the Russian destroyer coming straight at them at about five miles distance.

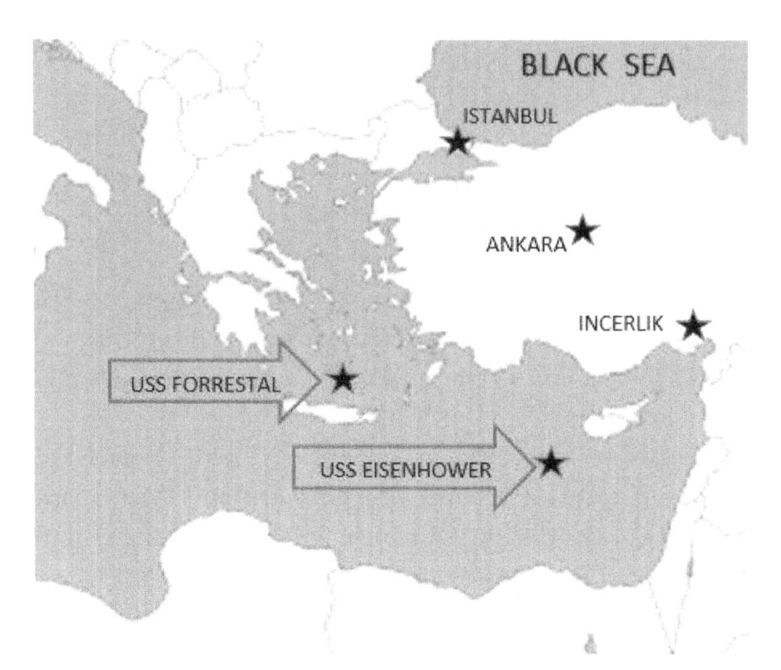
BLACK SEA
ISTANBUL
ANKARA
INCERLIK
USS FORRESTAL
USS EISENHOWER

CHAPTER # 17

The XO interrupted him. "Skipper, Seal leader wants to see you."

"What is it, Lt.? Are your men ready?" Kaar queried as the Seal leader came to him.

"They are all go. Sir, we are going to be dead in the water for a long time. Ivan may put some swimmers in the water to harass us. Muffle the sonar, foul the props."

"Yes, Lt. you are right. We can drop some concussion grenades to scare them off."

"What about we pull the same thing on him? He won't be expecting it."

"I doubt he will stop. He won't need to for swimmers. Will he?"

"No Sir, he won't need to stop. But he will have to be real slow."

"He will slow to about 2 to 3 knots as he passes so he can see what we are doing, then he will go past, turn around and came back by at the same speed. He will continue that until we move. But I sure need that bastard off my ass tonight."

Turning to his second in command."XO, where is his playmate, Taco?"

The Captain was referring to the second destroyer, The MARSHAL TACANISH that had shadowed them up until a few days ago when it was relieved by their current uninvited escort, The ADMIRAL STENKOV. Taco and Stink to the sailors on *Carl King*.

The XO immediately left the bridge for the Combat Information Center (CIC) next to the bridge.

"That is plenty slow to put swimmers in and retrieve them." The Seal Lt. continued.

"If he doesn't stop, then our swimmers can't do anything. Plus, that is too many in the water. It could be a real mess if they run into each other. The concussion grenades will hurt our guys as much as them."

"You are correct only to a point, Sir. We won't put swimmers in the water, we will just put one. Me. Your swimmers are repair guys not trained for fighting down there. And they fix things. I tear things up. I can do it better alone."

"What about the concussion?"

The XO returned and interrupted, "Latest we have is Taco in Odessa 36 hours ago."

"Damn, I need to know where he is." Kaar replied.

The Seal Lt. continued, "Concussions only hurt up to about thirty yards. I can stay at least fifty yards away."

"OK. So you are in the water. What good is it if he doesn't stop?"

"If he is dead slow, I can get in close. At that speed, he won't make a wake and there will be almost no suction into the screws."

A sailor came to the XO and talked into his ear so as not to disturb the CO's conversation.

"What will you do when you are there?"

The XO injected, "A Hawkeye just popped up out of Ankara. Complete array in eight minutes."

The Captain turned to the XO, "So COMSIX had one of his radar birds in Ankara. Maybe he can find Taco."

"I have a prop net on my scooter." The Lt. informed the Captain.

"You brought your scooter?" The Captain said with surprise. "Bring your water skis too?"

"How can you wrap the prop if it is moving?" The XO asked.

"I am having the engineering Chief attach a dead soft cable to my spear gun arrow. I can shoot it through the prop. Prop will be turning so slow it won't break the cable. Once the cable catches, it will probably snag the spear on the rudder and snap it off. The prop will wrap the cable and slowly pull my prop net in until it fouls around the prop. The scooter is neutral buoyance so I can just wait for Ivan to come to me."

"What about their swimmers?"

"They will stay within ten feet of the surface so they can see our deck lights to follow in. I will be down at thirty to forty feet. They won't be looking for me. Even if they were looking, they wouldn't see me because it is too dark. I can see them as the lights will silhouette them. Once they know you are tossing the grenades, they will return and get picked up at Ivan's next pass. They will be on the surface for the retrieve. We know they will be on the far side. I can work from this side and I will be down twenty-five feet. I figure she draws about eighteen to twenty."

"I believe that class is twenty-six and a half feet." The XO interjected.

Seeing he wasn't going to dissuade the Seal Lt., he decided it was time to stop the discussion. "Seems very risky and it left a lot of things to chance. I don't...." Before he could finish, the Lt. interrupted.

"Excuse me, Sir. This is a dangerous business we are in. Risk is everywhere. You are taking a chance Ivan will approach to the side where you want him."

Commander Kaar thought for a moment. He spoke as he turned to look at the approaching Russian. "Comrade, you drew the short straw tonight. We have a Seal here that is determined to get you a one-way ticket to the Gulag. XO you heard the plan. Any problems?"

"No, Sir."

CHAPTER #18

By the time the Seal leader and the XO had left the bridge, the tender was being lowered over the side. The seal boats were already in the water and slowly motoring away from *Carl King*.

Commander Kaar went to the hatch by the CIC. "Is that Hawkeye on line yet?"

"Just came up, Sir." The Lt. Commander in charge of CIC answered. "Taco is west of Sevastopol, about thirty miles."

Ten minutes later, the XO returned to the bridge. "Seal boats away and the swimmer in the water with his toy."

Messenger approached the two. "From Fleet, satellite saw an explosion on the beach."

"It has really hit the fan now." The XO ruminated aloud.

"We really have all of our marbles on that Seal." The Captain mused in reply.

"I am going down to see how the deck is doing." The Captain explained. "XO has the conn."

As he disappeared down the ladder from the wing, he heard the standard reply by the XO, "I have the Conn. Captain leaving the bridge."

When he was halfway to the deck party, the first concussion grenade exploded in the water near the stern of *Carl King*. He looked to see the Russian destroyer was some two hundred yards away and beginning to turn for a return pass. Two more concussion grenades went off, one closer to the bow and one midship. This would continue randomly every six to ten minutes until they were under way.

After talking to the deck officer and the chief for a few minutes, the Captain returned to the bridge. He stopped by the CIC first.

"Anything new?"

"Plenty." Came the reply. "We got an AWACS up out of Incirlik ten minutes ago. He sent the Hawkeye over northwest Turkey to watch the western front. AWACS is going east near Batumi. Taco out of Odessa, turned to a southwest heading making 25 plus knots."

"What is the ETA for Taco at Point B?" Kaar asked the CIC Officer.

The Officer turned to his plotting board. "Just over two hours, a little before daybreak."

The Captain turned and stepped onto the bridge. "Captain on the bridge." Was announced by the sailor standing nearby.

A statement from the XO followed this, "Captain has the Con."

Kaar retorted, "I have the Con."

The Russian destroyer was making a second slow pass. "How long should it take Nelson to get back on board?" he asked the XO.

"Having a scooter, ten, maybe fifteen minutes. Hope he did his thing this pass."

"Get the tender up close. Give him a written message, no radio for this. I want to send the tender west. See if it will draw

Taco down to it; keep him away from Point B. If Nelson was able to slow down Stink, that will leave Point B area clear from the south. Tell the tender to proceed due west at about 8 knots until further notice. Wait until our Seal is out of the water to head out. We need to move as soon as the scooter clears the water." The Captain instructed as the XO left the bridge.

Twenty minutes went by agonizingly slow for Commander Kaar until the seaman, wearing a headset for onboard communication, said, "Swimmer alongside on the surface."

The Captain walked over to the helmsman. "Be ready on my command, all ahead one half and set a course due north." He turned to the seaman with the headset. "Tell the Deck Chief they can use a light if they need. Time is an issue for us. Let us know as soon as the scooter is clear of the water. As soon as the scooter is clear, send the tender."

"Scooter clear." Came the seaman's voice after a few minutes. Then a minute later, "Tender underway."

"Helm, all ahead one half, set course due north. Navigation plot us a course to Point B and give it to helm. Helm adjust to new course from navigation."

The XO returned to the bridge. "The tender is gone. Everything looks good. We gave them three cans of fuel, some sandwiches, water and weather gear."

"Where is the Seal?"

"He is getting dry. I sent him to the wardroom to get some hot soup."

"I am going to CIC to watch Ivan's interest in the tender. Then I am going to the wardroom to talk to Nelson. XO has the Conn." As he entered the passageway aft to CIC.

It was almost ten minutes before the plotting chart showed the Russian destroyer from Odessa make a southerly turn. "He is going for it." The Captain said to no one in particular. He went to the sailor at the plotting chart. "How long until he intercepts the tender?"

After a moment of calculation, the seaman answered, "About two hours at current speed."

"And where is Stink?"

"He didn't waver at all, still making his passes."

The Captain left CIC to continue to the wardroom.

Kaar entered the wardroom where Lt. Nelson was sitting drinking a cup of soup. He had already changed out of his wetsuit.

"How you feeling? Getting warmed up?"

"Fine, didn't get that cold." The Lt. replied.

"How did it go?"

"Better than expected. They had three swimmers down towing a prop net with buoyance bags attached. They were at about ten feet, I was below them at thirty feet. When the first concussion grenade went off, they stopped and surfaced to have a little parlay. They remained there until the next grenades went off. Guess that convinced them the show was over for them. They went back to the net and put a small hole in one of the bags for air to slowly leak out. The three then swam back to their point of retrieval." The Lt. took a big swallow of soup.

"The small leak caused the net to slowly sink. I was very near to it so I let it come down to me, and then I was able to hook it and tie it to my scooter. To compensate, I can increase the buoyance of the scooter. I cut the leaking bag loose and tied a new air bag to the net. The net quickly stabilized when I got the bag filled correctly and I could cut it loose from the scooter. By this time, I could hear their ship approaching. I surfaced to get a look, then went back down to reposition. I had to do this every two minutes. The bow passed me by maybe thirty some feet. By the time the stern came near, I was in place some fifteen feet away and right at the depth of the props." The Lt. finished his soup.

"They had a tow cable on their net. I had changed my arrow from my prop net to their cable. I was able to shoot the arrow over the shafts in front of the props. The prop immediately wrapped the line and slowly pulled the net in. Once the net was moving, I cut my bag loose."

The Captain finally spoke. "So you wrapped their own net around their prop with no trace of us?" A rhetorical question.

"Was wearing gloves, Sir, no fingerprints." Nelson replied with a grin.

"What are the chances of it staying?"

"No way of knowing until he revs up."

"We may just give him that chance before long. We have a Hawkeye up and the Air Force put up an AWACS. You are welcome on the bridge, Lt."

"Thank you, Sir. I will be along shortly. Still nothing new on my boys?" Another rhetorical question.

The Seal Lt. stopped in CIC to look at the display of all the locations of the sea and air traffic. He pointed to two icons north of their location. "Are these my boys?"

"Yes, Sir. Those are only approximate, though. They aren't being seen by radar and they aren't transmitting a signal." A sailor replied.

"That is good. They aren't supposed to." He replied in acknowledgement of the seaman's information. He stepped into the passageway leading to the bridge.

The Captain was the first to see the Seal Lt. He turned to his XO. "John, here is a man that is trying to send three more to the Gulag."

"I thought they could get a group rate." The Seal replied.

"We can laugh now, but I have trouble feeling sorry for them." The XO continued. "Everything is about the same Lt., we are doing fourteen knots. Stink has dropped back to a station two miles astern but is keeping pace now. How much drag do you think that net will offer?"

"Don't really know. Looked similar to ours, but I couldn't get a feel for the weight. They probably got it off the shelf at Walmart where we get ours."

"Don't you buy in bulk from Costco?" Came the quip from the Captain.

"The net won't be felt until the revs get to about forty percent. Below that speed, it will just put a little drag on the prop."

The XO continued, "The props will be a little out of sync power wise. At higher revs, the efficiency will drop significantly. The prop will be out of balance and begin to vibrate. The entire ship will feel it. High revs for too long will cause a bearing to wear uneven and bigger problems."

CIA OPS

A GUARDED tranquility settled over the group until another time line on the screen changed to yellow. It was the Beach 3:45 notation. The clock showed 3:40. Everyone watched and seemed to do their own silent countdown. As expected, when 3:45 came, the notation became red and began flashing. Nothing else on the screen changed.

Katie nudged Andy. "Nothing up there changing is a good thing? We still at the no news thing?" It was more of a statement than a question.

A composed tension remained in the room for the next few minutes until someone approached the supervisor and handed him a piece of paper. He opened it and read it. He handed the paper to Agent Sanak with one hand as he picked up the handset and punched the buttons.

After reading the note, the agent come over to Andy and Katie. "Satellite image picked up small explosion and fire on the target beach. Your boy has guts. I just hope he didn't leave them there."

About this time, one of the CommOps turned to the supervisor. "Navy update. Both seal boats in water heading north. Two and half hours from beach."

All eyes went to the wall monitor. It struck Andy and Katie at the same time. The icon for *Carl King* and Bogey #1 had not moved for a long time. Just as Andy was about to ask about this, the supervisor stood up as another man approached. This was obviously his superior.

They conversed for a moment, then the supervisor returned to his chair. The other man turned to Andy. "This your guy? I had thought about going on vacation this week, should have done it. Guess we all make poor decisions."

Andy smiled and offered a small nod as the man turned away and left the control center.

Although the tension remained, a general calm again settled around the control module and those associated with it. However, from time to time, everyone in the room looked at the wall screen in front of them.

CHAPTER #19

THE BLACK SEA

The realization that point 'B' would no longer be their bus stop didn't change Brady's thinking that it must still be their destination. He would go there, then head due south. He would rather take his chances on the open ocean than with the greeting party that he was sure had gathered on the beach. Andy, he knew, would send the cavalry. Anyone searching for them would hopefully start at the known waypoint and work from there. The logical direction would be south, as far from trouble as possible. Savas had told him he had about three hours of fuel at full throttle. The speed he had used going in was much slower. Brady figured he had about another two and a half hours of fuel at half speed.

The woman and her daughter split a sandwich. Dmitry refused the food, but took a few swallows of water. There was nothing Brady could say to him. He knew not a word of Russian.

As things settled down, Brady learned the woman knew a few words of English. The daughter had a larger English vocabulary but could not really put a sentence together.

However, he was able to communicate with the girl. She was sixteen and her brother was fourteen. He learned her mother was a nurse. She had spent some time with the army in Afghanistan at a hospital until her husband had been killed. She then returned home to be with her children.

In just over an hour Brady marked point 'B'. Using the GPS, he put them on a heading of 180 degrees. A few minutes after leaving the waypoint, the engine sputtered. Within ten seconds, the engine died. Brady reached for the fuel tank; as soon as he tried to pick it up, he knew it was empty. He ran his hand around the sides of the tank until he felt the hole, then another hole in the opposite side. The last spray of gunfire had put a hole in the tank. Half of their fuel had leaked out. He touched the boat next to where the tank was; the air cell there was not inflated. The bullet had gone through the boat, through the fuel tank, and was most likely the bullet in the woman's leg.

Being dead in the water and only thirty-seven miles from shore with daylight coming, Brady decided it was time for him to call the cavalry. He hoped that Andy was tuned in. He reached for the satellite phone.

CIA OPS

ONE COMMUNICATOR at the module in front of them suddenly sat up and began writing. After a moment, he turned to the supervisor. "SatCom from point. Voice message. Giving danger and abort code repeatedly and randomly."

Andy turned to Sanak with a questioning look. Before he could ask, the CIA agent gave an answer. "A direct voice communication via satellite from your boy, he is point. There are two codewords. Cannonball is for danger and apple is for abort. He is giving both."

Katie replied before she could stop herself, "So much for the no news thing."

"When we get back, remind me to wash your mouth out with soap." Andy replied, then turned to Sanak. "What does that mean?" They could feel a stir in the room among the mounting tension.

"Makes no sense to us the way it was random and repeated. Your boy always talk like that?"

At the same instant, a light went on in both Andy's and Katie's heads. Andy answered. "Only when he wants to. Can you play that for us?"

The agent leaned to the supervisor and said something, then gestured for the two to step closer to the CommOp. They heard Brady's voice. "appleappleapple" in short quick cadence followed by a slow drawn out "c a n n o n b a l l......c a n n o n b a l l......c a n n o n b a l l......." then again back to the rapid cadence, "appleappleapple." "Play it again." Katie commanded.

The speakers again ran Brady's voice.

Katie spoke to all around. "Those are code words alright but not what you think. That is an SOS. Apple is a dot and cannonball is a dash. He is going to send more. He is giving us time to digest this."

With an ear to ear grin, Andy spoke, "Katie, this is scary. You think too much like him."

A voice that seemed somewhat familiar came from behind them. "I would think any comparison to this guy would be a supreme compliment."

Andy began to answer as the two turned to the voice, "Knowing him would....." Andy stopped in mid-sentence as they saw why the voice was familiar and what the stir in the room was. Andy then continued. "Mr. Vice President."

The Vice President replied, "I do want to know him, and soon."

"I believe there will be a long line that wants to visit with him, Sir."

Katie then interjected. "Not sure he will get out of this place with his head."

"I think I can smooth a lot of that, remember I had an office upstairs here at one time."

"I believe he will need all the help he can get." Andy replied.

The visitor faced Katie and put his hand out to her. "I am pleased to meet you and you are?"

Katie shook his hand without missing a beat. "I am Katie Reese. It is very nice to meet you. Kind of the wrong circumstances to make friends."

"We make friends wherever we can. And you are." As he offered his hand to Andy.

"Andrew Phillips, Assistant Director of the DSA."

"Ah, so this is your man."

"He was until today. Now I am not so sure."

"You might be right, but not like you think. A lot of organizations will want him. The crew here may make a lot of fuss, but they will take him in a second."

"They already had their chance way back after Vietnam. We want to keep him." Katie intervened.

"He worked with them, then?"

"Not really Sir. They spent a lot of time with him, though. Do you remember the story about the guy that escaped from the VC and walked out of Vietnam?"

"Heard the rumor, sounded like a whopper of a sea story that kept growing?"

"We just got a SOS from that sea story." Katie offered.

The speakers on the communication module came alive

again with Brady's voice. Katie turned to the supervisor. "That will be the same message, SOS."

They all listened until Brady had completed the same message. Then Katie offered, "There will be two more communications from him. They will mean nothing, just gibberish. He will be trying to confuse anyone eavesdropping."

The Vice President asked, "How do you know?"

Andy replied, "Like I said before, they think too much alike. Should see them in a think session when they get on the same wavelength, I just sit back and marvel at what they come up with."

"I would like to see that."

"Stick around. I think we are having one now by long distance."

Over the next few minutes, Brady sent two more communications. As Katie had predicted, neither made sense. It was just random; apple and cannonball mixed with various non associated words.

After a couple more minutes of silence, Brady's voice again came through the speakers. Brady used the two words to send a message in Morse code. The CommOp copied them as dots and dashes. When Brady was done, the CommOp quickly translated the message to letters and turned to the supervisor. "Out of fuel. One critical injury. I can't make out the word here. Comes out BS then forest gal, then more that makes little sense, the letter y then, the man said the letters, h o m b r e c i l l o s."

Andy began in a thinking tone. "Forest gal...."

The Vice President spoke from behind Andy. "Does he speak Spanish?"

"Yes Sir, fluently." Andy replied.

The Vice President asked the CommOp to read the letters

again. After which he said, "y hombrecillos- - - and little men."

Katie's voice exploded. "Forest gal and little men. Snow White and the Seven Dwarfs."

~

THE ROOM WAS dead quiet for a moment until Katie broke the silence. "BS, Point B. South. Snow white and the seven dwarfs. Seven. He is seven miles south of point B."

The supervisor turned to her. "How do you know it is miles, not kilometers, nautical miles or statute miles?"

"It is nautical miles. He is on the ocean. He will use whatever fits the situation."

The Vice President quietly said to Andy, "You were right, I am glad I stuck around. How well do these two know each other?"

"Only at work, Sir. They both have great marriages."

"My wife is close to that, but I am glad she can't read me that well."

"I have the same problem." Andy replied, as they both laughed.

The supervisor spoke to another CommOp. "Get this to COMSIX and *Carl King*. Out of fuel. Severe injury. Seven nautical miles south of point B."

Katie then stated matter-of-factly. "He is done unless something changes. His message is out, either we have it or we don't. Nothing else he can do."

The Vice President turned to the supervisor. "What are your contingencies for rescue?"

"The *Carl King* is the only thing around. They can't get there before daylight. There is a Russian destroyer on their tail. He will see them being taken aboard. Will cause a huge incident. The Russians will not want this asset to get away."

Andy added, "Where are the Seals in the small boats that left *Carl King*? They were heading that way. They can do maybe sixty miles an hour."

"Still over an hour away. It will be daylight by the time they get back to *Carl King*."

Katie pleaded, "You can't just do nothing."

"Mr. Vice President, you know the system. This decision is over my head."

Very serious now, the Vice President replied. "Get on the horn and get it going up the chain. The President is aware of this mission."

About ten minutes later, a CommOp turned to the supervisor. "Not our problem now. The Navy has it. They already had two seal boats near Point B."

"Who in the hell did that?" The supervisor stated to no one.

Andy added, almost boastful. "I know the two good men that did that." He was thinking of Adm. McGrew and Cmdr. Kaar.

"I guess that makes three people I need to meet." added the Vice President.

"You will not meet three finer, Sir." Andy stated matter-of-factly.

CHAPTER # 20

USS CARL KING

A messenger came on the bridge and handed the Captain a piece of paper. “From Fleet, Sir.”

The Captain read the message then handed it to his XO. “I guess it is time to make him vibrate. Is Taco still on intercept with our tender?”

The XO turned toward the CIC until the Seal spoke. “I was just in there. He is heading on a very southerly course.”

“We are going to put your boys to work now, Lt.” The Captain said as he turned to the sailor at the helm. “Helm, slowly increase speed to all ahead full. Maintain course. Navigation, keep us heading direct to Point B.”

The XO read the message aloud. “SatCom from Loner. Out of gas, critical injury, seven miles south of Point B.”

“Where do you think your boys are by now?” The Captain asked.

“Plot has them a few miles south of there. That is only a guesstimate.” The Lt. answered.

“We need to get this location to them. But Ivan will pick up anything we send.” The XO stated.

"I can get it to them. Where is our radio? We are on Channel 4." The Seal quickly replied.

The XO took a small radio off the table and handed it to the Lt.

Into the radio he began. "OK, kids, get your ears on. We tear em up and our construction cousins build em. You know those construction boys. OK, let's go have a party. Wrong way Dallas Forty. Throwing bones, you win. Marty's fantasy won't happen."

"You guys speak a different language." The XO offered.

"I think they will figure it out. The construction boys are CBs. They will get the B out of it and know Point B."

"Yeah, that one is easy for Navy." The XO answered.

"Go party means we are going to meet someone. The next is the toughest one. The movie North Dallas Forty. They will come up with south from 'wrong way'."

Cmdr. Kaar interjected, "Yeah, and all Navy knows throwing bones is dice, and you win is 7 or 11."

"Correct, Sir. And they need to go seven. One of our team members back at Sig. Name is Marty. His fantasy is to sleep with twins."

"Very good, 'twins won't happen. Would eliminate the eleven." The XO exclaimed.

"I hope your guys are as clever as you are, Lt." The Captain replied.

"I believe they have trained me well." Nelson replied with a chuckle.

The captain turned to his XO, "John check traffic in the area and get an ETA for us at point B"

The XO left the bridge for CIC.

An agonizing fifteen minutes passed until a messenger came to the Captain with a message. Kaar read the message and turned to the Seal Lt. "Need another message to your guys, Loner can hear voice hailing them. He doesn't trust who it is. Have them hail Gentleman Jack. Guess Loner is a Jack Daniels drinker."

The Lt. spoke into the radio. "We hear voices in the night. Hail Gentleman Jack."

~

The Black Sea, Seven Miles south of Point B.

"JACK DANIELS, this is the US Navy. Jack Daniels."

"We are to your northwest." Answered Brady.

"Give us another shout, Jack."

"Not far, more north now."

"I see 'em Fly." Came another voice from Brady's left.

In less than a minute, the two seal boats had Brady's boat sandwiched between them.

"Who are you guys, Seals is my guess? And how did you get here?"

"Navy Seals Sir. Off of the USS *Carl King*. I am petty officer first class Horton. I go by Fly. My partner riding the bow is Manny."

"Seals, I didn't hear of that part of the plan."

"Just flew out yesterday afternoon."

"Which of you is the best Medic?" Brady asked. "We have a fourteen-year-old with a severe chest wound. He took a bullet through his right lung. Got the external bleeding stopped. Lady with him is his mom. She is a trauma nurse. Has a bullet in her leg. Guy in front is our asset. He has a couple of nicks. The other female isn't hurt. Get them in the boat with the best medic. How far away is *Carl King*?"

"Dink is our medic in the other boat. Let's get them in there. You and the asset ride with us and those three go with Dink and Shooter." The Seal directed.

"We need to transfer some fuel into the tank here. How

far is *Carl King*?" Brady asked as the injured boy was being transferred.

"Don't know Sir. She was dead in the water when we left. We have been hitting between forty and fifty knots for the last couple of hours. *Carl King* has Ivan on his six. Communication has been minimal. We were told to not transmit."

"I have a SatCom. Is directional, but I have kept it to a minimum. We need to get all four of them in that boat. I will ride with you. We need to offer some diversion for Ivan. Could be very dangerous. Your bow rider needs to go with them, too."

The other Seal piped in. "That's not gonna happen."

"Can't let you do it." Brady argued.

Petty Officer Horton commanded. "Sorry sir. Not your boat, you are our guest. If Manny wants to stay, he is with us. Now, what is your plan?"

During the discussion, the teenage girl had not followed her Mom, but had made her way into the other seal boat. In her broken English, she explained to Brady that without her in the boat, it would go much faster. Her brother needed to get to help as fast as possible. One Seal confirmed they would probably go six to eight knots faster without the weight.

"OK, get them to *Carl King*. We are going to wait twenty minutes, then give a radar image for Ivan to follow. We will tow it northwest a few miles. Try to keep them away from you. Will do it for an hour, then head south. If you get to *Carl King* before that, have them direct us."

"Got it..........." was all Brady heard as the engine on the Seal's zodiac went to full throttle?

Brady turned to the remaining boat. "Fly, do you have one of those metal lined exposure blankets in your emergency supplies?"

"Yes Sir. Keep it to help prevent hypothermia if we fish somebody out of the water."

"Great, get it out." Before he could finish, the other Seal, Manny, was handing it to Brady.

"Manny, come over here into this boat, please. I need help with this." In the dark, and with the element of urgency, neither of the Seals had noticed Brady was only using one arm.

As Manny transferred into the boat next to Brady. "Your arm is hurt. What happened?"

"Took a bullet in the shoulder. Fly, do you have any type of tape or small line?"

"How about duct tape?"

"Duct tape! Really?" Brady exclaimed.

"I am from Georgia. Never leave home without it."

"OK, Manny, take the oar and wrap the end of the blanket around the paddle end. Use the tape to keep it there. Let the rest of the blanket hang. After our little beach party, I am sure Ivan is looking for me. Don't want to give him too much radar image or he will know something is wrong. Just give him a little hint to get him looking away from *Carl King*. We can tow this for maybe an hour before anything gets to us. We need to give them twenty minutes. Then Manny hold up the blanket as high as you can for about fifteen seconds every two to three minutes. When we cut loose to go south, you need to secure the tiller straight ahead and put the engine in forward at idle. Tape the oar to the engine cowling with the blanket up in the air. Give Ivan something to continue tracking. Be alert, if we see a mast light we will need to break off immediately."

CHAPTER # 21

USS CARL KING

"What is the status of Stink?" The Captain inquired of CIC.

"He increased speed to match us until we hit nineteen knots, then he slowed back to fourteen knots and is maintaining that." Came the reply.

The Captain turned to look in the direction of the barely visible mast light of the Russian destroyer and thinking out loud. "Have a pleasant stay in the Gulag, Comrade. Send us post cards to let us know how you are enjoying it."

"He will probably try to stay as close as he can to see what we are doing." The XO replied.

From the bridge communicator. "Sir. Stink just went active with his offensive array."

"Sound battle stations." The XO ordered.

"Two of the MIGS over Kiev turned south and went sonic." Came the communicator's voice.

"Ike...Err Eisenhower put up a flight of four Hornets headed this way."

"Holy Shit, what are we into?" The XO asked rhetorically.

The communicator continued. "Four Falcons from

Incirlik jumped up and turning north. Two just went sonic. The other two are going to ride shotgun for the AWACS."

"What is ETA for the sonics?" The Captain asked.

After a moment, the reply came. "MIGS will get here two minutes before the Falcons."

Again the communicator, "The Forrestal put up four Tomcats to shotgun the Hawkeye over west."

"COMSIX must have had them all on deck and with the brown shoes in place." The Captain mused aloud.

"Didn't take long for the Air Force to jump in either." The XO added.

The communicator, "COMSIX has a tanker ready to go at Ankara. Incirlik has a tanker on the runway."

The XO, "Sir, our gear is hot. Activate our offensive array?"

"NO NO, Ivan has only flipped a switch. He is trying to provoke us. He knows he is in deep shit. Let's not stir this pot any more than it is. Defensive to the max."

The bridge was as quiet as a church basement for the next three minutes. The communicator's voice broke the tension. "Stink shut down his offensive array and the MIGS have dropped back to cruise."

"What about our gang?" The Captain asked.

The two Hornets maintained sonic until they were closer than the MIGS, then dropped to cruise.

"Good call Skipper." The XO stated. "Put that fire out."

"Let us hope it stays out. Don't need those four up there playing tag. Nelson, what would be the status of your guys?"

Communicator reported, "Radar is picking up faint image near point B. Too weak to identify or track."

"I just checked the plotting chart. All speculation. Give my boys ten minutes to find 'em, then another ten to transfer. Then having them making forty knots. That shows we have closed to about twenty miles."

"XO. Secure from battle stations, but remain at general quarters. Turn on the forward mast light. Get a man on each wing of the bridge with a light. Aim only forward and flash every five seconds. Help those Seals find us. Closing at seventy knots, they should see us soon. Get a lookout up top."

Voice of the communicator, "MIGS have turned and are maintaining a position at coast east of Sevastopol. The two Falcons turned back over land and the other two are staying with the AWACS. Tomcats are about twenty minutes from the Hawkeye. Hornets are continuing to station over Ankara. The two Falcons that went sonic will need fuel as soon as the Hornets get there."

"We dodged that bullet; now let's get those Seals on board." The Captain spoke. "XO recall the tender. Return them to where we dropped them. They make a good radar image; we'll find 'em."

The Seal Lt. returned from CIC to the bridge. "My boys should be on us any time now. Skipper."

"Where is Stink now?" The Captain inquired.

Voice of the communicator, "Stink still steaming at twelve knots fourteen miles astern. Mast lookout sees faint red light forward at ten degrees port. About a mile."

"Flash that mast light, see if he responds." The Captain ordered as he picked up his binoculars and went to the port wing. Closely followed by the XO and the Seal Lt.

A moment later, the communicator reported, "Lookout says the red light flashed. He can see white wake now. But only one wake."

The three officers were straining through their binoculars. The Lt. spoke first. "I see the wake now, only one."

The Captain stepped back off the wing onto the bridge. "Helm, all stop. Boat coming alongside to be taken aboard. XO rally the deck party to port side. Get everyone aboard and haul the boat. Get the corpsman and his gang there.

Nelson, get down to your men and find out where the other boat is."

The Captain hollered through the passageway to CIC, "Let me know when Stink is eight miles."

Communicator again, "Boat secure alongside. One person coming aboard in a sling. Stretcher going down."

Returning out to the port wing to watch the activity on the deck, the Captain saw the Seal Lt. separate from the deck party.

The communicator hollered, "Stink at ten miles."

Lt. Nelson, now next to the Captain, "Sir. Fourteen-year-old boy took a bullet through the chest, difficult breathing, probably collapsed lung. External bleeding stopped. Woman has a slug in her thigh. Asset was nicked by two shots, minor scratches. Loner and sixteen-year-old in our other boat, they stayed there to make a decoy image. One passenger was lost on the beach. Fatal automatic weapon fire there. "

"Where is that damn boat now?"

"That is the radar image you are getting. They are putting up an image for Ivan. Wanted to keep him away from this boat. After they separated he was going to wait twenty minutes before throwing image. They will then tow Loner's boat northwest for one hour unless they see mast lights. After one hour, they will put his zodiac on autopilot with sail up to give a radar image. They will come due south from there at max speed. If possible, we need to give them directions and time."

The Captain went to the sailor with the headset, "Tell deck party I need corpsman's assessment of the wounded ASAP. And let helm know as soon as the boat is clear of the water." Then turning to the helmsman. "As soon as you get the word, make us ahead one half."

Kaar turned to go into CIC, "Come with me Lt. Let's help your boys and their loose cannon passenger."

Once in CIC, he asked a couple questions and assessed the situation. "Lt. you need to let your guys know Taco is southwest of them about an hour. Seems he broke from our tender and took Loner's red herring."

The Lt. returned to the bridge and thought a minute before he picked up the radio to give this information to Brady and the Seals.

"Have an update on the game. The Tribe is still down. They are at home tonight. Five runners across home plate. Weather report says thunderstorm heading in from direction of Bennetville, about an hour away."

He sat the radio back on the table. The XO was next to him. "I can get the picture. Tribe is Indians, at home is Cleveland. Don't get Bennetville."

"One of the other Lts. on our team is from Columbus. Ohio State everything. His name is Bennet."

"Got it. Columbus is southwest of Cleveland." The Captain interjected. As they felt the ship begin to thrust forward.

The XO continued, "Corpsman says the chest wound is critical. Doesn't know about internal bleeding. Kid's BP is low. He is typing the blood now. Has fluid bag going. Bullet entered back and exited front, probably shattered a rib. The woman with the leg wound is his mom. She is a trauma nurse."

"OK, great, with daylight about one hour away. I have four in a defenseless zodiac north of me an hour, my tender southwest two hours. Critical injury that needs to get south immediately. A pissed off Ivan with an itchy trigger finger south of me and Ivan's playmate northwest about an hour. Not to mention both teams of brown shoes looking for something to do." The Captain ruminated out loud.

"Helm, ahead full. Come about to port to course 225 degrees. Navigation will give course changes. Navigation, keep us away from Stink by at least five miles. Once past him set heading direct towards Ankara."

The XO inquired, "Where is the tender? Will he catch us?"

"Doubtful, but we will get him later. They are not in danger. Nelson's boat is the one in danger. They are going to just have to get out of Dodge and take their chances in the open until we can get back to them. It's a big ocean. We need to get that boy to help."

The Seal Lt. added, "At max speed they have about three hours' fuel left. They can get another hundred miles, at least."

"Lt. get in CIC and watch their back. Tell them when Ivan is close. XO get a message to fleet, one Ivan can read. 'engine room damage, severe injury. Steaming south to get in range of medevac.'"

Carl King made a few course changes to avoid and confuse the crippled Russian destroyer.

Lt. Nelson came back to the bridge and picked up the radio. "Update on the weather report. May need to call the game. Thunder and lightning from Bennetville now less than twenty minutes away. Thunder heads are at 25000 feet."

"When one knows what to listen for, your message is pretty clear. The 25000 would be compass direction of 250 from them." The XO stated.

"Yes Sir. They will separate immediately and take a south-easterly course for about fifteen minutes, then come due south. Do I need to direct them away from Stink?"

The Captain answered, "Wait and see what he does when he has a track on our new heading. He will probably try to intercept until we get past. See how long he follows. If he believes we are doing medevac, he may not follow. As soon as he gets some daylight, he will stop and let the swimmers untangle his prop. How long will it take to free the prop, Lt.?"

"Not too long. They can do it with bolt cutters. They won't need to use a cutting torch. Swimmers in the water, free the prop, then retrieve swimmers out of water. A little over an hour, unless the Captain wants to retrieve the net. That could take most of another half hour." The Lt. answered.

"Oh, he will want the net." Kaar replied. "I know I would."

"If he puts the same three swimmers in the water, he won't get it." The Seal Lt. answered.

"The KGB ass onboard won't let just those three go in the water, suspicious bastards that they are." The XO continued, "May not let any of the same ones go under."

Communicator broke the conversation of supposition. "*Deniz Esen* signaled permission to leave port at 6 am."

The Captain inquired, "Has Taco changed course?"

"I will get the status of both." The XO said as he went into the passage to CIC, emerging back out in less than a minute. "Taco maintained course and speed. Stink turned to us but is now falling behind."

"Navigation, give helm a course direct to Ankara." The Captain ordered.

Communicator's voice. "From Fleet Sir. Air Force medevac chopper coming out. Their range is greater than one of our birds. Bringing trauma doc from Forrestal. He is on his way to Ankara in a COD. Medevac will be waiting for him. His ETA is about 30 minutes. Maintain present course, AWACS will bring him to rendezvous."

"XO, get one of our pilots up here." The Captain ordered.

They felt the ship make a slight turn to the left as the helm responded to the new course from navigation. One of the LAMPS pilots stepped onto the bridge, followed by the XO.

"We have an Air Force medevac coming out. Is there enough space for him to land and will he land on a ship?" The Captain asked the aviator.

"His bird is larger than ours. But if the wind stays calm, then I would say yes, he will land. He hauls rescue jumpers around; they train and live for the tough stuff. Those guys are good and seem to have brass balls."

"Glad to hear that. Let's hope he proves you right. You need to be on the hanger deck when he gets here. You can talk him in."

"Yes, Sir."

Messenger handed the Captain a paper. He read it, then hand it to the XO. XO reading, "SatCom from Loner. 'Know the route, will catch the same bus home.' How the Hell is he going to do that? As you said Skipper, it's a big ocean. No radar or directional guidance for them to find each other."

The Captain answered, "I agree, but this guy has continually amazed me for the last six hours."

The Lt. added. "Sir, the woman with the wounded leg speaks a few words of English. Once on board, she was able to use hand gestures and a few words to get the corpsman to understand her. Loner took a bullet to his shoulder. His left arm is useless. She bound it to his side. He is in a lot of pain."

"Holy shit, is this guy Superman?" The Captain asked rhetorically.

Time seemed to drag as *Carl King* continued on a southwesterly course as the eastern sky began to give up its darkness to the breaking dawn.

The communicator broke the silence. "CIC has the medevac about fifteen minutes out."

"Get the patients up to the hangar and let the deck crew know we are bringing a bird down in a few minutes." The Captain ordered.

"All ready Sir. Our pilot is talking to Air Force already. Guy is going to set her down." XO replied.

"Helm, maintain course, slow to ten knots. Prepare for full stop." Then mostly to himself, "Let's help this guy all we can.

Don't give him a moving target." Again to be heard, "XO what is Ivan up to now?"

Two minutes later, the XO emerged from CIC. "The MIGs went back down at Kiev. Stink has come to a full stop. The Loner's red herring image disappeared from radar when Taco was just a mile or so away. It looks like he ran a search pattern for a while. Now it appears he is heading our direction. Still a lot of air and small ship activity near the coast west of Yalta. AWACS will get the medevac to us and then he is being relieved. We will have a new Hawkeye from Ike."

"Lt., can you let your boat know what Taco is doing?" The Captain asked.

"Yes sir, let me think a minute."

The Lt. then spoke into the radio. "Thunder and lightning reached the ballpark, but looks like a line of storms extends all the way to Dixie."

The communicator spoke. "Sir. Telex message to *Deniz Esen*. All contracted cargo to be loaded. Delay may require a change of loading pier. Stay on course direct to Varna. How is fuel problem, still making black smoke?"

25 Miles South Of The Crimean Coast

TOWING the smaller zodiac at such a leisurely pace made for a very comfortable ride; the two-foot swells gave the boat a gentle rocking motion. This gave Brady time to talk to their passenger. As they talked, she became more comfortable speaking English. Although broken and sketchy, she was able to tell Brady much about herself and family. Her name was Lena. She was sixteen years old. Her brother, Ruslan, was fourteen. Her mother's name is Raisa.

When they were quiet for a few minutes, Brady saw the Russian teenager had fallen asleep in the bow of the boat.

"Manny, warm up the engine for a few minutes, leave the prop in the water and tighten the lock to keep the direction straight ahead. Our time may be about up. We may have to separate in a hurry." Brady said to the sailor in the smaller zodiac trailing a few feet behind.

The Petty Officer at the tiller of the zodiac yelled for both Brady and the Seal in the other boat to hear. "Lt. says trouble less than twenty minutes away from southwest."

"OK, Manny secured the oar to the engine cowling." Brady then turned to the Seal next to him. "Horton, do you have any small charges with timers?"

"Yes Sir. Have a six-pack."

"Yeah, I know. Never leave home without 'em." Brady joked. "Give two of them back to Manny."

Then turning to the other boat. "Manny, set one of these at the transom right next to the engine and put the other in the bow. Set the timers for fifteen minutes. Let's give Ivan a little show but not leave anything for him but some debris."

While the Seal in the towed boat was getting the boat ready to be released, the two boats came to a stop. When all was set, he put the idling engine in forward and hopped into the larger boat. The small zodiac slowly pulled away from the larger boat.

As Horton opened the throttle and turned the boat to the southeast, he said to Brady. "We will head southeast for about fifteen minutes, then turn due south. May get a little bumpy."

Brady pulled the GPS from his bag. After a few minutes of manipulating the instrument, he held it up to Horton. "I am guessing *Carl King* headed south for a medevac. We are on our own for a few hours. We need to get as far away as possible by daylight. The line here is the track the freighter I came in on will be taking. When you get to it, follow it west.

Maybe we can find him before Ivan finds us. With daylight on us, the visibility should be good. Keep us south of the track eight to ten miles. Ivan will keep expanding his search radius."

With his GPS in the hands of the sailor, Brady took out his SatCom radio. He would let the folks back home know his intentions. In his apple-cannonball Morse code he sent 'catch same bus home. Know route.'

CHAPTER # 22

USS CARL KING

"Sir, medevac bird is secure on hanger deck. Doc is assessing injured. Pilot is a gal."

Kaar chuckled to himself, "Ask brown shoe if she has brass ones."

"Corpsman had them stabilized. All are being loaded now. Should be able to liftoff in less than five minutes." The communicator continued.

"Very well, permission to go when ready." The Captain replied. "Helm, when he...Err she is away, turn us north at 25 knots. Navigation, give helm a course to our tender. Then give the tender a course to intercept."

"Sir, AWACS is being relieved by a Hawkeye from Ike. His escorts are headed back to Incirlik. They released the Hawkeye out west from station and it is returning to Ike. The Tomcats are going home. All four Hornets are setting down at Ankara for a while."

The XO entered the bridge. "Medevac is away. The doc seemed pleased but wanted to get them back ASAP. Air Force says we owe them a few hundred pounds of fuel. Pilot said all of Europe is socked in with cloud and fog, can't get a fixed wing medevac flight up. Said she is still heading for Ankara but may get routed to Istanbul."

"OK, let's go find our tender. I'll be in the radio room."

The Captain entered the radio room. "Get the AWACS driver on the horn for me, please."

A moment later, an operator handed a headset to the Captain. "Got him for you, Sir."

Kaar adjusted the headset over his ears. "This is the Skipper of the *Carl King*. Want to thank you for your help this morning."

"Glad to help, had a training exercise with your guys over the Med today. Guess we got it done before breakfast. Sure did light things up down there for a few minutes." Came the reply.

"Minutes... seemed like hours down here."

"Made us pucker a little, too." Replied the AWACS pilot.

"Gave them a good bedtime story back home.

"Got the word medevac can't get out of Europe. Big daddy sent his G4 out of Portugal to act as medevac. Your ground crew gang at Sig probably had a great time tearing up the inside to refit for a medevac. The G4 ETA to Istanbul is a little over an hour. We have rerouted our chopper there. We will stay with her 'til she has the beacon from there."

"Big daddy heard you call him that." Kaar answered, smiling.

"No one here said that. You did a gutsy thing there today Skipper, congratulations. "

"Have a nice breakfast, Colonel. *Carl King* out."

~

34 Miles South Of The Crimean Coast

Having only one useable arm, Brady was not very stable standing in the moving boat. However, sitting he was able to help the Russian girl keep her balance. Lena stood toward the rear and Manny stood in the bow. Both had binoculars and were constantly scanning the horizon of the empty ocean. The visibility was good, so Horton kept them on a course some ten miles south of the intended track of the freighter. The two lookouts were watching for anything on the northern horizon. If a ship was spotted that was not their freighter, they would alter course to stay as far away as possible.

Lena stood very straight and stretched to her greatest height. Having a limited English vocabulary, she excitedly exclaimed. "dirt air, dirt air." Then pointing toward the horizon.

Brady had learned earlier she didn't know the word 'smoke'. She understood 'dirt in the air'. The Seal in the boat's bow immediately turned his binoculars to where she was pointing. Horton reduced the speed.

"Hint of black smoke on the horizon."

"Just enough speed to keep steerage. Need to get a direction track on the smoke as soon as possible." Brady said what they all knew.

After the Seal watching the horizon said, "Just let out a big puff of smoke."

"Keep the time of that." Brady instructed Horton. "Lost my watch."

"Shouldn't ever leave home without it." Horton quipped.

Both occupants with binoculars continued to scan the horizon in all directions while keeping their primary focus on the smoke. They could now see the tiny silhouette of a ship.

After a few minutes Lena exclaimed, "Big dirt."

Manny turned his attention to the direction. "Another big puff of smoke."

"How many minutes Fly?" Brady asked the boat operator.

"Right at fifteen minutes."

Manny spoke, "I see a stack on the horizon to the Southwest."

"Can't be the *Carl King*. It's too soon." Horton answered.

"If he isn't heading for us, we are OK. He won't see us outside of five miles. And then only if he is looking."

The next few minutes became very tense as it was determined the second ship was heading somewhat in their direction.

"Big dirt, big dirt." Lena excitedly exclaimed.

"Another big puff." Manny followed immediately.

"What about the time?" Brady asked to Horton.

"Right at fifteen minutes." Came the answer.

"Turn to intercept him, Fly. That is our ride. Savas is giving us a signal."

The Seal jammed the throttle open and turned the boat toward the silhouette on the horizon north of them. Both Manny and the girl fell from the sudden movement. "Sorry gang, let's get off this ocean."

It took about twenty minutes for the Seal's boat to get near the freighter. They could see the ship was slowing. When they were about two hundred yards away, the boarding ladder was being lowered. As Horton eased the boat next to the platform at the bottom of the ladder, Manny threw a line to a crewman on the platform. The big ship was at a standstill.

Manny helped Lena onto the platform first before helping Brady maintained his balance onto the platform. Manny then returned to the bow of the boat and attached a cable from overhead to a hauling ring on the bow. Horton was doing the same to two cables at each end of the transom.

Both Seals grabbed their gear and jumped onto the platform as the *Deniz Esen* wench above began to haul the boat aboard.

"Hurry please, we need to clear the deck and get underway." Savas encouraged the group from the deck at the top of the ladder.

Brady followed Lena up the ladder to receive an enormous hug from Savas, until Savas realized he was hurt. "What did they do to you, my friend?"

By this time, Lena was in a conversation with two of the crewmen. "We call on many Russian ports; most of the crew speaks some Russian. Is she your asset?"

"I'll explain later."

"Yes, we must get you off the deck. To my cabin please, all of you. The crew will take care of your boat."

As they entered the Captain's cabin. "Please sit down." He was especially cordial to the young Lena. He said something to her in her language that made her smile.

"First to your injury."

Brady quickly explained the situation. His injury probably needed no more attention until he got to a hospital.

"There should be hot food for you in the galley by now. When I knew it was you, I put a beer in the cooler. When I saw four, I put four in the cooler." Savas said with a slight nod of the head. "We are not prepared for this many guests. Our only cabin is the one you used. We can give you blankets and bedding to use on the floor of the crew lounge. I assure you it is very clean, my wife, you know. If you would like, you can shower." Savas offered.

"Let Lena have the cabin I was using." Brady replied. "I don't think I could laydown, anyway."

Savas then explained his offer to the girl in Russian. This brought a bigger smile to her face.

Later that morning in the Captain's cabin, the two were

talking about the situation. "The girl showered and is asleep in your cabin. I guess the two Navy Seals are also sleeping?" Savas stated to Brady.

"Once they were convinced there was nothing more they could do, they each had a beer, then bedded down."

"That brings us to what more can we do."

"Any word on where *Carl King* is now?" Brady asked.

"I sent word you were all aboard. *Carl King* is some hundred miles southeast of us. Don't want her near us now. We are probably still under some suspicion."

"The heavy smoke was a real help. But won't that and you stopping cause concern?"

"Normally yes. Your controller in Istanbul sent a telex asking if we still had problems with the smoke. It would seem like that had been a problem. When we stopped, I sent a telex back to the office that we were stopping to change a fuel filter. That took care of the smoke problem. Seems to have worked, as the Russians have not approached us. They have a destroyer less than thirty miles away."

"We are continuing to Varna as planned. We can't use the crew injury to get them to pick you up. *Carl King* used that to get a medevac for some injuries. Must have been for the rest of your party."

"We can't go into port with you. Didn't you get searched in Yalta?"

"You are correct. But we have a new plan. In a few hours I will notify the office I am having some steerage problems. As it gets worse, it would be too dangerous to enter harbor without tug assistant. Tugs are very expensive for foreign ships. We will stop to repair the hydraulic leak. We can sit dead in the water doing repair until after dark. Once it is dark, we will put your boat back in the water and the four of you will motor at 165 degrees for two hours. I have exact coordinates for you to meet *Carl King*. You will have to find her, can't use homing signal. The mast light can be seen for fifteen miles at night. But you will have to go to her. To identify when you are close, she will have two flashing lights facing forward. She will be making five knots so you can catch her."

"Think I have had enough of small boats for a while, but that sounds like a plan. Savas, you have done this before."

"Time for you to get some rest. If you would like my bed or sit here in a chair. Your choice. I will not disturb you until it is near time to leave. We will have a meal for you."

CHAPTER # 23

Brady finally got comfortable enough sitting up to fall asleep. The exhaustion overcame the pain. It felt like he had just fallen asleep when a lot of running and shouting throughout the ship brought him fully awake and alert.

Savas stuck his head into the cabin. "Hurry my friend. A Russian destroyer has turned and is heading our way at high speed. He will be here in about twenty minutes. We must get your boat and the four of you off the ship."

Looking at the porthole on the cabin wall. "It isn't dark enough yet. Can we get away soon enough?"

"No, it will be too light when you get on the water. He will see you with the daylight left. You will have to play cat and mouse, you being the mouse. With the seas this calm, he will come alongside to board."

"He can't board you. This is international waters."

"If you want to do business with Russian ports, you play by their rules. He will ease up on the lee side of the seas. You must maneuver your boat around the bow of the ship to stay away from him. Stay close to our hull. Cut the engine and use the oars to stay close."

"How did he get so close?"

"We have had him on radar all afternoon. He had not been tracking us. It looked like he was heading to Sevastopol. He was about twenty miles away when he suddenly turned to us and went to speed."

"What about your repairs? If he boards, they will see nothing happening."

"The repairs are complete. We have a damaged hydraulic seal to show him."

They stepped into the twilight on the deck. The rest of Brady's party was there next to their boat. Lena ran to them when she saw them.

Savas explained. "She woke up a couple of hours ago. She came to me to ask if she could stay on this ship, because she is afraid for her safety; is terribly frightened to get on an American Navy ship. They will feed her only the garbage, the sailors will be drunk and will all rape her. Then, before they reach port, she will be murdered and thrown overboard."

"Quite a propaganda machine. Poor Lena."

"I told her I know the American Navy. None of that is true. She will be treated like a princess. I told her the other two with her were American Navy, the baddest America could produce. She didn't believe me at first, but seemed to come around finally. She does trust you. You came onto the beach while under fire to help them."

"I think she exaggerates some."

"Really, what about your shoulder and her grandmother and brother? She thinks the only thing missing is your white horse and hat. I am kind of thinking that, too."

One of the crew handling the boat said something to Savas.

"We don't have time to lower the ladder. We can lower the

others in a sling, but with your arm, you can't use a sling. You are going to have to ride down in the boat. Sit in the middle, stay low and don't move around until you hit the water. One guy will go with the girl to keep her in the sling. Remember, she barely trusts them, but you she trusts completely. Oh, and she asked if the warship will have peanut butter. Good luck my friend. Don't come back this time." Savas ended with a laugh and a slap on Brady's good shoulder.

"U.S.Navy can't operate without peanut butter, popcorn, and ice cream." Brady replied.

From within the small boat, Brady watched as the boat descended along the side of the ship. Before he felt the boat hit the water, he could see Manny and Lena being lowered over the side. Just as the boat touched the water, he saw Petty Officer Horton leap from the deck into the water near him. It seemed Horton had barely hit the water before he was climbing into the boat. By the time he had released the cables from the transom, the other two passengers were freeing themselves from their slings. Manny released the bow cable as Horton started the engine and eased the boat toward the bow of the ship.

As the darkness descended, Brady felt better about their chances of avoiding detection by the Russians. It was shadowing and dim enough they were able to ease around the bow as the Russian destroyer crossed the stern of the freighter about a quarter of a mile away.

Using the oars, the two Seals kept the boat glued to the hull of the freighter near the bow overhang. Every minute of darkness worked to their advantage. It was still not dark enough for them to not be seen if they pulled away.

After about twenty minutes, which seemed like hours, they heard a voice above them, "Pulling away soon, move to stern."

From some of Savas' instructions to Petty Officer Horton,

they knew this meant the Russians had left the deck. They could start their engine but only use idle to move. As they neared the stern of the freighter, the bow of the Russian destroyer came into view a few hundred yards in front of *Deniz Esen*. They were able to round the stern of the ship before the Russian had a sight along the side of the freighter.

"We must get underway. Stay alongside for at least ten minutes. When you leave, don't make a wake for five or six miles." This was the voice of Savas.

Having been forced to separate from *Deniz Esen* sooner than planned, they had extra time until meeting *Carl King*. They were able to travel at a slower speed, which made for a more comfortable ride.

The four were sitting separated enough to balance the weight in the boat. Fly was in back operating the engine, Manny in the bow and Lena and Brady on the middle bench. The Russian teenager was right next to Brady. He could feel her tension. Brady took this time to explain Lena's fear to the two Seals.

When Brady was finished, Horton said, "I have a daughter." He reached out his hand to Lena.

She looked at Brady. He nodded to her. She reluctantly put her hand on Horton's. He slowly put his other hand on top of her's. He caressed her hand in a very gentle, fatherly manner. Brady could see a tear streak down her cheek.

Horton released her hand and went back to operating the boat. He then joked, "She has good reason. Every young girl should be afraid to be around a Seal. Especially that one there." As he nodded toward Manny.

"Not the ones that like peanut butter." Manny answered. Then Lena looked questioningly at Brady. He gave her a hug with his good arm, which brought a big smile to her face.

"We are at the assigned coordinates, but we are thirty minutes early. Do you see anything, Manny?" Horton asked.

"Still empty on the horizon." Manny replied.

Brady interjected. "Too early. They won't have any extra lights on yet. Will just be the running lights on the mast. Slow us down but continue south, maybe a little southeast."

After another ten minutes, Manny broke the silence. "I think I see a light dead ahead."

Another few minutes went by. "Definitely a mast light now, about fifteen degrees on our starboard bow."

"What is the distance?" Brady asked.

"Maybe fifteen miles."

"Horton, we better let her come to us. She should be turning on her forward signal lights soon. It is ten minutes until our appointment."

The boat slowed to a crawl, just enough speed to maintain steerage.

"The lights came on. Two lights on the bridge wings. About five miles."

They could all see the glow of the lights. There was some excitement among the three, but Lena got very quiet and still. Brady could sense her apprehension.

"Manny, use your light to flash at them, don't give a constant beam." Brady ordered.

Within a minute, the lights on the bridge wings went out, then flashed back on for a second.

When the small boat was about fifty yards from *Carl King*, an amplified voice advised them. 'We cannot go dead in the water, come alongside and match our speed. We will lower lines for the zodiac and slings for you.'

Horton maneuvered the boat next to the moving hull of the warship. Manny yelled to the sailors on the deck above. "Two need to sling together. One can't sling, need a boatswain's chair."

In less than five minutes, the four were standing on the deck of USS *Carl King*. Lena was clinging to Brady. Horton was explaining to Lt. Nelson, the XO, and the surrounding sailors about the Russian girl.

The deck officer yelled, "Chief, you have two minutes to lights out and four minutes to make the boat disappear. Have incoming eyes."

"Four minutes hell, we can't get the boat up here and deflated that quickly." The man running the deck crew answered.

Brady stepped over to him. "Chief, do you have a shotgun?"

The chief hollered to the deck officer, "Sir, get me a twelve gauge and shells from the locker. Tell them they have one minute." Then to everyone in general. "OK, get the deck cleared."

The XO said to Brady, "Come with me, please. Lt. Nelson, bring your two men along. Captain wants to see you in the wardroom."

They filed into the small room where the officers ate. One cook was there waiting for them with a pot of hot coffee and a plate with a peanut butter and jelly sandwich. He offered it to Lena. She let go of Brady's arm and laughed as tears came from both eyes.

Brady turned to the XO, "I think *Carl King* just hit a home run."

"We try. The Captain will be along shortly. See what the recon plane has in mind."

Over the next fifteen seconds, they heard five shotgun blasts. The chief on deck had demolished the floor and shredded the inflation bladders of the zodiac. The weight of the engine took it under immediately.

The XO smiled. "Have a seat. It may be a few minutes."

Once they were all seated, the cook brought the Russian girl a cold Coke. "Another home run." Brady remarked.

They had all about finished their cup of coffee when

Commander Kaar entered the wardroom. Before anyone could say anything, he spoke. First for the three Navy men. "Stay seated, gentlemen. You have probably had enough up and down for one night." He stuck his head through the serving window to the galley and said something to the cook. As he turned back to the group seated in the wardroom. "I am Commander Bill Kaar, Skipper of the USS *Carl King*. We are delighted you finally joined us."

Brady answered. "Not as pleased as we are to be here, Sir."

"How is everyone? I can see you're not so good." Looking at Brady.

"I am used to it now."

"Lt. Nelson, how are your men?" After a nod from each of the Seals. The Cmdr. Kaar continued, "Get them some chow and rest. Sorry about your boat. You can debrief them when you see fit. We will make Istanbul late afternoon. Orders are you all are not to go ashore until after dark. A C130 will take you to Sig. Dismissed."

As they stood to leave, the two Seals each gave the girl a gentle rub on the shoulder and a smile. She touched their hands and smiled.

As the three Seals left the room, Kaar shook hands with each one and gave them a 'well done.' He turned to Brady. "How do you think the girl will do? We don't have extra cabins or female facilities. We can give you two bedding and you can sleep in here."

She had finished her sandwich and Coke and was settling back against the corner when the cook came in with a bowl heaped full of chocolate ice cream. Kaar took the bowl and handed it to Lena.

"You really know how to charm a girl." Brady said

"Chocolate ice cream calms everyone."

"She will be fine if I am close by."

The Captain took a seat at the table across from Brady. "I am not to debrief you. However, is there anything of tactical importance I should know?"

"Besides the bodies on the beach? I returned small arms fire. Think I killed one walking patrol after he opened fire on the group. Killed Lena's grandmother. A small troop truck pulled up and began shooting, so I put an RPG in their gas tank. Don't know how many were in that."

"So that was the explosion the satellite picked up. No wonder Ivan was pissed. You popped them with an RPG with your shoulder like that?"

"No, the rest of our injuries came as we were pulling into the surf. Another walking patrol got there."

"Any other little things I should know?"

"Those are the highlights."

"OK Loner, I am not to get your real name. Of course you wouldn't give it to me, anyway. But you look familiar."

"I should. I'm not the real Loner; just a last-minute replacement. I'm not one of the spooks. I am actually, or should I say was until yesterday, an agent with the DSA. My real name is Brady Kinin. We crossed paths a few years ago when you came down to Mayport. You were with COMSURFLANT. There were some threats to your ships planning port calls in the Caribbean."

"Yes, I remember you. Now I know how you pulled this off. You were the guy that walked out of Vietnam."

"Guess I will never live that down."

"Live it down. Wait until this rumor gets out. CIA can whisper all they want. You have an entire crew that knows what went on out here. The stuff they don't know they will make up. Get used to it. Mr. Kinin, I and the crew of *Carl King* salute you for what you did."

"Thank you, Sir. Got in over my head. You all seemed to

be in the right place at the right time. Somebody made some good calls, and I think that points to you, Skipper."

The Captain pulled a paper from his pocket. "Almost forgot about this with her being so quiet, not used to quiet around here for the last day. The XO and yeoman did the best they could with a Russian translation book. Her brother and Mom had surgery in Rome today. Both are doing well. Her Granddad is probably in Virginia by now. Air Force came out to us and hauled them all to Istanbul. COMEUR sent his G4 there. Took them to Rome. Your mission controller must speak Russian. They sent him to meet them at Istanbul airport and escorted the Granddad. CIA wouldn't let him off American property."

"Mission controller is a she. We knew she would be in hot water for letting me go. They wanted her back there for a good ass chewing."

"Well, she is probably enjoying it right about now."

The Captain handed the paper to Brady. Brady pulled his hand away, "you give it to her." Brady used his good arm to tap Lena's wrist. As she sat turned, the Captain handed her the paper. She slowly unfolded the paper. As she was reading it, tears flowed from both eyes and dropped into what remained of the ice cream in front of her. She whipped the tears away and gave a laugh of relief.

In her best English. "Brady, I be not afraid now. Captain, Sir, thank you to you. Have very nice ship. Very clean. I like it much. Savas tell me you Navy good. I do work please to thank you."

The Captain smiled at her and gave a courteous nod. "Not on this ship. You are an honored guest."

She looked at Brady questioningly. He spoke. "You are Princess here." Brady paused as he thought. "Cinderella. Not work."

She looked at the Captain, but couldn't speak. Tears again

streaming down her cheeks spoke for her. She tried to finish her ice cream around the tears.

Kaar spoke to Brady, "Since you are in more of a sharing mood than I expected. I was told this would not be a hot mission. Automatic weapon and an RPG seems like they didn't tell you it wasn't hot."

"My host on the *Deniz Esen* felt that was a bad idea. He supplied the fire power. If he wouldn't have put them in my boat, I would either be in a box six feet under the Urals somewhere or decorating my cell in the Gulag."

"Our Seal Lt. has arranged for your reservation at the Gulag to be used, probably by more than one."

"I was busy. I must have missed something here."

"I have a story for you." Kaar replied.

Brady and Kaar talked for another half hour. During this time, a corpsman came in and undid the bandage on Brady's wound, cleaned and replaced the bandage. The Captain excused himself while Brady busied himself arranging the blankets and pillows for himself and Lena. He would probably sleep very well tonight thanks to the pain medication injection the corpsman had given. He had taken the offer of the medication to help him sleep. Not due to the pain so much as to how he was going to explain this to his wife.

The XO stuck his head in. "Skipper forgot to tell you. Your wife will be waiting for you in Sig tomorrow night. She is coming back on the G4. Somebody has pull. Is COMEUR your uncle or something?"

Now Brady knew he wouldn't sleep well.

CHAPTER # 24

DSA OFFICE, OCTOBER

Brady returned to his office after lunch. This was one of the three days a week he went to the shooting range. He enjoyed the activity and the chance to spend some time with his Father-in-Law. His wife's dad managed the government range.

When Brady first got to the DSA, he was told of this particular shooting range. On his first trip there, he had met his future wife and her father, Art Jennings. He had talked to Cindi a number of times at the range over the first year before they ever went on a date. She was an avid shooter, thanks to her dad. Her job as an analyst with the National Security Agency did not require her to carry a firearm, but she enjoyed it as a sport.

Art was a retired Marine. During his career, he had done three tours in Vietnam, so of course he knew the story of the Army officer that had escaped and walked to Thailand with a broken shoulder. He knew the shoulder was so bad it had to be surgically repaired with a plate inserted. He had suspected Brady was the guy, but never directly ask. However, once he asked how a raw Infantry Lt. had been sent to Europe. Brady had just answered he went where he was ordered. After this last injury, the retired Marine had figured for sure it was Brady, the bullet hitting a plate in his shoulder.

Having been out of the shoulder cast for just a couple weeks, he was not yet confident in a consistent aim when using both hands. The left arm just did not feel quite right when extended to fire a weapon.

His shoulder surgery to repair the shattered collar bone had gone well. However, the bone had been shattered from the impact of the bullet on the steel plate that had been placed there after Vietnam. There was a new plate there now, but that had required the shoulder to be immobile for nearly eight weeks. Vigorous physical therapy and exercise had given him full mobility and normal use, but in fine motor skill he felt he was lacking.

He settled into his chair to see a pink message on his desk. There had been a phone call from Lena. He immediately dialed the number on the pink message paper.

Lena's voice answered. "Hello. This Lena."

"Hi Lena, I just got your message. How are you and everyone?"

"I would like to say fine, but we are not sure. Granddad is much....I am sorry very concerned. He is at work now, but wanted me to call because I have better English."

"Your English is fantastic. You sound like you have lived in Nebraska all your life."

"Thank you, Mr. Brady. We all work very hard with a teacher. Comes here every day. But this week we get new teacher, she not very good. The other teacher quit. We go out seeing things to practice talking. Mother and granddad learn all morning, then I and Ruslan learn all afternoon when they go to work. They both work two until ten. Granddad at railroad yard and Mother at hospital. He say moving trains the same whether in Moscow or Omaha. We quiz him all time on location of cities, where is Minneapolis, where is Charlotte, where is Tallahassee? He does very good. Mother is nurse aid at hospital, working on learning for her license to nurse. She is at a school for this in Chicago all week. Ruslan and I do test in few weeks to see if our English is ready for us to go to school. Old teacher says we will do very well."

"That sounds wonderful, Lena. But you said things were not fine. What is the problem?"

"Granddad think a few days past a car was following him, it was at the railroad office and he saw it in the street by our apartment. He called his man to call to explain. He gave them the plate number."

"That was a good thing to do."

"Yes, then that day we see a police car stop next to that car and talk to man inside. The car left and he not see it anymore."

"Sounds like they solve the problem."

"Just as we think. Then he see different car doing the same. Looks like same man."

This now had Brady's attention as he sat up at his desk. "Do you have the plate number of this car?"

"Yes, I have number from both cars."

"Give them to me. And keep your doors locked. Do not go out after dark."

"But grandfather and mother both ride the bus to work. Must walk the two blocks from bus stop at night."

"Tell Dmitry to be careful. I will call you back tomorrow."

"Thank you, Mr. Brady. We know you will help."

Brady hung up the phone and headed down the hall to Andy's office. Brady explained the situation. Andy concurred that something wasn't right.

Andy began, "Let me run those plates."

"With Offutt there in Omaha, we should have a detailed map of the entire area. Call when you have something."

Brady went to the file room to find a map of the Omaha area. He was back in his office studying the map when Andy came through the door. "Both cars are rentals. The first was rented three days ago at O'Hare. They turned it in yesterday in Omaha. They rent the second car yesterday in Omaha from a different company."

"Doesn't sound good. Same person rent them?"

"Don't know. Company in Omaha won't say."

"Can we get a copy of the license they were rented on?"

"Companies won't usually share that paperwork without a court order."

"OK Andy, now is the time to pull some strings. Use some Fed muscle."

"Can do better than that. Head of security at Glenview is Naval Reservist. His day job is police Lt. in Chicago. Just got off the phone with him. Has a judge that will sign the paperwork. It is being faxed to the judge; he will sign it then fax it back. They will fax it to the rental car company and they will fax back a copy of the rental agreement and copy of license. These companies are usually very helpful. They are just covering their ass. Should have it on our fax machine all in a couple of hours."

"Guess that is what a career in the Navy does for you. Teach you how to get around the system."

"I'm small time. Some guys have perfected it to an art. I don't have any connections in Omaha, so I will have to use regular channels."

Over the next couple of hours, Brady was busy learning all he could about Omaha. A town he had never set foot in. It pleased him to learn the head of Security at Offutt AFB in Omaha was someone he knew. Lt. Col. Bill Roberts had been the head of Security at Maxwell AFB when Brady had spent a few days there upgrading their protocols. Roberts had been good to work with.

About four o'clock, the secretary came into his office. "This fax just came in, Mr. Phillips said, to get them to you as soon as they came through."

"Thanks Gail." As Brady glanced at the copy of the driver's license.

He walked down the hall to Andy's office. "Shows his license to be from Oregon."

Andy took the paper and looked at it. "I think I can help with this." Andy began thumbing through his Rolodex. "Remember what I said about some guys having it perfected to an art? This guy is one of those. If he didn't invent networking, he perfected it. Is a retired flight line Chief, he knew a chief on every ship and at every command the Navy had. It seemed they all owed him a favor. He was Senior Chief Petty Officer of CINCLANTFLT, was tapped to be Senior Chief of the Navy. Didn't want to go to the Pentagon, so he retired; about the time I did. He took a job as head of aircraft maintenance for the State of Oregon. He is now director of all state aviation. I guarantee you he knows someone in every department and agency in Eugene, Oregon."

Brady returned to his office. After a few minutes, Andy called him. "Got the Chief. He said fax it to him and he will walk it over. DMV is about a block away. They are three hours difference there so everything is still going. He will call when he has something. Going to cost you a bottle of good bourbon, and he knows what is good."

In less than an hour, Andy was at Brady's office. "That was trouble we smelled. The Chief saw the original photo. The fax was so washed out from so many copies he couldn't be sure of the resemblance. He looked the guy up and called him. Family said he has been in long-term hospice care for the last two months, can barely get out of bed."

"Your Chief earned his bourbon."

"If he is going to do something for you, he will go the

extra mile. That is why his network is so effective. Had a bet with the Admiral once in Norfolk. He could get fresh Alaska salmon there before the old man could get a lobster from Maine. Salmon was on the old man's desk before UPS had picked up the lobster at the dock in Maine."

"Andy, can you get that original picture from Oregon? Get it to the FBI to see if they can get us a real ID. Also get me priority on the Air Force run from Andrews to Offutt tomorrow morning. I can't chance standby. I need to catch Cindi's dad before he leaves the range."

"Taking some real hardware? Do I need to tell them to leave the cargo bay empty for you tomorrow morning? Guess no sense in me telling you not to leave a body count in Omaha. Keep in touch."

Brady had learned to sleep when and where he could. The airplane touching down on the runway at Offutt AFB woke him.

As the plane eased to a stop at the terminal, a security truck rolled around the corner of the building and came to rest near the passenger stairs. When Brady exited the plane, he saw his friend Bill Roberts leaning against the truck.

"Col. Roberts, pleasure to see you." The two shook hands. "Guess you got my message."

"Good to see you, Brady. I figured this must be interesting with you coming on such short notice."

"I'll explain in the truck. That is my bag they are setting out now."

Brady explained the reason for his trip on the ride back to the security office.

"How is your relationship with the area law enforcement?"

The Lt. Col. answered with a smile, "We are out of the city, so not a lot of direct contact with the Omaha police other than some of our boys going up there and getting in trouble.

They are helpful and do a good job. The Sheriff is our first backup here. They respond very well, especially good if we have a troublemaker at the gate. The state police are good help as well. For the type of trouble you may be heading for, the state police will be just the ticket. I grew up in Grand Island, my brother is a member of the State Police SWAT team. They train hard and a lot."

"Your brother's crew may be what I need."

"I am always available."

"Not an Air Force problem."

"They do give me leave time. And I am also a sworn deputy sheriff here. I can carry anywhere in the state."

"I appreciate the offer, but I hope this is all for nothing."

"If you thought that, you would not be here. I would like to see the arsenal you have in your bag." Roberts said as his phone rang.

He talked a moment, then handed the phone to Brady. Brady talked for a few minutes, then hung up the phone. "That was my boss. Nothing back from the FBI on the picture. But he said the name was used for a plane ticket from Philadelphia to O'Hare the day the car was rented. I need a car to get into town. Where can I rent one?"

"There is an agency over at the terminal. I reserved you one when I got the message you were coming."

By the time Brady got the rental car and made his way into Omaha, it was the middle of the afternoon. Bill had given him good directions to the apartment complex that the Russian family lived in. He drove around the block twice, looking for anyone sitting in a car. When he saw nothing unusual, he drove through the parking lots of the apartments. He cruised very slow reading license plates. Neither of the two plates Lena had given him was in any of the apartment complex lots. Most all the plates were local or from one of the surrounding states.

CHAPTER #25

Brady parked in a lot across from building #4. He guessed the first number was the building. The apartment he was looking for was 72C. He would go to the nearest building to figure out the numbering. He walked down the hall of the first floor, then went to the second floor. His guess was correct. They marked the first floor doors 41 and the letter. They marked the second floor 42 and the letter. Apartment C was the third from the end. He did not feel the need to go to the third-top floor. Building 7 was in the next row of buildings and two buildings down.

As he rounded the corner of the building next to number 7, he saw the curtains at the balcony sliding door being closed. The glass door remained open with only the screed door closed. He got the slightest hint of the person closing the curtain. It looked like a man. The man appeared much bigger than the boy Ruslan and larger than he remembered Dmitry. Brady continued past the building without again looking at the balcony. When driving around, he had seen the sign for a pay phone on each building. He continued to building #9 to use the phone.

He knew the number from memory. As the CIA was still paying the expenses, he knew there would be no caller ID. The phone was answered on the third ring.

"Hello." It was a heavily accented and gruff.

"May I speak to Mr. Palov please? This is the immigration service." Brady replied.

"He is not here now."

"May I leave a message for him? Who am I speaking to?"

"He is at work. This is his son-in-law. Yes, leave message."

"I am arranging his work visa. I have his six-month extension. He will receive it in the mail within the week."

"Yes, thank you. Good bye." The line went dead.

Brady knew there was no son-in-law. He went back to his car to get his second S&W. He would then go back to the phone and call Andy. From between the buildings, he saw Lena, Ruslan, and a woman getting out of a car and go into building seven. He was too far away to catch them. But he remembered Lena telling him they go out with the tutor. He continued to the phone to call Andy. He got the answering machine. That told Brady what he wanted to know. There was no news on the picture. Andy would have waited for him to call if there was anything.

The sun had set now, and the light was diminishing. He went to the corner of building eight and slowly looked around the corner at apartment 72C. There was a dim light on behind the curtain. The curtain and door remained as they had been

While standing there, Brady suddenly had the sense that someone was very near him from behind. Without turning, he slowly moved his hand inside his jacket for the butt of his S&W. He quickly turned as he ripped the gun from under his jacket.

Before he could bring his gun up. "Brady, Brady. Whoa, partner. I am with you."

The dim light didn't matter. Brady recognized the voice of Lt. Col. Bill Roberts. He was wearing black cargo pants and a black tee shirt with a black combat jacket.

"Sorry Bill. What I have seen has me real jumpy. Looks like you are dressed for a party."

"You have reason to be jumpy with what I learned. Andy called. The FBI got a make on the picture. He is an enforcer with the Russian Mafia in New York."

"Damn. These kids are in real trouble. He is in the apartment with them." Brady went on to explain the situation.

"With Russian nationals at the gate of Offutt, this seems to be my problem, too. I have three men with me. Two by the entrance and one at the rear of the complex. I also called my brother with the state police. He put the SWAT team on standby. Waiting for our call. Guess I need to make that call."

As they were talking, the woman that had entered the building with Lena and Ruslan left the building, got in the car and drove away.

"That is the new tutor. She is part of them. Don't call, they have Dmitry somewhere. We need to find him. Could one of your guys follow her? She may go to him?"

Roberts gave some orders over his radio. "OK, Sgt. Maxwell will follow her."

Brady thought for a few minutes as they both watched the apartment.

"Bill, do you have any small listening devices? I don't know how many there are in the apartment. I can get on the roof and drop one down to the balcony. They left the door open."

"I can get a unit here in thirty minutes."

"OK, do it, also how about tracking devices that can be attached to a car?"

Roberts again got on his radio and gave some orders.

While waiting, the two went into building eight to find a

way onto the roof. The buildings were all the same. Roof access would be the same. It appeared the only way to the roof was going to be from the stair landing at one end of the building. Standing on the rail, he would be able to pull himself to the roof. By the time they had established getting to the roof, Roberts had a call on his radio.

"The unit with the electronic gear is here." Roberts said.

"Have them bring it to us on foot. Then have your men go around the lot here and attach a tracking device to any vehicle with plates from the New York area. Won't be very many."

In less than ten minutes, Brady was on the roof above apartment 72C. The listening device was on the end of a long cord so he could drop it to the level of the balcony. The cord plugged into a transmitter and also had an earpiece. Brady put the earpiece in to listen. The transmitter would send everything to the control van to be recorded.

There was no talking in the apartment. It was eerily quiet. Suddenly, the earpiece came alive with the voice Brady had heard on the phone earlier. He was speaking Russian, but there was no other voice Brady realized the guy was talking on the phone.

Leaving the listening unit in place, he removed the earpiece and made his way back off the roof. Once to the ground, he ran to the van where Roberts was monitoring the recording.

"Bill, is all of this being picked up here?"

"We are getting it all real clear."

"I was just trying to find out how many were in there. I need to get his call translated. Going to the pay phone."

"Wait, I have a portable phone in my car."

The two jogged to Roberts' car. He pulled the phone from the front seat and handed it to Brady. "Just dial the number like normal." He instructed.

Brady dialed the phone and held the receiver to his face. On the second ring, his wife answered.

"Hi Hon, how you do'in?"

"Brady, where are you now?" She asked with trepidation.

"In Omaha, where I told you I would be."

"Yeah, like you were in Turkey for a few days. Then I get a call from Andy to meet you in Italy with your shoulder half blown off."

"I love you too. I need your help, and it is a real hurry up thing. Like now."

"OK. What? You sound serious."

"This is truly life or death, Cindi. I have a recording of half of a phone conversation in Russian. I need it translated now. Don't have time to go through the channels. Do you know somebody in the Russian section that you could lean on?"

"I can call Mandy. She is good. Father was with State, posted in Moscow. She lived there through Jr. High. Then after college she went to Moscow with a news bureau for three years. She really knows the street language."

"I have a very good recording. We can patch it to her. Nothing secure, any phone is OK."

"I'll call her right now. How do I get you? The caller ID didn't register."

"Here is Bill. He will give you the number to call me back."

Brady handed the phone to Bill Roberts. After a quick greeting, he gave her the number of his portable phone.

Roberts carried the phone as the two walked toward the electronics van. The technician told them there had been very little conversation. But he was able to distinguish between two male voices.

"Bill, do you have the equipment to tap on to their phone line?"

Roberts looked questioningly at the technician. "If I can get to the connection box, I can probably figure out which line and connect to it. Sir."

"Can you hook it up to record the conversation?" Brady asked the man.

"Yes Sir. Just like the one on the roof."

"OK, do it." Roberts ordered the man.

As the tech gathered the equipment and left the van. "Brady. You know this won't be admissible as evidence."

"Yeah, a bad case or dead bodies is an easy choice."

One of the other Air Force security team came to the van. "We have been all over the lot. Found one car with Connecticut plates. We tagged it. Two cars with Pennsylvania plates. Didn't tag them, but we can. Found a panel van with New York plates. Tagged it and strange as it may seem, Martin found one door unlocked."

Roberts skeptically replied. "Really. And Sgt. Martin, of all people."

"Yes Sir. Guess he is just good....er I mean lucky that way. Anyway, the van is loaded with artillery. Four automatic rifles, two shotguns, and half a dozen hand guns. Clips and ammo everywhere. We didn't disturb anything. Can go back and get them."

Brady quickly responded, "No, leave them. You did right. We don't want them to know we are here. We have got to let them lead us to Dmitry. If this bunch suspects anything, they are prone to kill the hostages, then shoot their way out."

The portable phone rang. Roberts answered. After a quick conversation, he turned to Brady. "The woman went to the airport, turned her car in at a rental desk, then checked in for a flight to Chicago. What do you want him to do?"

"Come back here. There is a park we passed a few blocks back. Have him go there and wait."

Roberts relayed the message, then hung up the phone.

Brady took a twenty-dollar bill from his pocket and handed it to the security man. "Sgt. there is a quick stop a couple of blocks down the street. Will you please go there? Get all the super glue they have and then some bubble gum and honey. When you get back, get the lucky Sgt. Martin and any of your guys around handy. They have too much fire-power for us; we need to even things a bit, without them knowing it. Get in that van. Use plenty of glue into the top of each spare clip. Remove the clips from the guns and do the same; then replace the clips. If there is a round in the chamber, remove it. Chew the bubblegum. Put some gum and honey in the firing mechanism of each gun. They won't know there is a problem until they try to use them. The only fire they will have will be what they are now carrying. And if Sgt. Martin happens to be lucky enough to find the trunk of that car open, check it. If there is stuff there, do the same to it."

"Yes, Sir." The man said with a smile.

"What if those are the wrong vehicles?" Roberts asks.

"OOPS." Brady replied as Roberts' phone rang again.

Roberts answered it, then handed it to Brady.

Cindi began. "OK, I got Mandy. She is waiting for the recording. She'll catch it on her answering machine. Here is her number. 1-.........."

"Thanks Sweetie, got to go. Love you."

They heard the dial tone and then a ringing from the speaker of the equipment in the electronics van. The tech came jogging up to them. "Easy to find. They marked the wiring panel with the apartment numbers, as I suspected."

They all listened to the conversation now being recorded. Both ends of the conversation were in Russian. While that was happening, Brady explained to the technician about sending the recordings to the gal in Maryland.

The current conversation lasted less than two minutes. "Send her that recording first. That may give us more information." Brady instructed.

Brady and Roberts walked back over to look at apartment 72C. The curtains and the door on the balcony were now both closed. "Guess we don't need the listener on the roof anymore." Roberts remarked.

"I'll go get it down."

"No, you need to be over at the van. I'll have Sgt. Martin do it. See how lucky he is with that?"

"Seems to be lucky at the right times."

"Yeah. It is nice sometimes. I told him I just don't want to know."

When they got back to the van, the tech said. "Your translator called. Said she got the recording. Will take her about two minutes for each minute of recording to write it down. She will call back."

"Can you record her when she calls?" Brady inquired.

"Not a problem, Sir"

After what seemed like an eternity, the phone rang. Brady grabbed it. "Hello Mandy?"

"Yes, Brady, I have it for you. Rather sinister. Not very nice men you have there. Russian mafia is my guess."

"Read it to me exactly. We can record it here."

"I won't give it to you verbatim; I'll change the grammar to English usage. And identify which caller is talking."

Brady looked at the tech. The tech gave him a thumbs up. "OK Mandy, we are recording."

They listened to her voice relay the conversation. It was sinister. It made Brady forget about the first recording.

When she was done. "Get to work, boys. If you have anything else, I will be here all night. And Brady, for Cindi's sake, don't come home with any bullet holes. Having a gal hang around a hospital is not how you show her a good time."

"Something I should know about here, Brady?" Roberts asked good-naturedly.

CHAPTER # 26

After listening to the translated conversation two times, they learned that Dmitry was being held somewhere. The man with Dmitry was in charge of the Russian thugs sent to Omaha. The two brutes in the apartment had the teenagers. They were to wait until after midnight before bringing them to their grandfather. They also learned that two more Russian henchmen would arrive later. One of those arriving later seemed to be the most vile.

At one point in the recorded conversation, the thug at the apartment asked if Dmitry was cooperating at all. The boss answered that he wouldn't say anything other than he hated Russia because of our kind of people. But the old man would talk once the child molester arrived, and Dmitry would have to watch as they plunged a screwdriver through his grandchild's eye. The old man would hear the scream for the rest of his life, all ten minutes of life that remained.

Brady had known with the Russian mafia involved, this whole family would be dead by morning.

"Nice bunch came calling." Roberts said.

"We know when they are leaving here to go to Dmitry.

Once we get there, we won't have much time. They will move quickly and get out of town. It'll be difficult because we know nothing about the location. So we can't make any plans."

"What about the SWAT team now?" Roberts asked.

"Yeah, might as well. They won't have time to set up, but at least they can be back up and do a perimeter. Don't let any of the Russian tourists get away."

Roberts used the portable phone to call his brother. When he got off the phone, he told Brady. "He said they have to inform the Omaha police, because it is on their turf. Plus, they don't want a routine patrol officer driving into the middle of something. They'll keep patrols out of the area unless they get a call."

The next few hours went by agonizingly slow. It was well after midnight when the two Russian teenagers were hustled out the door of the apartment building to the parked van. They both had gags on their mouths and their hands were bound together.

The first thug to reach the van opened the side door and shoved Lena in. He turned; grabbed the younger brother and shoved him in on top of the girl. The door was gently shut and the two men got in the van.

Brady and Bill were in the security director's car. Brady was driving while Bill handled the radio communication with the van and the other security car. He was also now on the mobile phone with the State Police Swat Team.

They waited until the van had left the lot and turned onto the street. The security van would track the two thugs and their victims from two to three blocks back. With the sending device on the out-of-state van, they didn't need to be too close. One of Robert's men was driving the Security van while the tech sat in back monitoring their movement.

It took about fifteen minutes before the van turned into a drive and pulled up to the gate. The man on the passenger side got out and went to the gate. He unwrapped the chain and pushed the gate open. When the van was through, he shut the gate and wrapped the chain around as it had been.

Brady and the security van had stopped about a block away with his lights off. From this distance, they could see the gate being closed.

"That is the paddock entrance to Ak-Sar-Ben. The horse racing track." Bill told Brady.

The tech's voice over the radio, "They have gone to the far right corner and stopped."

Brady moved the car to the same gate. "Tell the State Police to do a perimeter around the area best that they can. Have your men in the car to get the van driver and follow us onto the grounds. Tell the tech to remain in place and let us know if there is any movement."

A couple of minutes later, the second security car pulled through the gate. Driving with their lights off, they drove through the stable area and stopped a few buildings away from the corner. The tech had told them the building that the van stopped at was the Jockey ready room.

Brady explained to the four Air Force Security men. "I am guessing 6 or 7 men. They are very well armed and very dangerous. There will be the boss and at least two inside with the hostages. That leaves three outside to guard the place. If there is a fourth, it would be just a guess whether he is inside or out. So be ready for anything. I want each of you to take a side of the building and the back. They will be standing in the shadows. Use your night vision scopes and move slowly. They will probably have two at the front and the other one or two at the back somewhere. We will give you three minutes to get around the building before Roberts and I approach the front. Don't make any commotion. I don't want those inside to hear anything. Their first instinct would be to kill the hostages."

The senior sergeant asked. "What if they move to the front or go inside a back door?"

"If they go inside, there is not much you can do. If they come around toward the front, do what you need to do."

The three men jogged into the dark. As they moved around buildings to their places, they saw the van and a car parked next to the building. Brady and Roberts slowly made their way to the side of the building closest to the front of the target building. Brady went to one corner and Roberts to the other.

Before leaving the apartment complex, Brady had retrieved his bag from his rental car. From the bag he had armed himself with his K-Bar knife, a nine millimeter with a silencer, and his two identical S&Ws. He had given Roberts an extra clip for his sidearm.

When the three minutes were up, he peeked around the corner. He had to focus on the shadows for a few seconds before he could make out the figures of two men; then focused a while longer, looking for a third figure in the shadows. He did not want to expose his night vision scope this close. He was afraid there might be some reflection off the lens.

One of the men was against the building Brady was next to, about ten feet from him. He was leaning with his shoulder against the wall, looking away from Brady. The other was near the door to the Jockey ready room. Both men appeared to be carrying a rifle of some sort. The two men were carrying on a casual conversation in Russian.

With his K-Bar in one hand and his silencer attached nine millimeter in the other hand, he eased around the corner. He inched his way up to the thug leaning against the building.

He brought his knife to the man's neck, "Don't make a sound or......"

Before he could complete his warning, the man began a

yell. Brady plunged the knife into the man's throat. He left the knife there and stepped away from the struggling man as he was gurgling and sank to his knees.

Brady quickly transferred the gun from his left to right hand. The guard near the door had raised his gun toward Brady. There was a slight hesitation, and the man began to exclaim, "Aw Der..." Which Brady believed would translate to somthing like 'Aw sh...'.

The two slugs Brady put in his chest cut his words off.

Brady waited in the shadow directly across from the door to see if they had heard the noise inside. While waiting, Roberts joined him.

"You didn't give me much of a chance to help."

"All in the timing." Brady replied.

"I guess your bubble gum and honey trick saved our butts."

Brady moved to the door. Roberts stayed in the shadows to cover him.

Brady slowly opened the door and stepped in. He was in a dimly lit room. It seemed to be a supply room of some sort. He could hear threatening voices from the next room. They were talking in Russian.

He went to the door of the supply room and eased it open a crack so he could see into the room. Dmitry was bound in a chair toward the far end of the room, facing toward Brady. The two teenagers were also bound to chairs facing their grandfather, but about ten feet closer to Brady.

One thug was standing next to Lena, holding one of her hands on a table. There were some other instruments, as well as a gun, on the table next to him. In his other hand, he had a pair of pliers. It appeared he was about to pull one of her fingernails out. The gag had been removed, so Dmitry could hear her screams. The other thug was standing next to

Ruslan, toward the far wall. He was holding a gun pointed at the boy.

The man that seemed to be in charge was standing in front of Dmitry, yelling at him and pointing to Lena. Brady could not see the wall next to his door to know if there was a fourth man in the room. He would just have to take his chances, assuming there was a fourth man.

He felt he could take out two of them before they could react. The one in front of Dmitry would probably not react quick enough to get a shot at Brady before he could move out of sight. The unknown fourth man would be the most dangerous. He would take out the first two with the silencer, then go to his S&W. He could maneuver the shorter gun much easier.

Brady aimed through the crack at the man toward the far wall. Brady put the first bullet in the side of the man's head. The muffled sound from the blast only made the other two men turn their heads slightly, but it caused neither man to react instantly. Then when they saw their colleague begin to fall, they realized what was happening.

The man next to Lena dropped the pliers and reached for the gun. His hand had just reached it when Brady's readjusted aim put two bullets in his chest. Brady dropped the gun and got the gun from his other hand. He pulled the door open as the man near Dmitry moved to his right and pulled a gun from his beseallt. He fired twice at the open door before Brady's three shots struck the man in the shoulder and chest.

Brady stepped back away from the door, fully expecting someone to come charging through with a gun blazing. After a few seconds, when nothing happened, he went back to the door and slowly looked around. There was no one else in the room.

He could see the relief in Lena's eyes when she saw it was him. With one hand now free, she was struggling to get her other hand free. Brady picked up a knife from the table and cut the bindings on the three.

Roberts had yelled at him, and he had answered that everything was secure in there. Roberts and one of the other security men came into the room.

"You really made a mess here. Only found one around back. When he heard the shooting, he ran around the building right into one of our waiting guys. He took a nasty blow to the head. Will be out for a while. They have him cuffed and his feet bound."

"Bring him in here and put him in that storeroom. Call the SWAT team and let them know they can stand down. Ask their commander if he can meet me at the gate in five minutes. And you can release your tech van. Have your men bring the cars up as well."

Brady calmed Dmitry down enough to ask him some questions.

The men had told them nothing. They wanted Dmitry to tell them the location that he had moved the weapons to last summer. They kept threatening him and his family. Dmitry recognized the man questioning him. He had seen him around the rail yard and storage facility in Moscow. His name was Vosov, a mid-level KGB official. Although not the Director, he was one of the people in charge of security for the weapons being transferred to Afghanistan. Brady also got the phone number for Dmirty's U. S. Marshal contact.

Brady told them to go home and get some sleep. The security man would stay with them until he was relieved later in the morning. He promised them he would stop by a little later that day.

They finally got the three in a security car and heading back to their home with a security man driving. Brady asked the other two men to watch the prisoner while he and

Roberts went to the front gate to meet the State Police commander.

"Lt. Groves. Thank you for your support this evening. I can't tell you what to do, nor am I asking you to do anything you are uncomfortable doing. However, this will be logged as a training exercise by the DSA. If you were to log it as such, you will save yourself a mountain of paperwork and possible investigation proceedings into the events. In the event of an investigation, you will be backed 100% by the truth of what really happened here. By this afternoon, your superiors will get a call convincing them this was training. There will be a $20,000 grant for training and equipment in appreciation for your help. There will also be $2000 for any overtime pay your department sustained tonight. These same arrangements will also be offered to the Omaha Police."

"I believe it will take me a couple of days to get a report written up on this. Will that be long enough to still the waters?" The SWAT Team Commander replied.

"Plenty of time Lt., you don't know how fast these people work sometimes. Here is my card with my office number. On the back is the name of my boss if you need something in a hurry. Thank you for your help."

CHAPTER # 27

Brady and Roberts returned to the other corner of the stable area. The two remaining Air Force security men had moved all the bodies inside. He had arranged with Roberts to let his men help maintain security in the area. Roberts would return to Offutt to keep things as normal as possible.

"We need to keep all of tonight as quiet as possible. I would prefer to not have anyone else around here. I do not have a contact for the proper folks to take care of this. My boss should be in his office in about an hour. I can let him get the ball rolling. Until then, I believe I'll go to that convenience store I saw a few blocks back to get some coffee. What can I get for you gentleman?"

Both men gave Brady their preference for coffee and snack.

When he returned, "Bill, you need to head back to base. Can you run me by the apartment complex to get my car? Things should be settled down there by now. I'll try to get some more information from Dmitry."

On the drive back to the apartment, Brady used the

portable phone to call the contact number Dmitry had given him.

After the second ring, a voice came on the line. "Your contact code, please."

"I don't have a contact code. This is Agent Brady Kinin with the Defense Security Agency. I need to talk to a supervisor."

"I need your contact code, please."

"I need a supervisor............" The line went dead before he could finish.

By the time they got to the apartments, it was about 5 am. He again used Roberts' phone. This time to call Andy at the DSA offices.

Andy answered on the fifth ring. "Andy, glad you're there."

"Just barely. You calling this early gives me a bad feeling. I surmise someone didn't want to play nice."

"It was interesting. I am on a portable phone, wanted to see if you were in yet. I am going to call you back from a pay phone in about twenty minutes to give you a sketchy report then. In about an hour, Lt. Col. Bill Roberts will call you on a secure line and fill you in completely."

Brady gave a brief hint of the night's events and finished by saying. "And get me on the hop back home tomorrow." Brady broke the connection.

Brady went up to the apartment and the security officer driving him left the parking lot for the Air Force Base.

Dmitry did not have the contact code. It was in his wallet. He had lost the wallet sometime during the night.

Brady stayed a few minutes, then left the apartment. He stopped at a pay phone to call Andy and give him an overview of the evening. He continued to the Air Force Base to call Andy on a secure line to get the process started for the CIA to clean up the mess at the racetrack. Then he would return to the track to be with the two security men until a crew arrived to take charge of the situation.

Brady left Lt. Col. Roberts' office after a long talk with Andy on a secure line. He knew Andy would get things rolling immediately. Bill Roberts gave Brady his portable phone to take with him.

By the time he got back to the racetrack, it had been almost three hours since he and Roberts had left.

As soon as he approached the gate, he sensed something was not right. The gate was standing open. He drove onto the grounds, then stopped his car at the same spot they had parked last night. He cautiously approached the building where he had left the Air Force security men. When he peeked around the last corner, it surprised him to see nothing. No people, no cars. The Air Force security car and the two men were gone.

He eased the door to the jockey room open. It, too, was empty of people and bodies. However, the blood and mess were still there. He holstered his gun and ran to his car.

He knew this was not a clean-up by a CIA team. They left no mess.

Speeding out of the grounds toward the apartment, he was able to dial the portable phone.

He got Bill Roberts on the phone. "Bill, your guys at the track are gone."

"Yeah Brady, they just got back here. Said they were relieved by a team of FBI folks."

"What about your guy at the apartment?"

"Haven't heard from him. Is there a problem? You sound pretty excited."

"Can you call your man at the apartments?"

"Only if he is in his car."

"Give him a try."

After a minute, Roberts came back on the phone. "He left

there about ten minutes ago. FBI relieved him as well. What's the problem, Brady?"

"Those weren't FBI. They probably have the whole family again. I am heading to the apartment now. Call you soon." Brady broke the connection, then dialed Andy.

By the time he reached the apartment, he had explained it all to Andy. Andy would call the FBI; this was a kidnapping with a very short time limit. They needed all the help they could get.

Using very little caution, Brady went to the apartment. He knew what he would find, nothing.

Back in his car, he returned to Roberts' office at Offutt Air Force Base. He called Roberts to tell him to keep the three security men there. The FBI would want to talk to them immediately.

Thirty minutes later,Brady entered the Security building at the base. The three security men were sitting in the break room with Lt. Col. Roberts. They looked like three whipped puppies.

"Gentlemen, some very good credentials fooled you. If you had not been fooled, you would be dead now. They would not have taken the time to explain much. There were guns pointed at you while you were talking. These guys usually don't take the time to talk. They shoot first. So you did the right thing. We would still be right where we are now, but without your presence."

The three all began in unison to answer. Brady held up his hand. "Guys, I am thrilled you are here. The FBI will be here sometime soon to get statements. They are going to want to know anything you can remember about the guys and their vehicles. If you don't remember clearly, you don't. No information is better than bad information. Whomever they send may be somewhat abrasive, but they just want your help. You are not in trouble. You did an excellent job for us tonight."

Brady pulled a chair out and sat at the table. "Do you remember how many cars you put tracking devices on?"

"Just the van and the one car with Connecticut plates."

"Bill, do you know if your techs took those back off the vehicles? I looked around the lot when I was there. The Connecticut plate was gone."

"We got the one off the van at the track." One of the security men answered.

Roberts spoke to one of the security men. "Call Sgt. Miller. Wake him up if needed. Find out if they got it off the car at the apartments."

The man left the room to return ten minutes later. "Miller said they didn't know there was another one."

Brady sat up immediately. "What is the frequency of that device?"

Lt. Col. Roberts spoke to the same man. "Get Miller over here pronto."

"Yes Sir. He lives off base, will take him a good half hour to get here. Hinkle, the reservist is in the barracks here on base."

"OK, go get him. Tell him what we need."

As the man left, Brady got to his feet. "Bill, I need to use your phone. Let Andy know we may have a break."

Brady completed the call to his boss. He and Roberts sat there talking for a few minutes before the phone on Roberts' desk rang. Roberts answered, then listened and wrote something on a notepad. "Yeah, bring him over with you."

Handing the note to Brady, "There is the frequency for that device. Fairly common, most Federal agencies use pretty much the same ones."

Brady called Andy to give him the frequency. The FBI could begin monitoring it immediately. But the range was only eight to ten miles. The group had well over a two-hour head start. Would be like looking for a needle in a haystack, very fitting in the middle of Nebraska and Iowa.

By morning, nothing new had materialized. The FBI had taken their statements and searched the apartment and race-track. They had determined there was a seventh person at the track. He had probably gone up into the grandstand when he saw what was happening, had used the pay phone there to call, waited for the new group to show up, and then left with them.

The lead FBI Agent seemed to understand the urgent nature of the situation and the time constraints. There would be no ransom call or any offer to release the captives.

The tracking frequency was being monitored in Omaha by the police helicopter, using a search grid of the city. The State Police were doing the same over the suburbs. Nebraska and Iowa State Police were monitoring the Interstates with their fixed wing planes. Missouri and Kansas were cooper-ating but were a little slower in implementing their action.

The only description they had was a late model sedan with Connecticut plates. The Iowa State Police were also watching traffic on I-80 heading east over the Mississippi River into Illinois.

With nothing for him to do in Omaha, Brady took his scheduled flight back to Andrews. Sitting was not good for him. He at least needed to be with his think group of Andy and Katie.

Over the next two days, the three had tried to make sense of the problem.

They had agreed that with the information Dmitry had given Brady; they had a few days. The man confronting Dmitry had been from Moscow. This left the slim possibility that the operation was KGB sanctioned. However, they unani-mously felt the KGB was most unlikely. The KGB would not use the Mafia as there was a lack of control and security. Also, if it was a KGB operation, they would have sent someone more versed in interrogation. The three felt fairly certain these were KGB officers, but it was a rogue operation.

They also concluded the operation was to be kept as secret as possible, only the few involved were to know. It would take a few days for the Moscow group to get someone else to the U.S. to complete the affair.

These agents were operating on their own. The KGB did not take favor on an agent suddenly wanting time off and leaving the country.

Most likely, the agent traveling would use a false passport and identification. Therefore, they felt trying to monitor the airports was a waste of time.

The three also discussed how the family had been located so rapidly. Andy made a few calls to the State Department.

The placement of the family in Omaha, at jobs they could be traced to, had also been explained. After the CIA had gotten all the information from Dmitry, they placed the family with the State Department for political asylum. Because none of them had Russian government security jobs, they did not consider them to be a risk. Therefore, the security about their location was rather loose. He was a railroad dispatcher and she a nurse, so they were openly placed into society at jobs they could most easily fit into. It gave them a high priority for placement, therefore jobs materialized surprisingly fast.

CHAPTER #28

Sunday afternoon Brady was loading the car to head to the harbor for an afternoon sail with his wife. It would probably be the last pleasant weekend for sailing before the weather closed in for the winter. Cindi hollered out the door. "Brady, you have a call. A Bill Roberts says it is important."

Brady sprinted to the phone. "Bill, what ya got?"

"Unbelievable luck, Brady. You remember our reservist that was here? He completed his 2 weeks this weekend and left to go back home. He's an installer for the phone company, lives and works in a small town in central Iowa. Against the regs, but he unknowingly had one of our tracking monitors in his car. They accidentally do that sometimes, track a girlfriend or wife. Anyway, as he gets near town, the light on the unit flashes, indicating it is getting a signal. By the time he gets in town, he is getting a strong signal. He drives out of town in another direction until he loses the signal, then turns around and goes back. Same thing, real strong signal in town. He knows calling me means he is in trouble for having the unit. But he realized the bigger picture and remembered what you had said about the serious nature of this."

"Did you tell him to not tell anyone or to try to locate the car? That will only get him killed. Especially do not involve the local law enforcement. They won't have a prayer against these guys."

"Yeah, he said he did nothing but call me."

"Where does he live?"

"A small town northwest of Des Moines. Perry, Iowa."

"That receiving unit does not triangulate, does it?"

"No, it just gives a yes or no. Will get weak on the fringe of reception, eight to ten miles."

"OK. Thanks Bill. Sit tight. I'll take it from here. And give that guy a promotion. He may have saved the lives of three good people that deserve to live."

"I can probably forget he had the monitoring unit with him. But to put a star by his name without the explanation would just raise questions aimed at us both. We would both suffer. You work in it too, it's an unforgiving system."

"You're right Bill. But, it is people like you that make it tolerable. Thanks Buddy, I owe you and this guy big time."

"Not me. I am just the messenger. Remember 'Don't kill the messenger.' The other side of that coin is don't kiss the messenger. Let me know if I can do more."

Intuition had told Cindi to bring stuff back in from the car. They would not be going sailing. She was setting the last load on the kitchen table when Brady hung up the phone.

"I am going to Iowa. I believe we've found the car." He told her.

"That didn't sound like the FBI." She questioned him.

"And that is exactly why they pay you the big bucks. You're a good analyst. Can you throw me a bag together, please? I need to try to get on a flight. I'll explain on the way to the airport."

Brady got busy on the phone with the airlines. He was able to get a flight out of Baltimore to Chicago in time to get the last flight of the day from Chicago into Des Moines.

He then made a call to Cindi's father. The retired Marine that ran the shooting range. "Gunny, I need a favor from one of your regular customers. I need a scanner that will receive the signal from a tracking unit and will do it with a directional indicator. And I need it now; I have a flight out of Baltimore in two and a half hours."

"Yeah Brady, I know just the guy. Al Samly. Retired from the Corps a few years after me. He is with the U.S. Marshal Service in Baltimore. Al was in shooting Friday, talked about he had duty this weekend. He should be at their office. I'll get right back to you."

While Cindi finished putting a bag together, he went to the basement where he kept his array of arms. He gathered his usual, the two Glocks and his K-Bar knife. He took a few more loaded clips than usual. They were all place securely in a separate case he could lock. With his Federal Agent ID, he could take them on the plane, but he preferred to declare them as such and carry them in the case. Carrying a weapon on his person made other passengers nervous if they happen to see something.

Cindi's father had called back. His friend knew just what Brady wanted. It was slow at the office, so he would bring it to the airport for Brady. Al would meet him at the ticket counter with the unit.

On the way to the airport, Brady explained the situation to his wife. Then ask for her help.

"Can you get into your data and tell me what, if anything, you have on Perry, Iowa? Can't figure out how they landed there, of all places."

"Sure, I'll swing by the office after I drop you off. Call me when you get to Chicago. I doubt any of it will be classified, just general information, if anything."

Cindi stopped at the curb in front of his airline. As soon as he was out of the car, she pulled away. As Brady approached the ticket counter, he saw the government agent waiting. His Marshal Service badge was clearly visible. They shook hands, and the man gave Brady the unit in a small carrying case. Brady thanked him. "No need for thanks. I held that wife of yours on my knee as a little tyke. Her Dad and I ate a lot of mud together."

Using his federal agent credentials, Brady was allowed to carry all three items on with him. His personal bag and the tracking monitor fit in the overhead storage. He kept his gun case on the floor next to his feet.

During the layover in Chicago, he called home. Cindi answered on the first ring.

"Hi, what did you find for me?"

"Much more interesting than we had expected. Nothing classified but unusual and interesting. Perry is a normal farming community, except it has one large industry. There is a large pork slaughterhouse and processing plant there. A few years ago, they began bringing in labor from Mexico, all legal. The town now has a relatively large Latino population, enough so that a Latino around town is commonplace. Nothing unusual to the locals. Because of this anonymity, the Mexican gangs in the bigger cities of the Midwest send their people there for a few weeks if they need to hide them from trouble. They can just be around Perry without drawing attention. It appears when they are there, they are model citizens as long as they are left alone. They don't seem to mingle a whole lot with the local Latinos. Just go there to lie low for a few weeks, then leave. Other than that, we have nothing."

"That is interesting. The gang connection must be the answer. The Russian gang has somehow tapped into this. Call

Andy at home and tell him what is going on and this stuff about Perry. Tell him not to send the FBI. Let me see what is going on."

"OK. Be careful. I love you without the bullet holes. Don't bring any home to get sympathy."

"I thought that is what you loved about me, having lots of fresh sore spots, so it is easy to get my attention."

"It is easy to get your attention in other ways that are more fun."

CHAPTER #29

By the time Brady arrived in Des Moines and got his rental car and directions to Perry, Iowa, it was after ten o'clock. It took him most of an hour to get to the small farming community.

Waiting until he was well into town before he pulled into the parking lot at a feed store. He took the tracking monitor from the case and activated it. He held the unit above the dashboard and rotated it to see if it was giving directional data. After three passes, the needle always centered in the same direction. Now satisfied, he could locate the car.

Using just the directional information, it took him about twenty minutes to locate the block and street the signal was coming from. From one street over, he had deduced it was the fourth or fifth house from the corner. He put the unit away and drove down the street at what he felt was an appropriate speed for this neighborhood at about midnight. He felt he could only make one pass without raising suspicion. If this was what he was thinking, there would be someone watching the street. Probably someone watching the rear of the house, as well.

When he was getting near the fourth house, he saw the glow of a cigarette from the dark front porch of the fifth house. In the driveway was a light colored late model sedan. Brady continued down the street a few blocks before turning around. When he was a couple of blocks away, he turned his lights off, then pulled to the curb near the corner.

He had a pretty good view of the front of the house. Using his military grade night vision binoculars, he could see the man sitting on the front porch. He had found the car, but was this where Dmitry, Lena, and Ruslan were being kept? He believed they were there because of the guard on the porch.

He sat there watching and trying to formulate a plan. He decided the best time to make a move would be just after the guard changed. The new guard would have been asleep, a little groggy, and not very attentive. He needed to be ready to move when they changed, since he wouldn't know their rotation schedule, i.e. two hours, three hours, or four hours.

It was coming up on three hours before there was any action around the house. A light in the front room came on, followed by a porch light coming on. This was not a normal changing of the guard. Some more men came onto the porch.

Some of the men were carrying what looked to be suitcases and duffel bags. They carried them to a car parked on the street in front of the house. They were four Hispanic looking men. Three of the men got in the car, the fourth went back to the porch. A light-haired man came out of the door and the two men talked for a few minutes. He handed the Hispanic man something. The Hispanic then returned to the car and the four Hispanics drove away. It appeared their services were no longer needed.

Brady was rethinking his plan. The lights stayed on at the house. He could see an upstairs light was also on. There was too much light for him to approach the house. He could get to the cars on the street without being seen, but he would never be able to get across the yard. It was most of a half hour when another set of headlights turned onto the street. It pulled to the curb area recently vacated by the previous car.

This was a dark SUV. Three men got out and were greeted by two men from the house. Brady had removed the light from inside his car. He got out of his car and worked his way along the parked cars until he was one car from the SUV. He could hear the voices, they were speaking Russian.

Now Brady understood. This was the Russian from Moscow they had expected. The Russians had rented the house and guards from the Mexican gangs. The Mexican guards were no longer needed and were sent away. Now he knew his time for action was very short.

All but one man went into the house. The man took a seat on the porch. They turned the porch light off. This gave Brady some advantage. However, the light from the front rooms cast a glow onto the front and side yards. Also, this guard was fully alert. Brady had seen the guy was carrying a machine pistol. Brady's Glocks were no match for one of these. Especially if the shooter did not panic. Even if he got the first shot, it would alert the rest of the group in the house.

Another light in an upstairs room came on toward the rear of the house. Normally for these older Midwest homes there were three bedrooms and a bathroom upstairs. They were getting everyone up.

The front door opened and one of the men that had just arrived came out and went to the back of the SUV. He opened both side swinging rear doors and reached into the back. He pulled a bag to the back, then closed the door on the street side. As he turned to close the other door, Brady came up behind him and gave him a debilitating blow to the back of his head with the butt of his knife. As the man slumped forward, Brady hoisted him into the back of the SUV.

The guard on the porch did not seem to be concerned

with the SUV. Brady went into the bag the man was retrieving and found what he expected. Among the things, he found a roll of duct tape and a coil of rope. He quickly wrapped tape around the man's mouth and eyes. Then used the rope to bind his hands behind his back and tied his ankles together. He used another piece of the rope to pull and secure his feet up as close as possible to his wrists. If he regained consciousness, he could not thrash around much to attract attention.

Brady took the bag and stepped around the open door. As he walked toward the house, he turned over his shoulder and spoke to the SUV. "Si Senior, now I hurry."

When he reached the porch, the guard stood up. "Hey amigo, I thought you all left. They leave you here to make some more tacos?"

Brady answered, "Si Senior." This was what Brady was hoping would happen. Having black hair and dark complexion, they would mistake him for one of the Mexicans. Ignoring the guard as he passed into the house, then hearing voices from upstairs.

He went through the house to the back porch. There, quickly cut a piece of rope and tied each end to the posts supporting the porch roof, about twelve inches from the bottom.

This was the section directly in front of the back door.

He went back into the house and up the stairs. The four Russians and the three hostages were in the front bedroom. Dmitry and his grandchildren were bound at the wrists, gagged, and blindfolded. When Brady got to the door, the man that appeared to be in charge looked up at him and said something in Russian. Brady answered, "Si, Senior."

He gave what seemed to be an order and two of the Russians left. The man came over to Brady and grabbed the bag. He again said something in Russian to Brady. Brady nodded, "Si, Senior."

The man turned and said something to the remaining Russian. This man then spoke to Brady in English with a heavy accent. "He wants to know where Nikos is."

Brady, not wanting to gin up too much rage, answered in broken English with a Hispanic accent. "He at car. Send me to you with this." Although being blindfolded, Brady sensed that Lena had recognized his voice.

The guy translated this to the man in charge. After hearing this, the guy in charge uttered what Brady guessed was a curse, then stormed out of the room.

"Nikos in trouble." The remaining man said with a malevolent grin.

The man was going to look for the guy Brady had left in the back of the SUV. When he got there, all hell would break loose. Brady eased toward the Russian while he was enjoying the thought of Nikos' predicament. With all of his force, Brady dealt a crushing blow to the front of the man's throat. This completely compressed and shattered his larynx. If he was ever able to regain breathing through it, he would never again use it to talk. The man went to the floor silently, with only labored gasps.

He used his knife to cut the bindings from the three hostages. While doing so, he instructed, "Be quiet, say nothing. Walk slowly and follow my instruction exactly." They each quickly removed their own gags and blindfolds. They followed his instructions exactly. With looks of terror mixed with gratefulness, none of them uttered a sound.

The man on the floor had gone into a violent fit of thrashing around as he could not bring any air into his lungs,this movement caused him to use up what little air left and his writhing quickly subsided.

Brady herded the three family members into the hall and

to a bedroom at the rear of the house. He opened the window and pushed the screen away, then helped each onto the roof of the back porch. Just as he put his leg over the sill, he heard the yelling from the front yard. He had the three move as far away from the window, then crouch down on the roof of the porch next to the house. "Stay here until I come for you."

In two steps Brady disappeared over the edge of the roof onto the backyard. He could hear the thunder of footsteps coming up the stairs. Then more yelling.

Brady hit the ground, rolling to break his fall. There was a shed at the back of the yard. He went to the shed, pushed the door open a crack, then moved into the deep shadow between the shed and the side fence. He stumbled over some garden tools and nearly fell.

All the lights in the house were on now. He could see people scrambling around downstairs. The man in charge appeared at the upstairs window they had used to get onto the roof. He looked out but did not lean out to look. Yelling some more, he went back toward the front of the house.

He had alerted them to the back of the house. Two of the men were coming through the kitchen. He could see one man running around from the front of the house on the walk between the fence and the house.

The two men from the kitchen hit the back door at full speed, splintering it off the hinges. The first man through took two steps, then hit the rope Brady had tied to the posts at about ankle level. This sent him facedown to the ground. His forward impetus had broken the rope from the posts.

The second man, unable to stop, stumbled over the guy on the ground. He almost fell, but was able to keep his feet moving forward and used one hand on the ground to keep him from falling. However, maintaining his forward speed caused his head to smash into the concrete birdbath. He slumped to the ground, motionless.

The first man was regaining his feet as the third man along the side of the house neared the back. Unseen by any of them was the clothesline wire stretched from the fence to the side of the house. This line caught the man running at full speed just below his chin. His momentum brought his feet, legs and torso to a horizontal position level with his head. He then fell to the concrete walk with the full weight of his body smashing his head into the hard concrete. Brady could hear the shattering of the man's skull.

The man that had tripped over the rope was now on his feet, he was looking for any sign of the escapees. He moved to the rear of the yard. Just before getting past the shed and out of Brady's sight, the man stopped and looked at the door. He slowly moved to the door. Using his gun, he gently pushed the door open; when nothing happened, he stepped into the opening. Reaching in to feel for a light switch, he was occupied, and didn't see or hear Brady come from out of the shadow.

Brady did not need to get close as he used the shovel he had tripped over earlier. Giving the handle a home-run swing, the flat spade met the back of his head at full speed. Blood spewed from the fresh wound as the man fell forward into the shed. His fate was probably the same as the man that had hit the clothesline.

There was one unaccounted for, the man in charge. Also unknown was the status of the guy he had left in the back of the SUV. And how long would the guy that hit the birdbath be unconscious? He quickly gathered the guns from the three and threw them under the shed. If the guy recovered, it would take him time to get armed.

Brady reasoned the last man would be watching the front of the house and the street, knowing the hostages would try to leave the area. Brady would have to get to a car. Going through adjoining properties would be noisy and cause dogs to bark. The Russian could go to the sound of the dog.

Brady moved slowly along the side of the house. The light from the windows had ruined his night vision. He could only see as far as the glow from the windows. It was difficult to see the cars on the street. He remembered seeing the electric meter on the back corner of the house near where the clothesline attached. Brady moved back to the rear of the house and around to the far corner. As was normal, there was a master fuse below the meter. He raised the cover and flipped the breaker. The house went completely dark.

Staying low and in the moon glow shadows, he moved along the side of the house, then around next to the porch. He moved to the front corner of the porch. As he stood to look over the porch rail, a brilliant light from over the hood of the SUV illuminated him.

Before he could bring the gun up and adjust his aim toward the light. "Brady. Is that you? I have who you are looking for."

"Aw crap Roberts. Be a little more gentle on an old guy. What about the guy in the back of the SUV?"

"Didn't know there was one there. Let me look. Yeah, he is still asleep."

"Turn the damn light off."

"Yeah, sorry." As the light evaporated from the front of the house. Brady walked over to the SUV where Bill Roberts was standing. On the street next to him was the last Russian. He was lying face down with his hands cuffed behind him. "Found him hiding between two cars there. Must have been waiting for you."

"Thanks Bill. Hold a minute, I need to get the family. They are terrified."

Brady went around the side of the house. A few seconds later, the lights in the house came on. Brady went to the edge of the back porch and spoke to the three on the roof. “It is safe now. Go back in the window and come down to the front of the house. I will be there soon. There is a friend there.”

Brady went over to the man that had hit the birdbath. He was not moving, but he groaned when Brady rolled him over. Brady retrieved the duct tape from next to the shed where he had left it. He pulled the man’s hands behind him and bound them together with the tape.

He moved to the body next to the house that had hit the clothesline. Brady confirmed he was dead. He then went into the shed to the one he had hit with the shovel. He was also dead.

He went back to the man that was now beginning to move. Brady pulled him over next to the porch, sat him up against one of the support posts. He wrapped tape around the guy’s head to cover his mouth, then wrapped tape around the man’s neck and the post.

Going back around to the front of the house, the three family members were standing with Bill Roberts.

“So what now, Brady?” Roberts began before the other three smothered him with gratitude.

It took Brady a moment to acknowledge them all and calm things.

“We have three dead. We need to get them into the house. Then we have two semi-conscious we need to manage. The one you have there I am not sure about.”

Brady took Roberts’ flashlight and walked to the man lying on the street. He rolled the guy over and turned the light in his face. “Dmitry, do you recognize this guy?”

Dmitry came over and with one glance, “Yes, he is KGB. Deputy Director of Domestic Security. His focus is security for movement of military people, equipment and supplies. He spends much time at the storage depot where I work. The man last week in Omaha works for this one.”

Brady asked Roberts to get his portable phone while he seated the three on the front porch. Roberts handed him the phone, Brady quickly dialed. He gave the handset to Lena. "Your mother will want to hear from you. Do not tell her where you are."

"How could she, Mr. Brady? We don't know where we are." The brother Ruslan answered.

The three kept busy on the phone while Brady and Bill brought the two bodies into the kitchen, leaving the third body upstairs where he had fallen. They brought the two now conscious Russians into the kitchen and securely bound them together with the tape and rope.

While working, they had discussed what to do with the KGB man from Moscow. Brady explained the theory he, Katie, and Andy had worked up. The guy probably took a few days off, then slipped out of the country on a false passport. He wanted to go through the guy's stuff in the SUV when they were done in the kitchen. He felt sure the CIA might like to visit with him, but he didn't want to leave him here with the others.

Finally, they had a plan. "So, Bill, how did you get here?"

"I called your house a few times, finally Cindi answered. Said she had taken you to the airport. You were on a plane to Chicago. She didn't know of your plans from there. I went out to the base and got a crash course in operating the tracking monitor in the van, figured that would be the fastest way to find you. When I saw a figure moving along the cars toward the house, I parked down the block. I knew that would be you. I left the van and came along behind the cars on the far side of the street. Didn't have any way of letting you know I was here, so I thought I best stay out of your way. Saw all the excitement around here, then this guy came out and got down between the cars. He was very intent on the front of the house, never heard me behind him."

"Well, I am glad you came. But isn't this a bit out of your territory?"

"Yeah, but I can deal with it."

"Help me get him into the back of the SUV, then why don't you head west? You can be there before reveille. None of this ever happened."

"That will work for me, make life a lot simpler. What are you going to do?"

"Am going to get the CIA involved as soon as I can get Andy moving. Need to use your phone again before you leave."

Brady dialed the home number for his boss, Andy. It was a few rings before a very groggy voice spoke. It was a few seconds after he recognized Brady's voice before he was wide awake. Brady explained the complete situation. He told Andy he was not sure where he would go with his passengers. And to tell the CIA he had a big prize for them, and to have a plane standing by in Chicago. He asked Andy to get him a quick response phone number he could use to contact the CIA. He would call later to tell them where to meet him.

Returning to Omaha was not a good option. This family would never see Omaha again. The mother had been moved to a safe house in Lincoln until the fate of her family was known.

Brady returned the phone to Bill Roberts and thanked him. He got the three family members in the SUV and left Perry, Iowa, heading south to I-80. East or west, he still was not sure.

He got on I-80 and went east to the junction with I-35, then turned south to Kansas City. Brady had formulated a plan.

About an hour after leaving Perry, he pulled off the interstate to use a pay phone and get gas. He placed another call to Andy, this time to his office. Andy answered on the second ring.

"Did you get the CIA stirring?"

"Yeah, it took a couple of calls to get to the right people. First two that I talked to weren't very interested. I finally talked to somebody that became very interested when I used your name. She knew exactly what was going on with the missing family. I told her they were safe with you for now. And that this information, for now, should be passed to only those with an absolute need to know. Let everyone else, including the FBI, continue looking for now. With the time estimate she gave me, they will have a Leer ready to go in Chicago in about another half hour."

"OK. In half an hour, call them for me, and tell them to send the plane to Minneapolis. And give me the phone number, and contact code. I will give them more instructions when they are airborne. Did she say who is to take charge of the family now?"

"Yes. They have a group that takes care of their high value defectors. This group will manage them. No one in their charge has ever been uncovered. When you are ready to turn them over, call this same number. They may need 12 to 24 hours notice, depending on where you are."

"Alright, tell Cindi I won't be home for a couple of days."

Brady completed the call and paid for the gas. He took the SUV back onto the Interstate headed for Kansas City.

He drove south for an hour before stopping again to make a call. The CIA Leer Jet should have been in the air for half an hour, heading to Minneapolis.

The phone was answered on the first ring. "Contact code please."

Brady responded, "Fly to me."

"What are your instructions?"

"Cancel Minneapolis, come to Kansas City. Go into a

holding pattern northeast of the area. More instructions to follow. Message complete." The line went dead immediately.

"Yeah, you too have a nice day." Brady muttered as he replaced the receiver.

Andy had given Brady an estimated time and location of the plane to the Kansas City area. Brady was waiting at a pay phone near the St. Joseph, Missouri, airport when he placed the call with the final set of instructions. He wanted the plane to meet him at the St. Joseph airport. The plane would be very close by now and could be on the ground there in a few moments. Even if someone was monitoring their conversation, there would not be enough time for them to rally an ambush at the St. Joseph airport. He figured he could meet the plane, turn over the Russian, and be away from the airport property in less than thirty minutes. From there, he would head east on a smaller highway, then work his way south to Interstate 70 and on toward St. Louis. He would stop in Columbia, Missouri, and get the family into a motel to get some rest. They could also get some new clothes and personal items. He would let the CIA group come there and get them.

DSA OFFICES, Three Days Later.

BRADY WAS in Andy's office, going over his planned routine inspection tour of some bases. The secretary buzzed in. "Mr. Phillips, you and Mr. Kinin are requested in the conference room immediately. There is someone there that wants to talk to you. I was told it is very important."

"OK, we are on our way."

They didn't know if it was a good or bad sign. Both men felt trouble was brewing as they reluctantly shuffled out of

Andy's office toward the conference room. As they passed through the administrative staff area, everyone there was trying unsuccessfully to suppress a smile. They met Katie in the hall outside the closed door of the conference room.

Brady smile at her, "You too? Sorry for whatever I got you into now."

Andy knocked on the door, then opened it slowly. As the three entered the room, a familiar voice greeted them. "I have had the pleasure of meeting you two, but now I want the honor of meeting your colleague." As the Vice President stepped toward Brady with his hand extended.

"I believe the pleasure and honor is all mine, Sir." Brady replied as he shook the Vice President's hand. They then exchanged all around pleasantries, with even a hug for Katie.

"May we all sit a moment and visit?" The Vice President stated as they took seats. A tray of coffee appeared on the table.

They visited for a good half hour. Then the Vice President said, "I know what all you have done over the past month or so. The entire group of you. Of course, the CIA is not prone to even say thanks, much less keep you informed of the ongoing status of what you have done. I believe you deserve to know a little more. You three all have the clearances for what I am going to tell you."

"Yeah, the need to know thing." Katie piped in.

"Right Katie, but anyway. The Russian you gave to the CIA was indeed an Associate Director of the KGB. He had taken a few days vacation so he wouldn't be missed. The CIA offered him a deal. They got him back to Helsinki in time to get his flight back to Moscow on his false passport. He could return home and to work without being missed. In exchange for this, he is now a high placed double agent for the CIA in the KGB. He preferred this to a firing squad or the Gulag for life for him and his family."

"So it is truly as Dmitry told us. Dmitry moved and hid the weapons so well they cannot find them." Brady stated.

"Apparently so. They have no clue what that railroad manager did with the weapons. And speaking of the railroad manager. Appears the U. S. Marshall Service will employ him in Oklahoma City. He will do the routing and scheduling of their movement of prisoners around the country. The mother will get a job as a nurse at the VA hospital there. They will have identities showing them as U. S. citizens and being from a different European country. They have maintained a mailing address for them in Omaha. That cousin of his in Austria corresponds with him at that address. He should never know they are not there. He knows nothing of what they went through."

The visit lasted about an hour in total before the Vice President excused himself from the office.

PART III

CHAPTER # 30

'Overnight break-in at a downtown Houston engineering firm. Nothing of value taken, but they accessed some of their most sensitive data storage computers. Security measures within the software were not tampered with. Appears no other damage.' Houston Police Report.

Of course, nothing was taken, nor was there a break-in of the engineering company that did not exist. Just an address with a name on the door and a phone number to answer simple questions and take messages.

New Orleans, November

Luis lowered the small inflatable boat over the side of the Moroccan owned cargo vessel. It was moored at the grain loading docks on the Mississippi River between New Orleans and the Luling Bridge just a few miles upriver from

New Orleans. It was 2 a.m. on a moonless night. He only needed a small boat to get to shore, as he was taking just a medium-sized duffel bag. It had $50,000 cash in small bills, four sets of identification, one change of clothes and a 9mm S&W. He was carrying an identical 9mm in the cargo pocket of his pants. He wasn't expecting trouble, but he couldn't have common thieves or gangs interfere with the mission. Also, he had a forged permit to carry a concealed weapon. If law enforcement officers confronted him, he would not use his weapon. If confronted by lethal force, he and his team would surrender. The mission may involve some injuries, possibly serious. But none of the injuries would be by gun shot.

Luis had entered the U.S. several times over the last ten years. He had always flown in from various Central or South American cities using false passports. This time, his duffel bag had things that would not pass customs.

The river current would take him down to where he could come ashore near the New Orleans airport. It would be about two miles inland to the area near the airport. Getting there just after daybreak, the airport activity would have begun for the day. He would check-in to a motel as if he had just come in on an early flight. For the time being, he was Alberto López, business owner from Fort Worth, with Texas driver license and, of course, a gold MasterCard.

Getting a room at the La Quinta for two days went smoothly, as he knew it would. He had done it many times before in various American cities. He would sleep for a couple of hours, then go rent a car from one of the local companies in the area. The nearest Walmart would supply his needs for wardrobe and suitcase, mostly to satisfy the curiosity of the cleaning staff. He would spend the rest of the day looking for a more permanent location to use as a base of operations to conduct his mission. Hopefully, he could arrange something in the next two days. If not, he would need to change motels.

By early afternoon, 'Alberto López' was cruising the warehouse area near the cargo docks on the West Bank of the Mississippi River across from downtown New Orleans. He needed to rent a small warehouse type facility with some office space and restroom. It would need to be large enough to easily fit five vehicles and an eighteen wheeler. Hopefully, he could find one that had a small kitchen. This would be living quarters for up to eleven team members. Some members would be there almost a month, as the rest of his team intermittently filtered into the area. It would be ten days before the first two arrived. That would give him time to become familiar with the area and reduce the local curiosity as to the recent activity.

The next day, he had found a place just three blocks from the dock area. He had negotiated a six-month lease. However, they wanted the six months paid up front. He paid the six-month lease with a cashier's check that was drawn on a local bank. The account in the name of North Gulf Distribution had been active for the past fifteen years. It was supposedly a small company on the Mississippi coast. They would not need the place for six months, but demanding too short a lease might draw attention. Six months would take them thru Mardi Gras. It was normal for local groups to use such places to build floats for the parades.

Next he bought, with cash, a late model panel van. The mission plan called for three more of these vehicles, but they would not be purchased local. In fact, there would not be two vehicles acquired in the same state. He would take the bus up to Jackson in a few days to get another van. The following week, he would fly to Atlanta to get a third van and also pick up the first of his team. That would be Rodolfo Perez, one of his intelligence officers that spoke fluent English. Rudy was as fluent as Luis himself however, he still had somewhat of a Latino accent, unlike Luis, who had no hint of an accent. Luis could even throw in some Cajun or Texas twang if needed.

Rudy was flying in from Costa Rica on a Panamanian passport. The rest of the team would be Cuban military regulars, eight Army Rangers and one member from the Cuban Coast Guard. They needed this petty officer to navigate their landing party across fifty miles of open Gulf water. This seaman had been working with the team for the last three months and fit in very well. The team commander, Lieutenant Raul Salinas, had passable English skills and the first sergeant's English was adequate. Both had been working very hard on their language skills. The rest of the Rangers had virtually no useable English, except the one female, Elana Marquez, had been taught a few specific phrases. Another sergeant, Filipe Mendoza, had been living in the Cuban community in Miami for the past month. Hopefully, his English was much improved.

Luis had an uneventful week in the New Orleans area, making numerous small purchases of supplies. They made no large purchases that may draw attention. He also needed to be able to carry everything in his van; he did not want any deliveries.

During his time in the area, he had decided they needed a fifth van. One evening, he had taken the overnight bus to Houston to purchase the next van. He had slept well on the bus, then spent the rest of the early morning in an all-night coffee shop. It was mid-morning before the used car lots began their business day. The van was purchased with cash, and Luis returned to New Orleans that afternoon. He left the direct route of Interstate 10 at Lafayette to go south through the coastal bayou country. He needed to become familiar with the roads between Morgan City and Houma. Brady had given him the address in Morgan City, where the drill bits would be stored. He wanted to see the location himself during daylight hours.

The next day, his flight to Atlanta and the purchase of the fourth van were equally uneventful as his trip to Houston had been. Driving the recently purchased van, he met Rudy at the Atlanta airport. Together they drove to Charleston, S. C. In Charleston they bought the fifth van, all the vans were of different color and different make and style. Finding five different style utility vans of varying color was more difficult than Luis had anticipated. Family and sport vans filled the entire color spectrum, but utility vans favored white and beige. Near the Charleston harbor, they were to meet the Cuban Ranger Lt. later that night. He was coming off a ship in Charleston, much the same as Luis had done in New Orleans. The Lt. was bringing a couple of larger pieces of baggage that would not pass a customs inspection.

Luis and the Lt. would return to New Orleans and continue the reconnaissance of their targets and buying the rest of the materials needed. Rudy would drive the Atlanta purchased van to Tampa to meet Sergeant Mendoza, who was taking a bus up from Miami. They were then to get two more of the Rangers coming off a merchant ship as crew members, not to re-board. Rudy carried identification as an American contractor from Atlanta, and papers of the other three as documented workers from Central America. The four would then return to New Orleans.

In each city, they had managed to acquire a set of license plates from a parking garage. Always from a van of the same make and similar color to one of the vans they had already purchased. They would first take the plates from a vehicle on one floor and put them on the target van to replace the plates they wanted. People paid little attention to their license plates.The owner of the missing plates would most likely think they had fallen off and go pay the $10 for replacement plates with no fuss. It would probably be months before the van owner realized the plates on his van were not correct and reported the problem. By then, all the stolen plates would be at the bottom of the Louisiana marsh or the Gulf and the Cuban team would be comfortably back in Cuba.

Rudy arrived in Tampa as scheduled, however the Cuban sergeant coming from Miami never arrived. The mission demanded no communication during their time on U.S. soil. He met the two Cuban Rangers coming off the cargo ship as planned. Missing one member and having no way to trace him, the three others returned to New Orleans.

Luis and the Lt. had been busy renting U-Haul moving trucks on a daily basis from different outlets. Some they actually used to haul supplies to the warehouse, they needed some longer 2x8s. With all the trucks, they had copies of the keys made and kept each key tagged to match the identification number on the truck. They also made copies of the rental papers. They would need one of these trucks Thanksgiving eve, but wanted no record of having rented it at that time. On Thanksgiving eve, the night of the mission, the truck would be taken after closing time, then returned to it's original parking spot by the opening of business on the Friday after Thanksgiving. They needed to have several keys and trucks to choose from to be sure they could find one that wasn't rented.

They reserved a flat bed eighteen wheeler for a two-week period from a rental company in Mobile, Al. The missing Sgt. Mendoza was the experienced eighteen wheeler driver. It was decided for now that Sgt. Ochoa would drive the eighteen wheeler, but Lt. Salinas would ride with him. He would have to use the ID they had for Sgt. Mendoza. The pictures on all of their IDs were of rather poor quality, that was purposely done for such an event as this. Rudy would take the Lt. and Sgt. to Mobile to get the eighteen wheeler flatbed. Lt. Salinas'

English was very good, but since they were going to change the rental agreement, they felt Rudy's command of the language may be needed.

Rudy, Lt. Salinas and Sgt. Ochoa left the warehouse mid-morning. Rudy would change the estimated rental return time when he got there. They would return it the following weekend. He would need to know where to park it and leave the key if they returned after hours.

The rental agency was most cooperative. They hardly looked at the Lt.'s driving credentials, just made photocopies. He was told to park the truck in the lot anytime and drop the key and rental agreement in the slot in the door. The credit card would remain open until they returned the truck.

All went smoothly; their next stop was west of Mobile. A place there sold shipping containers. Rudy bought the best two twenty-foot units they had. The plan had them return to New Orleans after rush hour. By the time they had stopped for lunch and bought the containers, they got back to the warehouse about 6:30 p.m. The area was very quiet, with no traffic around the warehouse.

The Lt. and his two enlisted men were kept busy building support framing in one of the containers. They changed the numbers on the containers to be exactly the same. One ranger had been taught how to use a mixture of common chemicals to age newly painted surfaces.

Luis and Rudy spent many hours driving the roads of the coastal marsh of South Louisiana, around the town of Morgan City, and the roads around the Stennis Space Center in South Mississippi. They needed to know instantly where every turn and road went.

They were also keeping watch on an empty lot some ten blocks from their warehouse. The lot was perfect for their needs, had an eight-foot chain-link fence and gate. With no activity there, they would use this to have a rented forklift delivered the day before Thanksgiving, then picked up there the week after. They needed the largest electric powered lift as possible. The low noise of electric power was of most importance.

While they were becoming familiar with the areas, they had also been searching the small towns around New Orleans and Slidell for dental offices. They needed an office that was either in an individual building or small office building. The particular office needed to have poor or no security alarms.

When they located a likely office, one of them would then call the office to inquire if they offer nitrous oxide (laughing gas) for their patients. If the office had the gas, they would then ask for an appointment the week of Thanksgiving. They needed to find an office that would be closed the whole week of Thanksgiving. If the office was closed that week, the loss of their gas tanks would not be discovered until the following Monday. Their time schedule was such they would have to get the tanks early in the week. They would be very busy the last couple of nights before Thanksgiving.

That was one of the many things Luis liked and admired about America, a major non-religious holiday that was not political. A true celebration just to celebrate being themselves. In Cuba now, every holiday was politically motivated, Castro's birthday, Castro's takeover of the government, the glorious revolution and such. Fortunately, the overwhelming Catholic influence had forced the continued observance of Christmas and Easter.

Over the years, Brady had offered Luis many opportunities to move to the U.S. and gain citizenship; along with a sizeable sum of money. He never asked his friend Brady Kinin how much money nor where it came from. But his move to the Cuban intelligence service and his rapid advancement gave him the sense he could do more for his people of Cuba and possibly ease the burden of their forced lifestyle if he remained as a government agent. He would never betray Cuba; however, he would never accept the Castro regime as being real Cuba. He felt he could do more to thwart the Castro government in his present position than he ever could from the U.S.

Once he and Rudy had located an acceptable dental office, they would make a reconnaissance run. There would be little time the last few days before Thanksgiving. A recon trip would assure them of an office that met all of their needs.

They made the run one night long after business hours. The recon plan was to approach the office after dark to do a close inspection for the presence of an alarm system. Luis would park a distance away in a van with stolen plates attached. If no alarm was seen, Rudy would use his considerable skills of picking locks to open a rear door, then step in a few feet before quickly retreating into shadows toward the waiting van. He not only wanted to activate any door alarm, but also any motion detectors. He would remain hidden for a full ten minutes to listen for an alarm or the arrival of police from a silent alarm notice. If no alarm was raised, he would re-approach the building and again clean his feet good before entering. His next move was to find where the gas bottles were stored and what size bottles were there. He would check the gauges to determine the amount of gas in the bottles. They would need the larger size tanks that were close to full. Although easier to handle, the small portable tanks would not supply enough gas for their purposes. It wasn't until the fifth office Rudy entered that everything was acceptable for their needs. The office was a few miles out in New Orleans East.

CHAPTER # 31

NEW ORLEANS, SATURDAY BEFORE THANKSGIVING

Saturday was busy for the three man Special Forces team. They were fitting one of the ocean-going shipping containers with plywood against the walls and 2x8s running the length at 2 foot intervals. This was to attach framing and braces to support the mainframe terminals they would be shipping. All had to be ready Wednesday evening, as there would be very little time once the computer units arrived.

By Sunday afternoon, the eighteen wheeler was parked in the warehouse near the two 20 foot long containers. One container loaded with the leftover lumber scraps and pieces of plywood to give it some weight. The other container, with the interior support skeleton ready for the computer mainframes, was on the floor a few feet away.

Sunday was somewhat stormy and rainy. The wet muddy ground would slow their process of getting the nitrous oxide tank from the dental office. But they needed to get it done tonight, as this was not a good night for the rest of their team to come ashore. The small boat would not do well on the stormy seas.

After attaching stolen license plates to a van, Luis and Rudy crossed the river. They headed the few miles to New Orleans East and the dental office they had assessed as a good place to acquire the nitrous oxide tank. This office fit all of their requirements except the back door had only a small stoop, then a poorly graveled walk path to the parking area. Their shoes would pick up a lot of debris. They would have to take the time to clean and dry their shoes completely so as not to leave any shoe print or dirt on the floors

They drove past the building just before midnight. There was some light traffic on the street. Luis pulled around the corner to let Rudy out. He then continued down the street while waiting for Rudy's signal. Two long beeps on the small communication radios they had gotten at a hunting store. Luis would drive a large loop around the area.

Luis didn't want to stop or cruise the same streets this late at night. Doing such would draw suspicion. It was less than fifteen minutes when he heard the two beeps from the radio on the seat next to him. Luis slowly made his way back to the dental office. He turned the lights off as he pulled behind the building. Rudy immediately opened the back door and began to drag the heavy tank onto the stoop, as Luis went around to open the back of the van. When Luis turned around, he saw Rudy wrestling a second tank thru the door. Rudy pulled the door closed and made sure the lock was secure. They would have to carry the tanks so as to not leave a telltale groove in the soft gravel.

As Luis lifted one end of the first tank. Rudy explained, "I missed it the other night. They have a full tank in reserve. This one I checked the other night is now down to about half full."

"OK, load them both, quick."

It took less than three minutes to load the two tanks and leave the parking lot. Another half an hour and they were back in the warehouse. Two of the Special Forces men moved the tanks to another van that would haul them on their mission. It was easy to know which tank was full. It still had the steel cover cap protecting the valve and outlet at the top. Rudy told Sgt. Ochoa to attach their gauge and valve to the tank that still had the cap, move the cap to the other tank. The two tanks were quickly strapped down with the 250 feet of half inch plastic hose coiled neatly beside them. The hose was not yet attached to the outlet on the tank. On their trip, they would hold the hose near a heater vent of the van. When needed, the hose would then be soft and supple so it would uncoil easily and lay flat in the weeds.

Hopefully tomorrow night would be better weather. The ship bringing the rest of the Cuban Special Forces was fifty miles out in the Gulf, South of the Louisiana marshes. They needed a reasonably calm night for the five Special Forces members. It was a fifty-mile trip across open water in their small inflatable boat with a forty hp outboard. However, a light chop on the water would help mask the white wake they would cause. They had to come ashore in one of the next two nights.

South Louisiana Marsh, Monday Before Thanksgiving

THE PAST COUPLE OF WEEKS, Luis and Rudy had spent hours scouting the Coastal Marsh. They had found a lone fish camp near Grand Isle. It was isolated far down a side road and on the water, only about a mile up a small cut from the Gulf. As was common, the house itself stood up about ten feet on pilings. The gravel road led right to the water where the bank had been sloped down to the water. It looked as if it was used to launch the owner's fishing boat. They had sent the coded

GPS coordinates to the ship offshore. The ship's captain would pass due south of there as he launched the small boat and five Cuban team members.

It wasn't a great night for the small boat carrying the last group of Cubans, four men and one woman, to come ashore. Mostly low clouds from yesterday's stormy day remained, intermittently obscuring a quarter moon. The light breeze from the west over the Gulf gave the water a light chop which would make for a rough and wet ride. However, it favored the small boat's journey as it helped mask the white bow wake from the boat. For the occupants, it was not hospitable, it was a very rough ride and blew more cold spray into the boat. The four Special Forces members could stay low and turn away from the spray. However. the Coast Guard Petty Officer steering the boat had to continue facing the blowing spray. But they had to land tonight, as the weather forecast for the next few nights was worse.

A coded conversation on a marine channel confirmed the group of Cubans would leave the ship at 10 pm. It would take the small boat about five hours to cover the fifty plus miles. Luis, Rudy, and Lt. Salinas would each drive a van. Rudy took one of the other Cubans, 2nd Sgt. Pablo Alvarez, to handle the communications equipment. They would not need to leave until about mid-night. Luis and Rudy would leave 15 minutes apart. They would take separate routes until they got to Highway 90. Rudy would stay south of the river on Highway 90 past the Huey P. Long Bridge. Luis would take a bridge across to downtown New Orleans, then get on I-10 west until near the airport, turning south and working their way to cross the Luling Bridge to Highway 90. The Lt. would leave 45 minutes after Luis and take the same route. Rudy would leave first with the communications equipment as it would take them some extra time to set up the equipment.

Rudy and 2nd Sgt. Alvarez arrived at the fish camp at

about 2 a.m. Not wanting to leave any sign that they had been there, they were careful to not displace anything under the building or on the small porch facing the Gulf. Alvarez quickly scaled the house to get on the roof. He dropped a rope for Rudy to attach the bags with the communication gear.

Rudy assembled the tripod stand and mounted a radio that would send a directed homing signal. He then hoisted this to the roof. It was very low power, with a range of about ten miles. As a backup measure, it would give a higher power signal burst every 90 seconds. The Cuban on the roof then went about setting up a large night vision spotting scope. Once he saw the small boat, they could turn off the radio signal and guide them in with low-intensity light signals. The lights would be easily seen by the helmsman in the boat with his night vision goggles.

Luis arrived just as Rudy was activating the radio signal. The third van was to stay a few miles away until they called the Lt. After about 45 minutes, Sgt. Alvarez on the roof told Luis and Rudy that he had spotted the small boat. It was still a couple miles offshore and about a mile west of the entrance to the cut in the marsh where they were. Rudy shut down the radio beacon. The Sgt. on the roof manipulated the light signals to bring the boat to the entrance, then up the cut to the fish camp. When they entered the cut, Luis signaled Lt. Salinas using the same small communication radios they had used at the dental office.

By the time the small band of Cuban Rangers in the inflatable touched land all three of the vans were backed up near the launch ramp with their back doors open. The recently arrived Cubans had rehearsed this many times. However, the rehearsal had been for five members coming ashore. Six soaking wet shivering souls climbed out of the boat. The extra man was Sgt. Felipe Mendoza, the Cuban that had failed to meet Rudy in Tampa. The five went about stowing their gear in the vans, removing the motor and gas tanks, deflating and folding the boat. The boat took up most of one van. As soon as it was loaded, the Lt. and Cuban Coast Guard man left

The second van took all the other gear, including the communications gear. Luis, Sgt. Alvarez, and Sgt. Mendoza left in this van; they waited a good five minutes after the first van. The other four new arrivals went with Rudy in the third van. This van was equipped with a rear heater and had room for the group to stretch out after being cramped in the small inflatable for five hours. All the vans had sandwiches and hot coffee for the travelers. Five hours on the open water in November, especially tonight, had put a real chill in them all. This return trip was time for Sgt. Mendoza to explain to Luis his tardiness.

Luis did not rush Sgt. Mendoza, he let him finish a sandwich and cup of coffee and absorb some of the warmth the van's heater was spewing out. Mendoza poured himself another cup of coffee and then began.

Just a few days after arriving in Miami, the Border Patrol had picked him up. As Luis had trained him, he reluctantly revealed himself to be from Costa Rica. As an illegal immigrant, he was processed and then returned to Costa Rica. He made his way back to Cuba just in time to join up with the rest of the team before they embarked on the ship for the Louisiana coast. No apologies were needed for not notifying Luis. Because of the great secrecy to this mission, no system to communicate could be used. There was to be only one communication and only in one direction, the coded signal to the ship for the coordinates of the landing location. The ship was not even to acknowledge the signal.

After Sgt. Mendoza had satisfied Luis' intelligence officer suspicion and curiosity. Luis reflected on the team's performance tonight. He knew they had carefully chosen this team for this mission. They had trained very hard. Yet it still impressed him with the speed and efficiency they had shown. Even the Lt. had obviously trained with them. They all knew exactly what to do and when to do it. There was very little talk. The Coast Guard man had melded with the team perfectly, and the lone female held her part of the work.

They arrived back at the warehouse without incident, well before daylight. Sgt. Rolando Catalan was waiting at the warehouse to immediately handle the door. The vans were unloaded; the equipment cleaned and stored. By 7 am, the team was in their makeshift bunks and asleep.

They had purchased the gear and provisions for the group over the past two weeks in small increments at various grocery, sporting goods, and hardware stores. The team only needed to be fed for a couple of days. Ham and cheese sandwiches, potato salad, and various canned soups would be their staple. Rudy had bought a camping stove so they could cook eggs and heat the soup. There was also a coffee maker.

Only one trip to Walmart remained, 3rd Sgt. Elana Marquez needed civilian clothes, as she and Rudy were going to a Thanksgiving eve 'party'. Although not laid out as part of the plan, Luis would allow the lady to keep the new dress and shoes on her return to Cuba. He wanted to take her to a nicer place to buy her outfit, but could not chance it because of her very limited English vocabulary. That was the part of the plan that worried Luis the most, her limited English.

All the gear would be taken out to sea with them and sunk in the Gulf. They would stuff the bedding and tools in various Salvation Army collection stations. They would leave no trace of them in the warehouse except a few pieces of the wood after bracing the computer units. They would have no way of easily disposing of these pieces of wood.

The team spent the next couple of days going over the

pictures and maps Luis and Rudy had acquired over the past few weeks. Their physical training was limited to running and stretching. One of the Cubans that had been there with Luis and Rudy had calculated a circuit of the inside of the warehouse,14 laps were a kilometer. On one of his buying trips, Luis had bought a soccer ball. There was enough room inside to have a small field. None of the group left the building unless absolutely necessary.

By noon, all the new arrivals were awake and inspecting their temporary living quarters.

By early afternoon, the Lt. was sitting in one of the vans near the vacant lot they had selected, a few blocks from the warehouse. The Sergeant was in the passenger seat, waiting for the rental company to deliver the forklift they had contracted for a few days. They had already cut the lock off of the gate and replaced it with a lock Luis had bought at a hardware store.

When the flatbed with the forklift arrived, the Sergeant went to unlock the gate while the Lt. talked to the driver. They told him he could just park in the street to unload, did not need to back into the lot. The two helped as the driver secured the ramps at the rear of the trailer, then set about removing the chains and binders that secured the machine to the trailer. Once the chains and binders were hung on their storage hooks, the driver mounted the fork lift and easily backed it off the trailer. He pulled into the fenced area of the lot as the Lt. directed him. The driver asked them if they needed instruction on using the forklift. He was told they knew how to operate the machine.

They helped remove the ramps and replace them on the bed of the truck, signed the delivery receipt and the driver was gone. He would return Monday to pick up the forklift. The Lt. told him they would probably not be around Monday, but the gate would be unlocked.

They placed the new lock on the gate, got in the van, and returned to the warehouse. One of them would return on foot late tonight and move the forklift to the warehouse. Being electric powered, it was very quiet. Anyone wouldn't notice the noise at night, if there was anyone around to notice.

CHAPTER # 32

MILITARY AIRFIELD, CUBA, TUESDAY BEFORE THANKSGIVING, LATE AFTERNOON

Lt. Col Raul Ibarra was pre-flighting the old Beech Bonanza. The ground crew was topping off the fuel tanks in the wings as well as the auxiliary tank in the cargo area. He had checked the weather for his route from Cuba north out over the Florida Straits and up across the Florida peninsula. Because he would be flying at about a hundred feet to avoid radar detection, he would have to navigate by compass until he was near the Florida Keys. At such low altitude, he would lose radio contact with the directional beacon at Havana in less than twenty minutes over the water. He would not be able to receive the directional beacons from either Key West or Homestead Air Force Base south of Miami until he was within visual range of the Keys. This gave him about twenty minutes over open water in complete darkness.

Col. Ibarra, commonly known as Barra, had personally tested all his personal survival gear, even to packing his own parachute. When packing the chute, he had asked the most experienced parachute rigger on base to carefully monitor his job and re-inspect the chute. This one would be his only chance; if this chute failed, he would be too low to deploy an auxiliary chute.

Lt. Col. Raul Ibarra had been in the Cuban Air Force for almost eighteen years. He had not pushed to make full colonel as he wanted to continue to be on active flying status. He could fly everything in the Cuban air fleet, even the old, obsolete jobs like this resurrected Bonanza.

Barra had flown Luis Quiroz before, both on official business and some off-the-record trips. He liked Quiroz; the guy knew his stuff but readily took advice and even deferred decisions to those more versed on the subject. When he had presented Barra with the part of the mission that required air support, he let Barra do the research, work out the details and decide the best equipment for the job and develop the plan to carry out that part of the operation. Barra understood the mission and had offered very few alterations to what was presented to him by Quiroz. His part was the details.

Barra had chosen the old Bonanza as it was no longer in service, but could easily be made airworthy for a few hours. It could handle the five to six-hour flight with an auxiliary tank and not have to refuel. The engines could be modified to efficiently burn the premium grade automobile fuel they had stored for him in Tennessee. Normal aviation fuel was of a higher octane than highway fuel.

He had installed a new seat and new navigation radios. Also installed was an old communication radio with a recorder attached. A few other special accessories/modifications were fitted to complete Barra's specifications. The cargo/passenger door was changed to open inwards. They attached a sheet metal fin along the top of the body to change the airplane's exterior profile.

Drug interdiction air patrols took place along the southern border of the country. The U.S. did not closely watch for air traffic from Cuba. The island nation would not let private aircraft enter their airspace. Therefore, the U.S. knew very little drug trafficking was coming from Cuba. Also, the land based radar at Havana could monitor the U.S. drug airplanes. They were easy to identify by the pattern and altitude they were using. When the planes were further north is when Barra would enter the U.S. airspace.

Barra had flown into the U.S. a few times using this same strategy. He was to fly undetected, i.e. below radar from Cuba to the Central Keys. When he reached the area near Marathon airport, he would bring the plane in a gentle climb into radar space. It would look like he had just taken off from the Marathon field. Then, by radio, a flight plan would be filed with the FAA.

Once his flight plan was accepted, which was always without question, although sometimes the FAA would change his altitude by a couple thousand feet or his route by a few degrees east or west. He had a transponder that identified him as a Bonanza. The Bonanza would continue north on the submitted flight plan route toward Nashville. When near Nashville, as he descended, he would cancel his flight plan, as was required when reaching a destination. Flight plans used cities or areas, not specific airports. Once below radar coverage, he would turn to the exact coordinates of the isolated airstrip in west central Tennessee. Which ironically was near an area called Cuba Landing?

In mid-September, he and a top agent with the Cuban Intelligence Service had made a clandestine trip to central Tennessee to find a suitable landing strip. They wanted an unused and isolated strip where he could hide himself and the plane for a full day.

Barra needed to time his arrival just as dawn broke. The landing needed to be as early in the morning as possible so as not to be noticed by any locals. However, he needed some light to see the landing zone. This was a very dangerous landing as trees surrounded it and he would come in with his engine off to reduce noise. He had been there on the ground, but they always looked different from the air. Ask a Navy or Marine pilot. The deck of an aircraft carrier looked huge when standing on it, but when approaching it in the air at 150 mph, it looked the size of a postage stamp.

The flight went as planned. The weather had cooperated, keeping the dirt landing strip dry and hard. This was a real blessing as once his forward momentum stopped, he would have to move the plane to cover by hand. As the day lightened, he saw the dilapidated barn they had readied. It was in the tree line at the edge of the cleared area. It was probably where an airplane was parked when the strip had been used. The cold weather in central Tennessee had stopped the growth in the whole clearing. When they were there a few weeks ago, the two had spent time knocking down the weeds on the strip. However, the area between the strip and barn was still congested with some sizeable weeds. They had purposely left these to help hide the spot where they had buried some locally purchased and filled fuel tanks. He needed to get the old Bonanza into the structure, then as best he could cover it with the Camo netting he had brought with him.

The plane and pilot needed to remain hidden during the daylight hours. He would not take to the air again until about 5 that evening. It would be about a three-hour flight to the Stennis Space Center. Engine noise or being seen at take-off was not really a concern; he would never be here again.

Along with the buried fuel tanks, there was a hand pump. Barra had also buried, along with the tanks, seventy-five feet of hose to use in refueling the plane. This was the premium grade automobile fuel the engines had been modified to burn. He also had a bedroll and would try to get some sleep. Sleep may not come easy as he continually went over his mission for that evening. It was apprehension, not from fear as much as concern. He was constantly playing through everything in his mind to make sure they had not overlooked something. He would be busy for a few hours digging the dirt off the buried tanks and pumping the fuel into the plane.

The night ahead held some very dangerous elements for him. After takeoff, he would climb to eight thousand feet on a southwesterly heading. He again would use the radio to file a flight plan from Nashville to New Orleans, identifying his aircraft as a Cessna. He had a transponder that identified him as such.

Once at altitude and heading, he would continue until he was past Hattiesburg, Mississippi, then begin a descent and close his flight plan. He would drop below radar coverage and fly a holding pattern until he received the signal from his countrymen at the Space Center. When he received the signal, he would have to find and land after dark on a very poorly lit field. He would be on the ground about fifteen minutes, then takeoff with as much engine noise as possible to mimic a takeoff with a very heavy load. The old Bonanza would fly south out over the Gulf. He was to again stay below radar, except he was to make two mistakes by 'accidentally' rising into radar detection for about thirty seconds each time. This first time was just eight to ten miles after takeoff from Stennis, then again about twenty minutes later. They wanted the Americans to be able to go back and track his course.

After another forty-five minutes, he would be clear of the off-shore rigs. He was to contact his recovery ship. It would be a private yacht crossing the Gulf. When near the yacht, with the autopilot active, he would set the various explosive timers, open the rear door and exit the plane with his minimal ocean survival gear. The plan was for him to splash into the Gulf as close to the yacht as possible. They would have a skiff deployed to retrieve him in a matter of a few minutes. He would be equipped with a short range homing beacon and low-intensity strobe light.

The autopilot would maintain the Bonanza on course heading and altitude. By the time the first timer went off, causing a small wing/engine fire, the Bonanza should be within sight of the deep water oil rigs in the Gulf. Thirty seconds later, a recorded distress call would be sent from the plane. The recorded voice was very panicky and continued transmitting for another thirty seconds until the second timer set off the larger explosion to destroy the plane.

The rigs and commercial shipping would monitor the distress call. Someone would surely witness the fire in the sky, then moments later, the fiery explosion. However, any boats at the rigs would be too far away to be of any assistance in a search and rescue effort. Search and rescue would not begin until daylight some eight hours later. The pieces of the Bonanza would be secure at the bottom of the Gulf by then. That was the plan.

It impressed Barra with the amount of detail Quiroz had put into this mission. All Barra knew was something of vital importance was being stolen from the Americans at the Stennis Space Center. His flight was a diversion.

The Americans were to think the stolen cargo was being removed by his flight. The plane had engine trouble over the Gulf, caught fire, exploded and everything went into the water. If the Americans believed this, they may not continue an intense search for the items. If the plane was ever recovered from the three to four thousand feet of the Gulf, it would take months. They would see it was a red herring, but by then the successful conclusion of the mission would be history.

New Orleans, Wednesday

Throughout the day Wednesday, the Cubans were told to get as much sleep as possible, as the next two nights would be long and strenuous. But they all knew that. They had selected each one for this mission because they were Rangers and could operate under stress with little sleep.

By mid-afternoon, Luis and Rudy were each in a van on the streets. Each had a Ranger in the passenger seat with a high-powered scope. They were out scouting the various rental yards to find one of the U-Haul trucks they had previously rented. One for which they had made a duplicate set of keys. The second lot Rudy went to had one of the trucks parked, the Ranger with the scope confirmed the number on the body. It was almost 4 o'clock and the person operating the facility was closing, just as Luis had planned. He had only rented from small Mom and Pop operations; he felt they were very likely to close early the day before a major holiday.

Because they wanted to keep communications to a minimum, he could not talk to Luis to let him know he had located a truck. He did have the small sport radios they had used previously. He pushed the button twice as a signal. The units had a very short range.

He and his passenger returned to the warehouse. No need to scout his other assigned lots, as they would be further out of the way. If Luis did not hear his signal, he would return after scouting all of his assigned lots, or finding a truck. By 4:30, Luis had also returned to the warehouse. He had found a truck on the fourth lot he scouted. When they compared the location of the two trucks on the map, the one Rudy had found was better situated for their purposes.

About 5:30 p.m. the first van left the warehouse, two more vans would leave at 15-minute intervals. They had fit all the vehicles with the stolen license plates they had acquired in Florida and Georgia a couple of weeks ago. Sunset was near, but it would not be dark enough for them to be around their destination until at least 6:15. It would take them a good hour to get to the Stennis Space Center on the Mississippi gulf coast.

Rudy drove the first van with the female Ranger, 3rd Sgt. Mestas and the Lt. as his passengers. The Lt. had experience driving mid-size trucks.

Rudy would take the Lt. to get the rental truck they had spotted earlier. When they neared the rental lot, Rudy turned down a side street. He was barely to a stop before Lt. Salinas was out the back of the van. When Rudy heard the door shut, he proceeded on at a speed acceptable for the neighborhood. The Lt. would approach the rental truck on foot, staying in the shadows. He had a small bag carrying another stolen license plate and some tools to use to switch plates. However, he would not change the plates until he was on a back road in Mississippi.

Rudy continued around the block, then turned to continue the direction they had been going. He preceded a mile or so before turning around. As he approached the rental lot from the other direction, the truck with Lt. Salinas at the wheel was pulling onto the street ahead of them. They both knew the route they were to take to get across the causeway to Slidell and then the Mississippi coast. Rudy would follow the rental truck a mile or so behind. If Lt. Salinas was stopped, there would be nothing Rudy could do to help, however they would know of the situation. This truck was an important part of the mission tonight. Salinas could speak excellent English. His Georgia license and other identification were very good, but the altered rental agreement for the truck would probably not pass scrutiny.

CHAPTER # 33

NEW ORLEANS, THANKSGIVING EVE

By 6:30 darkness had sufficiently descended on the Mississippi Coast for the team to begin to deploy. Two of the Rangers had rigged all the vans with a switch on the dash that would allow the driver to disengage the rear brake lights. They did not then want the brake lights to be seen when stopping.

Stennis Space Center was a major facility for America's space program. It was a test site for the rocket engines. An eight-foot chain-link fence marked the perimeter; it was topped with three strands of barbed wire. The main gate had a small guardhouse. Workers and visitors used this gate. There were five auxiliary gates spaced around the facility. These were all secured by chain and heavy padlocks, but could be easily opened to allow truck traffic on or off of the facility.

Infrared sensor eyes monitored the fence, mounted at every third post. Magnetic sensors monitored the gates, mounted adjacent to each other on the gateposts that would swing open. These were all controlled in the central security area in the main building. They were going to have to open one of these gates to gain access to the facility.

Rudy stopped near one of the gates along the east side, 3rd Sgt. Mestas was quickly out the side door of the van. Rudy proceeded slowly down the road. He knew that at this same moment, 2nd Sgt. Catalan would be stopping to let 3rd Sgt. Lorenzana off at a gate along the western perimeter. They equipped the two men at these gates with battery operated magnets. And one of the small communication radios.

The magnets in their units were very powerful. A plate could be placed between the two sensor magnets of the security system attached to the gates. When the unit was turned on, it would disrupt the magnet field between the two security magnets, giving an inconsistent reading at the monitoring station. To the person watching the control panel, it would look like a short in the system. If the system had an audible signal that was activated, they would most likely turn the system off, or at least not believe what it was telling them. For the purpose of the mission, it did not matter. They just needed to get one gate open without causing alarm. The two Sgts. would not activate their units until they got the signal on their radios. Three short beeps.

The van with Luis driving was also near Stennis Space Center. Driving with his lights off, Luis drove down the road toward the main entrance. He stopped about half a mile from the guardhouse. The remaining two Cubans quickly exited the van, taking a small bag of tools and the full nitrous oxide tank. 3rd Sgt Rojas was of a particularly muscular build, but it would still take two men to carry the heavy gas tank most of the half mile in twenty minutes.

The van driven by Rudy pulled to a stop about ten feet from the guardhouse. As the guard exited the small glass sided building, Rudy opened the door of the van and stepped out. Rudy and his passenger, Elana Marquez, were both dressed in casual evening clothes. He had on navy blue trousers with a gray open collar shirt and a dark green sport coat. Elana was wearing the party dress Luis had taken her to Walmart to purchase. All of the other team members were in their black combat fatigues.

Rudy was relieved to see the guard was not armed. He had his 9mm automatic next to his seat, but knew this was not a mission by force. Luis had absolutely insisted on not using force. Only Luis and Rudy were armed for use in case of complete breakdown of the mission and eminent deadly danger. They were to surrender before causing serious injury or death to any American.

The guard had a very pleasant manner. “May I help you, Sir?”

Rudy walked to the front of the van in the bright headlights. He saw some movement in the shadows next to the guardhouse. His team there was doing their work. He had to keep the guard occupied and turned away from the guardhouse for at least three minutes. “I seem to be lost; we are going to a party this evening. I have never been around here before.”

“Where are you heading?”

“Just a minute. Let me get the map I was given.” He returned to the passenger side of the van. Elana rolled down the window and handed him the folded paper. “Here is the map dear.” She said in perfect Cajun style. One of her few practiced lines.

As Rudy turned around, he was startled to see the guard had followed him to the window. He couldn’t let the guard engage Elana in conversation. But before he could move the guard back to the front of the van. “Good evening mam, sorry about you being delayed to your party.”

“Yes, thank you Sir.” Not a line she had learned, but she

had worked on the words. Thankfully, she had put them together correctly.

Rudy ushered the man back to the front of the van into the bright lights. He fumbled with the map as he spread it flat on the small hood of the van. "We are looking for this address. Was told it was before Diamondhead."

The guard stepped closer to the van and squinted at the paper. "Aw, need my reading glasses. On the counter in there.", as he began to turn back to the guardhouse. It had been less than two minutes, Sgt. Alvarez would still be working and not see the guard approach.

"Sir, do you have a ladies' room I could use?" Came a voice from the passenger side as that van door opened, and Elana stepped out. Rudy was in complete surprise; her language training had been very limited. They had trained Elana only on the scripted phrases. This was not anything they had schooled her to do or say. Her diction was very Cajun.

The guard turned back toward her. "I am sorry, mayam, we are closed for visitors. I can't let anyone on the property without an ID."

"Are you sure? I could really need to go." Rudy needed to end this, as her phrase was a little off.

"Get back in the van Honey, we can find a store down the road." He spoke to the guard. "Know where we might find one open tonight? When she needs one, she needs it in a hurry. I can get directions there." Out of the corner of his eye, he saw Sgt. Alvarez move away from the guardhouse and back into the shadows.

The guard smiled. "Yeah, I understand that. Got three kids myself. Jameson's place should still be open. Mile or so on down the road. Enjoy your party and have a Happy Thanksgiving."

Rudy offered a thanks and a wave to the man as he

climbed in the van. He backed around to head in the direction given him. He was careful to not let his headlights shine in the direction Sgt. Alvarez was heading.

"Elana, what can I say? You saved the mission."

"We are a team, Sir. And no, I am not pregnant and no, I don't need a toilet." She said with a wry smile.

"We need to go there, anyway. I'll ask directions and you go in the ladies' room. Just in case the guard goes by and asks about us."

After pulling away from the small store, Elana got in the back of the van and changed into her black fatigues. She carefully folded the clothes Luis had gotten her. They were very nice, and she was so surprised and much appreciated that he had told her she could keep them. They would be in Rudy's luggage when he flew out of Atlanta in a couple of days, just as he had arrived.

Rudy recognized her appreciation of the clothes. "Fold them nice and put them in the bag. We can put them here on the floor between the seats so no one will set or step on them."

She was impressed by how both Luis and Rudy had treated her as one of the team, yet still discretely acknowledged she was a woman. No wonder they were good intelligence officers in the field. They really understood people. If her officer in the Special Forces unit treated her this way, she might be inclined to stay in the unit. But being married and having a child, she knew it was time to leave the military.

CHAPTER # 34

From the shadows some 200 feet away, Sgt. Alvarez watched the guard re-enter the small guardhouse and close the door against the November chill. During the time Rudy had kept the guard away from the building, he had drilled a small hole through the side wall. He had then inserted the end of the black tubing from the nitrous oxide tank. The tube was held in place with some plumber's putty. Alvarez slowly opened the valve on the tank to fill the guardhouse with the gas. Normally, when nitrous oxide is administered, it is mixed with oxygen. Not having oxygen as a supplement, this was the one part of the mission that exposed an American to injury. There needed to be enough gas to put the guard asleep for a few minutes. Alvarez needed to watch closely for him to fall asleep.

It took a good ten minutes for the guardhouse to fill with enough gas for the guard to become still. He threw a small rock at the window. The guard did not move. Alvarez ran to the small building and opened the door, allowing a rush of oxygen rich air in. Sgt. Rojas would have turned off the flow of gas by the time he reached the door. If he was in time, the guard would arouse in four to five minutes, would think he had just dozed off.

While at the guard house Alvarez turned off the switch that controlled the perimeter security system. As soon as it was off he waved to Rojas, Rojas then gave the three short beeps on the communication radio to signal the men at the gates to activate their units. Alvarez waited thirty seconds, then turned the system back on. He stepped out of the building and shut the door. As he moved away, he heard the sleeping guard sputter and wheeze. He was OK. Luis would be pleased. Staying in the shadows, the two Cubans moved quickly down the road toward where they had been dropped off earlier that evening. They were to continue until they came to a waiting van.

If the magnetic units at the gates were activated while the system was on, it was more likely to show the problem. If the system was off, when it was turned back on with the interruption active, it would not be able to diagnose the problem. Once the perimeter was checked by a guard, they would assume it was a short somewhere in the wiring.

Luis was parked on another side road about a mile from the main building. He had both night vision and regular binoculars. He did not need the night vision unit to see a guard leave the main building and get into a security vehicle. The small truck drove to the perimeter road, then turned east along the inside of the fence. Luis was sure Sgt. Mestas would see the lights heading his way. The Sgt. would remove the magnetic unit and take himself into the ditch and the shadow of the weeds across the road from the fence. He would remain hidden until he heard the truck leave. Sgt. Lorenzana at the West perimeter gate would continue disrupting the signal. Using the two separate locations, they could keep the appeared malfunction continuing.

Sgt. Mestas heard the truck stop and the door open. He

was well concealed in a direction away from the beam of the truck's headlights; the guard was using the truck's lights so he could see the gate and magnetic sensors. The Sgt. could see the guard inspect the gate and wiring. As he was returning to his truck, the guard radioed that "Gate 2 is secure."

He remained lying in the ditch until he heard the truck leave to continue making a round of the perimeter, checking each gate. After a full two minutes, he rose above the road to scan the area, then cautiously crossed the road and moved back to the gate. He reinserted the plate between the security magnets and turned it on. He knew that in a few minutes, Sgt. Lorenzana would go thru the same routine as the security man reached that gate.

Sgt. Lorenzana, at the next gate, saw the headlights of the truck turn the corner and head toward his location. He removed the magnetic pad from between the sensors and retreated to the weeds in the ditch across the road from the gate. He could hear the truck stop at the gate and the door open. Sgt. Lorenzana remained lying flat in the weeds for a good five minutes until he heard the truck pull away from the gate. After a few more minutes, he made his way back across the road to the gate. This time, when he inserted the pad between the sensors, he used the roll of black duct tape to secure it in place. The roll of tape was then used to secure the sending unit to the gate pole just below the sensors. This unit would remain in place and active until either the batteries ran out or the security officers found it. In either case, they would be long gone from the area. The batteries were good for eight hours.

Just as he was securing the unit to the gate, Rudy's van pulled up to the gate. He ran to the van and jumped into the open sliding door. The door was quickly and quietly closed, and the van turned around to retrace the direction it had come. All lights were still off. When away from the perimeter fence, Rudy turned the lights on and continued on their planned route to the far side of the Space Center.

Rudy arrived at the east side of the compound. As he slowed to turn along the fence line, he switched the lights of the van off. He slowly approached the east gate. In the dark, he could see Sgt. Catalan's van parked in the open gate. Sgt. had used the bolt cutters to remove the padlock on the gate. Rudy could barely make out the silhouette of the third van Luis was driving; it was about halfway across the compound to the building housing the mainframe computers. At the gate Mestas had joined Luis.

The remaining group would wait here until Luis signaled them on the small radios to come across. As soon as he stopped, Rudy got out of the van. Sgt. Marquez slipped over into the driver's seat as soon as Rudy was out. Rudy went to Sgt. Catalan's van. He got in the passenger seat as Lorenzana took the bold cutters from Catalan; then got in the passenger seat that Marquez had just vacated.

Sgt. Marquez slowly moved her van back down the road. When she turned on the main road, she turned on the lights. She had a specific route to drive for up to an hour. Her first destination was along the north side of the fence to drop off Lorenzana with the bolt cutter. Lorenzana would hide in the ditch near the fence in case things went wrong. He would need to open the fence for St. Mestas or any of the team to escape.

The van she was driving was now a backup vehicle in case it was needed. The planned route did not take her along the same road in the same direction. She was to drive a few miles away, then slowly work her way back toward the Space Center on a very circuitous route back to this open gate. It would be during the last half hour of the mission when the team may need her van.

Luis moved his van slowly around the airstrip and across

the compound. The auxiliary operations center he was heading for stood about two hundred yards from the safety/security building. That was a long narrow building; one end of the building housed the two fire/rescue trucks and the contingent of on duty fire brigade. The other end was the center of the security force. He knew the security night shift consisted of three, two in the control center and one at the gate. The shift changed at ten o'clock and reduced to two; the gate being closed and locked. With a 10:00 shift change, their mission needed to be completed by no later than 9:15 to avoid detection by any early arrivals for shift change.

He stopped the van close to the building on the side, away from the building housing fire/security. He and Sgt. Mestas slowly made their way around the building, assessing the doors. They wanted to find the door Sgt. Mestas felt might be the easiest to get open. Sgt. Mestas had been working for months, practicing dismantling numerous types of locks and latches. All the doors had the same type of lock. The door on the side of the building facing the Security building was wider than the others. All the doors had a small security light above them. They could easily access the bulbs as there was no housing to protect the bulb, only the metal cover to shield the bulb from rain. While there, they would disable this bulb. If a security guard was to come out, they may see the light out and not expect anything wrong if nothing else was happening. Luis bent over slightly and braced himself with his hands on his knees. Mestas used Luis as a platform to stand on while he slipped a rag around the bulb and unscrewed it until connection in the socket was lost and the bulb flickered off.

They would need the extra width of this door to remove the mainframe chassis. They decided that they would make the initial entry through the door on the far side. Once in the building, they could disconnect and dismantle the machines before opening this more exposed door.

Sgt. Mestas got his small bag of tools from the van and began working on the lock. Luis got back in the van and pulled away from the building. He would move to the far side of the airstrip. This left Sgt. Mestas isolated if the door triggered an alarm opening. Luis did not like this part of the plan. However, there was no sense jeopardizing himself and the rest of the team. The mission would fail, but the team could still execute their planned exit of the country.

From the van parked at the east gate, Rudy was watching the progress around the auxiliary operations. At this distance, he definitely needed the high power and the night vision. He watched as the van moved along the road away from the building. He quickly adjusted his view as his real interest was on watching the end of the other building housing the security offices. If a security officer left the building, he was to signal Mestas and Luis on the small radios each were carrying. Mestas would have to do the best he could to run toward the north fence line. Rudy would signal him again when the security officer got near an opening with a view that might reveal Mestas' silhouette. The Sgt. was to drop to the ground and continue toward the fence as best he could. If he reached the fence, Lorenzana would have cut the wire for him to exit.

Rudy watched for a good fifteen minutes before he saw Mestas move rapidly from the building. That told Rudy that Mestas had dismantled the lock and opened the door a couple of inches. Rudy would wait to see if it triggered an alarm before moving his van slowly across the compound. Luis did not feel the buildings had alarms, as the general security of the compound was somewhat lax. There were no security cameras, and the guards were not armed.

Mestas waited in the tall grass for ten minutes before re-emerging and returning to the building. By the time Mestas was back at the door, Luis was pulling the van to a stop near the door. Luis and Mestas slowly entered the building. Using low powered flashlights, they explored the interior halls and doors. Halfway along the second hall, they found the room housing the computer mainframes. It was exactly what Luis had hoped for; an interior room with no windows. They could turn on the lights without exposing themselves.

Luis then had two signals to send. He pressed the button on the radio three times. Hearing the signal, Rudy increased his speed across the open area. That was also the signal Lt. Salinas would be expecting. The team in the van would make their way across the compound using the same route Luis had taken. Lt. Salinas would also begin to bring the rental truck nearer the Space Center.

The second was more than a signal; it was a voice communication. These were coded and short. The second communication he had done tonight. This time, however, there would be no confirmation, only one way from Luis. He picked up the French made military radio, keyed the button and said. "Ten minutes to Paradise." This told Barra he needed to land in about twenty minutes.

Circling in a low, slow holding pattern northeast of the Stennis Space Center, the pilot of the old Beech Bonanza turned a southerly course for the Stennis runway. He adjusted his speed to make his arrival in ten minutes.

Luis and Mestas began detaching the large frames from the floor and the support braces. Sgt. Alvarez would need to look at the wiring connections of the computers. They had trained him to disconnect the machines. In less than five minutes, the other team members were in the room, ready for instructions. Until the computers were powered down and disconnected, Sgt. Alvarez was in charge and giving instructions to each member as required. During a mission, the person in charge of a particular part was not the one with rank, it was the one Luis had designated in charge. It was the one with the expertise in the particular part of the operation.

After dropping the rest of the team at the building, Rudy turned the van back toward the small landing strip along one side of the Space Center. Although well maintained, this was not an active public airport, it was a U.S. Government facility, used only by permission and reservation. They turned the runway lights on only when needed. No one in authority felt there was any need for the lights tonight, as there were no flights scheduled; they thought.

When he reached the far end of the asphalt runway, he turned and stopped the van. Rudy got out and quickly place three small jack stands he and Luis had purchased at Pawn Shops over the last few weeks. Secured to the stands with black electrician's tape were two flashlights. The flashlights were pointing in opposite directions. He directed one up at about thirty degrees and the other was directed parallel with the ground. Being at the end of the runway, three were set to mark the middle and edges of the runway. The lights parallel to the ground were facing down the runway. These would let a plane taking off know where the runway ended. The lights angled upward could more easily be seen from the air to tell a pilot the beginning of the asphalt.

When he was satisfied that these three were set and turned on, Rudy drove the van back down the runway some five hundred feet. Here, he placed a stand on each side of the runway with one flashlight taped to each. He angled the flashlights on these down to the asphalt at about sixty degrees. The light would reflect on the asphalt enough for the pilot to know the runway width.

Rudy continued setting the stands every five hundred feet until he had placed all six sets to mark the runway width. Three thousand feet would be plenty for their purposes. He then parked the van two hundred feet past the last set of stands. A small communication radio that allowed him to hear both sides of the Luis' voice communication. He could not transmit, only listen. Rudy took the high-intensity emergency light and plugged it into the cigarette lighter receptacle. He stood next to the van with the light in one hand and a large, clear plastic rectangle on the other. Half of the plastic was tinted red and the other half blue. These would be held over the lens of the light, alternating the red and blue to help the pilot find the landing strip.

Rudy knew he would not see the plane as it was coming in low and without navigation lights. Now he would wait for the voice of the pilot before turning on the light.

Sgt. Catalan remained outside near the van, watching for anyone approaching the building. From the corner, he could see the building housing the fire and security. If some approached, he would signal the team inside, then head toward their muster point at the north fence. Hopefully, he would have enough time to be far enough away to not be seen. The team inside were to immediately vacate through the door they had entered. Luis would take the van and drive away from the building in somewhat a different direction. Scrubbed clean of fingerprints, he would toss his 9mm S&W into the tall grass. It may be weeks before they found it, but even then, it would be hard to connect with him. America was full of guns. Smart country, he thought. The rest of the team would remain on foot and head toward the north fence. Luis in his van was purely a distraction for the alerted security. He knew they would catch him, but all efforts by security at would direct him for the next fifteen minutes or so. Possibly, that would be enough time for the rest of his team to escape. They all knew what to do and Rudy would get them back to Cuba.

Luis knew this was not proper protocol for such a mission; he was the one that should be protected from capture. Actually, he should not be on the mission; at most, he should be at the warehouse. The pre-mission planning in Cuba had Sgt. Francisco Rojas driving the distraction van. Many had volunteered for this duty, Sgt. Rojas was chosen by drawing lots. Once at the warehouse, Luis had changed the plan to put himself in the van. These were good people he had been given. He would not sacrifice them for such a low value mission. Of course, General Espinosa did not see it as such low value. He was risking many people and resources. However, Luis felt this was a necessary part of a bigger plan his friend Brady had. That was the scenario that General Espinosa knew nothing about, but which Luis knew was of great value to Brady. He also knew his friend would not betray him. This bigger plan would not harm Cuba. If this mission failed, the bigger plan could not be continued.

It took Sgt. Alvarez about twenty minutes before he felt the computers were all disconnected and ready to move. By this time, the rest of the team had removed all the supporting braces. They had four separate units, each about five feet tall, three and a half feet wide, and two feet deep. The weight was not of real concern for them. The team had plenty of muscle. Especially the oversized Sgt. Rojas.

Luis had signaled Lt. Salinas to bring the truck to their location. Although they were going to have to remove the mainframes out through the most exposed door, they could not risk parking the truck in full view of the security building. He instructed Salinas to back the truck along the back of the building to the corner near the door. As he was stopping the truck, the first mainframe was being maneuvered out the door and along the side of the building. The rear door of the truck was pushed up as quietly as possible. They did not extend the ramp; they had enough people to lift the machine and slide it into the cavernous truck body. The four large computers would fit easily into the truck if placed properly.

When the first mainframe was being maneuvered out the door, they heard the expected voice of the pilot on both the radio Luis had and the earpiece Rudy was wearing. It was just nineteen minutes from when Luis had sent his message.

"Sight unseen." Came the voice.

As they had assumed might be, the pilot had not been able to distinguish the lights Rudy had set along the runway. They knew this would have been too much to hope for. Not to blame the pilot, he was very good and doing some very precise and difficult piloting. Landing on a dark runway without the use of his landing lights was only one of the very dangerous exploits that were expected of him over the next two hours.

Rudy pointed the light down the runway and slightly skyward. He held the 'ON' switch and slowly moved the plastic over the lens, moving from red to blue every second. After about twenty seconds, his earpiece crackled.

"Pretty, pretty." Came the voice of the pilot. This was the message that he had seen the lights.

Rudy immediately hit the 'OFF' switch. He jumped back in the van and headed for the building where they were loading the computers.

Just as he arrived, the rental truck, now driven by Luis, came out from behind the building. When Rudy turned to look back toward the landing strip, he could see the altered silhouette of the Beech Bonanza coming to a stop a few hundred feet past where he had been parked. Luis did not stop the truck, but continued directly to the plane.

The rest of the team got into the two vans, Rudy driving one and Sgt. Catalan the other. Both vans went directly across the compound and out the gate. They were to go back to the warehouse in New Orleans by separate routes, stopping only to change the license plates back to the original.

Luis stopped the truck near the parked Bonanza. The

pilot was walking across the asphalt after relieving himself in the grass next to the pavement; he had been in the air for almost four hours. Luis shook hands with the pilot. Luis had used him before on a few missions, none as dangerous as this. As Luis was only parked next to the plane for show, there was nothing to do except make small talk for the required fifteen minutes.

Luis liked Barra and was amazed at how calm the pilot was about the remaining part of his mission. Jumping into a dark ocean was not something to be taken lightly.

Luis timed their stay on the runway. He didn't want to rush it. When waiting, it was difficult to judge time. Fifteen seconds seemed like a minute. Since it was for show, it might as well be as believable as possible. If anyone happened to casually notice them, he wanted it to look as though they had enough time to be transferring a load from the truck to the plane.

When the fifteen minutes passed, Luis shook hands with Barra, wished him luck and returned to his truck. As he climbed into the truck, he heard.

"Voodoo Cantina, two weeks give you enough time." Barra phrased it as a statement more than a question.

It was too dark for Luis to see the ear to ear grin he knew Barra would be sporting, but he heard the short laugh. Luis did not attempt to answer, he just shook his head and smiled.

Luis moved the truck to the open gate. Sgt. was waiting to close the gate and replace the chain. When this was done, he swung himself into the passenger seat of the truck and Luis took the truck toward the I10 on-ramp and New Orleans.

Barra timed their exit from the Space Center. They needed to be long out of sight from there before he began his takeoff run. He would purposely rev the engines to appear he had a heavy load on takeoff. The noise may draw the attention of security. Didn't really matter if they saw him, nothing they could do to a plane already airborne. They might call the tower at Keesler to locate and follow the plane. However, even security wouldn't really know why they wanted it located. By the time they sorted through the red tape, Barra would have already given their radar a brief image.

Keesler and Belle Chasse in New Orleans did not have active fighter squadrons, they were all reserve. Certainly there would not be any training flights this evening. Military red tape was the same the world over. Would probably take at least two hours to get someone to authorize any such mission, and then the nearest active squadron was in Tampa. Even if they managed to get something in the air sooner, it would do the Americans little good. They would not shoot him down, very bad public relations. At most, it might only give another witness to the Bonanza going down. The chances of them seeing him exit the plane were very slim. His flight suit was dark green, and the chute was black. If they identified him, they would circle the Bonanza at probably ten thousand feet, almost two miles above him.

CHAPTER # 35

EAST NEW ORLEANS, 5:45 PM

About the time the caravan of Lt. Salinas and Rudy were crossing into Mississippi, the door of the warehouse was being rolled up. With all the lights in the warehouse turned off, Sgt. Mendoza was unseen as he gazed both directions on the street. There was no one around this evening before Thanksgiving to see him, anyway. He checked his watch as he climbed into the cab of the diesel Freightliner. He quickly pulled the truck and flatbed trailer with the neatly secured shipping container out of the warehouse and parked across the street. Leaving the engine running, he ran back into the warehouse to close the large roll-up door. No need to secure the battens now. He exited thru the side door and was back behind the wheel right on schedule. He had two minutes to go the six blocks to the receiving gate of the container shipping yard.

Sgt. Mendoza pulled his rig up to the receiving gate just as the guard was turning away from the gate after placing the lock. Mendoza flashed his lights and gave a quick hit of the horn to get the guard's attention. The guard turned, looked at the truck, shook his head no and gave a dismissing wave.

Mendoza swung down from his seat and hurried toward the gate as he pleaded with the guard.

"Come on Senior, it is just time. I need to get this unloaded."

The guard was not friendly or helpful. Even condescending. "Sorry Poncho. Not tonight. Gate closes at 6."

"Oh, please Senior. I got caught in traffic."

"Not my problem."

"I need to get unloaded so I can get back to Houston tonight, Thanksgiving with family tomorrow."

The guard seemed more sympathetic. "Sorry, no way can I let you thru tonight. Gate will open again Friday at 6 a.m."

"This is a terrible situation. I need to unload."

The guard walked to the gate where Sgt. Mendoza was standing. "I can't let anything thru after 6. Especially tonight. These guys want to get home for the holiday as well. If I was to let you in now, by 8 Friday morning the Shop Steward will have a grievance filed and by Monday I may be out of a job."

Not wanting to be too antagonistic, Mendoza accepted his fate. "Can I park my rig somewhere around safe? Maybe I can catch a bus home."

"Yeah, park it along the street here anywhere. Nobody will bother it."

"Will someone be around to watch it?"

"Not our job to watch it, but there is 24 hour security here in the yard. Someone is around."

"Here in the guard shack?" Mendoza asked.

"No, only one person overnight. He monitors the whole yard."

"How far to the bus station?"

"Pretty good hike across the river in Downtown. I can call you a cab."

"That would be nice. Thanks." To refuse a cab might raise suspicion.

Mendoza returned to his rig and climbed aboard. He backed onto the street, then went around the block so he could park the rig in just the right place. They had scouted this street, needing a place near the gate yet getting the least light from the security lighting of the yard. The nearest street light would not be functioning in a few hours.

After securing the rig, Mendoza walked back over near the closed gate to wait for the cab. They had anticipated this event. He would take the cab over to the quick stop on the Highway, then walk the mile or so back to the warehouse. He had plenty of time until the team returned from Mississippi. Would be very tempting to get a beer while at the store. He had acquired quite a taste for American beer during his recent stay in Miami. But he knew they were in the middle of a mission, even if his function was at a minimum for the next few hours.

Returning from the quick stop, Mendoza turned the corner from behind the warehouse. As he neared the building, he sensed something was wrong. There was no one on the street. However, he had heard a car a few minutes ago. When he got to the door, he saw that it was slightly ajar. He had been gone less than an hour. He was sure he had not left it unlocked. This was a mission in 'enemy' territory. He was too careful for such a mistake. As he eased the door open, he heard nothing. He stepped thru the door into the makeshift alcove. All the lights were still off and there was no sound. He waited a few more minutes, then carefully lifted one of the plastic flaps of the alcove wall. There was still no movement or sound. Mendoza knew the place in the dark as well as in light. He quietly approached a pile of equipment where he knew there was a flashlight. With light in hand, he quickly scanned the building, being careful not to allow the beam to shine on the edge of the roll-up door with no batting in place. It took him fifteen minutes to satisfy there was no one in the warehouse and nothing was missing or moved. However, he knew he would not spend his next few hours sitting and waiting for the team to return from Mississippi.

He could not take a chance that someone had been in here. They, for now, he, would need to dispose of all the gasoline supply they had stored for the boats to return to sea.

They could take no chance the gas had been contaminated. Mendoza began loading some of the five gallon gas cans into the van that remained. They would not need this van until about midnight, but it would need a full gas tank.

The gas would have to be dumped in various alleys and lots. He could only dump it in small amounts at any one spot. This night would be much busier than they had planned. First priority would be to empty one of the five gallon containers and get it refilled at the quick stop before it closed. Having gas to refill the van for the second mission was an absolute necessity.

New Orleans, 1 a.m. Thanksgiving Morning

LUIS PULLED the van out of the warehouse; the real plates had replaced the stolen license plates. They would again attach the stolen plates just outside of Morgan City. When the van had cleared the opening, they again played the usual routine of door security out. One of the Cubans immediately closed the large overhead door. Accompanying Luis in the van were two Rangers. One was the marksman, Sgt. Ochoa, and the other was a very muscular Sgt. Rojas, with a lot of lifting power. The other Cubans quickly placed the batting around the door to seal any cracks. Rudy was standing in the shadows across the street. Once the Lt. was satisfied everything was sealed, they were able to turn on a few lights. From across the street, Rudy looked for any light around the door. When he was certain the door was sealed, he came back across the street and entered the warehouse through the side pedestrian door. They had constructed an entry alcove inside this entrance using heavy black plastic to block light.

The Rangers reformed their work groups and continued to move the mainframe computers from the 'borrowed' rental truck. They now had the luxury of the forklift to lower the machines from the back of the truck and set them in the shipping crate.

As soon as the truck was unloaded, the Sergeant moved the truck to the large roll-up door, closely followed by Rudy in one of the vans. This van, too, had the real license plates attached. They turned the lights off, and the Rangers went about removing the batting and opening the door. When the two vehicles had cleared the door, they again rolled it down. They did not replace the batting, as Rudy and the Sergeant would return in half an hour. They turned a dim light in an inner room on for the time being. The Rangers would use this as a break time. They had been alert and busy for the past seven hours. Rudy and the Sergeant took different routes to the rental lot to return the truck. Rudy took a longer route to give the Sergeant time to park the truck and walk the two blocks back to where Rudy and the van were waiting.

Luis headed his van across the bridge to get on I-10. They would take it west until near the airport, then wind their way to re-cross the Mississippi via the Luling Bridge to Highway 90. Then take Highway 90 west-southwest for the hour and half trip to Morgan City. The traffic was light, although heavier than expected. Luis kept the van just under the speed limit; he did not want to attract any attention. Luis had his American identifications showing him to be a citizen, and the Rangers had their legal work visas, but they still did not want to be stopped.

Luis slowed the van as they neared Morgan City. At a dark stretch, he stopped and one ranger jumped out and quickly changed the license plates. He knew exactly where he was going in town. He had scouted the route one day a couple of weeks ago. Then the other night he and Rudy had driven over to do the route in the dark. He turned right off of Highway 90 into an industrial section that housed numerous businesses. All of which served the active field and offshore oil industry of South Louisiana. As he neared the building he slowed as Rojas cracked the door and Ochoa pushed the barrel of the high-powered air gun through. Luis waited for the Rangers order to stop.

"Aqui" came the word from the Ochoa.

Luis had no sooner stopped the van when he heard the release of the compressed air from the rifle. He quickly began a slow acceleration up to normal speed. Sgt. Rojas closed the door as the other shooter confirmed the air pellet had knocked out the night light of the supply yard. They proceeded down the street for a couple blocks, then turned to circle the area, then continued this for the next 20 minutes. They wanted to be sure the loss of light did not trigger some type of alarm or signal.

Once satisfied there was no one coming to check the light, Luis pulled the van to the double gate of the chain-link fence surrounding the supply yard. A chain looped around the adjoining pipes of the gates was for the lock. The lock hung on the inside of the gate. The muscular Cuban was first out of the van with bolt cutters and smoothly separated one of the links. Sgt. Ochoa was right behind him and opened one side of the gate while Rojas retrieved the fallen chain and hung it on the remaining gate. Luis pulled the van through the gate as Rojas jumped back in the passenger door. He quickly drove the van to the back of the building, out of sight of the street. The remaining Ranger closed the gate and wrapped the remaining piece of chain around the gates to look as if it was still locked. Checking for traffic, he then ran to the front corner of the building and buried himself in the shadows. Sgt. Ochoa was to remain there to watch for traffic on the street and whistle to warn his team members of any cars.

Luis and his partner knew exactly what they were looking for, the approximate size and shape of the stacked drill bits on a pallet. There would be two pallets, probably next to each other. They would have to use small low intensity flashlights. Even with the low-intensity lights, they could not take a chance of a passing car noticing, therefore the Ranger doing lookout would warn them of any traffic. After a few minutes of searching, they found two pallets setting near the back fence. The drill bits were each in their own small crate, the shape of a cube about two feet across. They were stacked two high, with eight on a pallet. One pallet was full, the other pallet had three already gone. Luis was pleased with thirteen. With the pallets located, he signaled Sgt. Ochoa to join them. It would take all three to lift the individual crates into the van. Luis backed the van to the pallets. They first moved the five crates to the ground, then placed the empty pallet in the van. They wanted to restack the crates on the pallets. Each crate weighed almost 100 pounds, so it was slow work, even with three of them. The muscular Cuban took one side of a crate, then either Luis or the Ochoa took the other side of the crate. The pallets had to be placed just right in the van for both to fit. It took almost 45 mins to get the pallets and crates loaded in the van.

When loaded, the Ranger doing lookout ran back to the shadows near the front of the building. Once settled in the shadows, he peered around the building and down the street both ways. There was no traffic. He gave one short whistle, then ran for the gate. He swung the gate open just as Luis drove through. Sgt. Rojas jumped out to help close the gate and set the chain. They replaced the link they had cut with a split link. They used another tool similar to the bolt cutter, but without cutting edges to compress the split link closed. Since it was on the opposite side from the lock, it would probably not be noticed immediately. Didn't really matter as the missing pallets would never be noticed or reported from this site Brady had leased. The two Rangers were back in the van in a matter of a few minutes.

Luis eased the van back on to the street and slowly sped up, heading back to Highway 90 for the return trip to New Orleans. Just a hint of light could be seen on the eastern horizon as they pulled up to the door of the warehouse. Sgt. Ochoa gave a double whistle and within two minutes the big door rolled upwards.

Once inside, the door was closed, and the batting again replaced. As was routine, Rudy was across the street in the shadows to confirm they were light tight.

As soon as the van rolled to a stop, the Cubans began a flurry of activity around it. They quickly and efficiently moved the crates of drill bits from the van into the waiting shipping container. While Luis had made the trip to Morgan City, the Cubans at the warehouse had secured the stolen computer mainframes into the shipping container.

The crates were stacked and secured in a matter of two hours, and the container was closed and locked with a banding seal.

They turned the lights off through the building, as it was now time for the team of Cubans to sleep. The American holiday of Thanksgiving was not relevant to the Cubans. The coming night would again be very busy for them.

CHAPTER # 36

THANKSGIVING NIGHT

By the time darkness had consumed the city outside, the Cubans were dressed and prepared for their evening's activity.

They had cleaned up the warehouse, leaving no trace of their presence except for some larger pieces of scrap lumber. The smaller pieces were placed in trash bags, along with all of their garbage. They would disperse these bags around the area to various dumpsters later that night. During the afternoon, Luis and Rudy had taken the tools and cooking utensils to several donation receptacles around town.

This night, they were to use four vans to make the trip through the marshes to the coast. All the Cubans except for Sgt. Mendoza, Lt. Salinas, Rudy and Luis would be returning to the waiting ship offshore. They needed the four vans to carry all the passengers and the Zodiacs, outboards, and pumps to inflate the boats.

The rendezvous with the ship was at four a.m. the next morning. Luis wanted them on the water by midnight or twelve thirty at the latest. Luis left the warehouse in the first van at nine thirty. Another van would leave every ten minutes. It would be at least an hour and half drive to the area near Grand Isle where they had come ashore earlier that week. Luis went first to be sure the fish camp was not occupied.

He had selected an alternative launch site about half a mile above the fish camp, just in case the camp was occupied.

As Luis passed the alternate site he had selected, it shocked him to see two pickups parked there. He slowed as he passed the area. There were two tents erected near the trucks. A group was camping there. This alternate site was now unusable.

Luis continued along until he neared the fish camp building. As he neared, he could see a light on at the cabin. He turned off his lights and pulled the van off the road about fifty yards from the building. He wanted to approach the site on foot to evaluate the situation. Time was critical to get his group on the water.

As he neared the elevated building, he could see there was a small light on under the building and a couple of lights on inside the building. There were four vehicles parked around the area and two fishing boats sitting in the bayou. Keeping in the tall marsh grass, he circled the building. From the front of the cabin facing the bayou, he could see in the window. The door was also open so he could hear. There was laughing and banter from the six men sitting around a table playing cards. Luis understood immediately. The anglers were heavily into beer and a poker game. He was running out of time for his group.

He returned to his van as the second van approached. This van being driven by Lt. Salinas. Luis had seen a fork in the short road to the fish camp, leading to a small clearing he could use as a staging area. He explained that he needed Salinas, being well over six feet tall, to get to the building and unscrew the light below until it went off, but leave it in the socket.

It was just a few minutes before Luis saw the light flicker off. He crept his van down the highway and onto the road to the small clearing. By this time, the third van had arrived. Luis left his van and ran back to the other two waiting vans. The third was full of the Cubans with a few pieces of equipment. He told everyone his plan. This third van had a somewhat noisy muffler and squeaky brakes, so he did not want to bring it any closer to the cabin. The driver, Sgt. Mendoza was to remain there to explain the plan to Rudy when he arrived in the fourth van.

On foot, Luis returned to the road and the clearing, with Salinas following in his van. Strung out behind them were the Cubans carrying the remaining equipment from the third van. By the time the last Ranger got to the staging site, Rudy had his van to the site as well. Sgt. Mendoza was instructed to return to the warehouse in New Orleans. Luis did not want to have an extra van parked along the highway for any period of time. The tall grass pretty well hid the vans in the staging area from the site of the highway.

The team quickly and silently went to work unloading the vans and assembling the equipment. They would inflate the Zodiacs there. The only reasonable access to the bayou was still the ramp area near the cabin. They would have to use it and take their chances that the group inside was too consumed with their beer and card game.

Carrying the inflated Zodiacs and equipment would be more time-consuming than had been planned. They had a total of three boats. The larger Zodiac the group had come ashore in a few nights ago, a small Zodiac with an outboard motor Luis had purchased a few weeks ago, and the third was a small inflatable to haul the hand operated inflation pumps and other equipment they felt should not be put in the trash or donations containers. This third would be towed a few miles, then deflated to sink with the unwanted gear. The remaining two Zodiacs with the Cuban Rangers would continue out to meet the waiting ship.

The hastily crafted plan had the smaller Zodiac going first, towing the small inflatable with the gear. Then the third larger Zodiac would follow. The outboard engines would not be attached to the transoms until the boats were down the bayou a few hundred yards. Less drag would reduce the amount of time they were passing near the cabin.

In less than ten minutes, the small inflatable was loaded and tied to the grass. They brought the smaller Zodiac and outboard to the ramp. They set the outboard engine and gas cans at the rear of the boat. Two of the Rangers boarded the boat and tied the line from the inflatable to a cleat on the Zodiac. With one on each side, they used paddles to quietly move down the bayou.

It was more of a chore for the remaining team members to get the larger Zodiac, engine, and gas from the staging area to the launch ramp. As the last of the gear was placed in the boat and the Rangers began to climb into the boat, they heard a voice from the direction of the cabin.

"Hey, what goin' on der?"

They all froze. Luis quickly responded, using his best Cajun. "Nih fishin, not ver good. Too much beer. Had pull to shore to peess."

"Ye, me too. Y'all need any more beer? We got plenty."

Luis motioned for the team to continue boarding the boat. "No, we goo plenty, too. Tanks eyway."

He could see the man return into the cabin. They pushed the over loaded Zodiac out onto the bayou. They would paddle down to the waiting smaller Zodiac and some of the Rangers would transfer to the smaller boat. Luis, Rudy and

Salinas quickly returned to their vans. They left one at a time in five-minute intervals, Luis being last.

They returned to the empty warehouse in New Orleans.

At the warehouse, Sgt. Mendoza had already begun his assigned work of moving the loaded shipping container from the warehouse to the flatbed of the eighteen wheeler. The rig was still where he had left it, near the gate of the port yard.

This was one of the most vulnerable times for the plan. If a random police patrol stopped him, it would be very hard to explain the moving of a shipping container at two in the morning. The original plan had Luis himself doing this, to not expose one of his team to prison time in the U.S. But the plan seemed smoother to have Mendoza switch the containers.

The large door to the warehouse was just wide enough to get the 20 foot container out. It was about five blocks from the warehouse to where the truck was parked. Although the electric forklift was quiet, the large machine with the container could easily be seen.

Mendoza stopped around the corner from the truck. Staying in the shadows, he moved near the truck to see if the security guard in the yard was near. He did not see the security pickup. While there, he released the straps securing the container to the flatbed. He went back and brought the forklift to the truck. He placed the container on the street near the back of the flatbed. With the forklift, he lifted the first container off the flatbed and moved it to the street near the front of the truck. He then raised the container from the warehouse into place on the flatbed. He did not take the time to place the straps on the container. No one would notice that. He would replace them in the morning when he returned to move the truck into the loading yard.

In less than thirty minutes, Mendoza was back in the warehouse with the empty container. His next task was to use the only remaining tool. This was a hand grinder with sandpaper wheel to remove the identifying marks they had put on the container and paint over the bare metal. This grinder, scrubbed clean of fingerprints, would be 'accidentally' left in the van when it was sold next week.

Mendoza was painting the container as the first van returned from the South Louisiana marsh. Within the next few minutes, the remaining vans were all secure in the closed and locked warehouse. Rudy inspected the work Mendoza had done on the container.

The rest of the night, Luis was as nervous as a nine tailed cat in a room full of rocking chairs as he waited for the signal from the ship that the Rangers had transferred successfully from the Zodiacs to the ship. It was not until after five am that the signal came. Luis immediately went from a pensive nervous mood to over flowing jubilation.

As it neared 6 a.m. Sgt. Mendoza left the warehouse to move the eighteen wheeler into the port yard. Luis again showed some anxiety until Mendoza and the truck returned a little before eight. Mendoza reported everything went as planned. Mendoza then climbed onto the forklift and loaded the empty container onto the flatbed. Luis opened the warehouse door for him to return the forklift to the vacant lot for the rental company to pick it up. Luis went with him to help with the gate. Both men were back in less than twenty minutes.

Luis had very little apprehension about the remaining parts of the mission. Rudy and Salinas were to sleep as soon as they returned from the bayou, however, they too could not rest until they got the signal from the ship. This hitch in the plan was one Luis could easily tolerate. They were both asleep by six. Luis and Mendoza fell asleep shortly after returning the forklift.

After a few hours of sleep, Mendoza and Rudy would

head to Mobile. They would stop at the place they had bought the container. Rudy would explain they wanted to sell it back as they didn't need two after all. How much money was not important. They just needed to be rid of it. They would then return the eighteen wheeler to the rental office in Mobile. Salinas would pick them up in a van to return to New Orleans. During that time, Luis would take one van to a used car lot and sell it for cash.

Luis would then take a second van to the Gulfport and sell it. Salinas would pick him up on his way back from Mobile.

By late afternoon, the four remaining Cubans were at the warehouse. Luis had driven by the cargo wharf to confirm the ship with their container had left. He was not disappointed. The ship had sailed, with their container, to it's next port of call, Colon, Panama.

The plan was for Salinas and Mendoza to take two vans to Houston. They would sell one van in Houston, then the two would continue to Laredo where the two would cross the border into Nuevo Laredo. They would drive the van south to Monterrey. The two would make their way back to Cuba after selling the van in Mexico. Because of the late start, it would be night before they got to Houston. This slight change of plans had them sell the first van in San Antonio the next day before continuing to Laredo and crossing to Nuevo Laredo.

Luis would remain at the warehouse to dispose of the remaining gear and equipment. He and Rudy would drive the last van to Atlanta and sell it there. They would fly from Atlanta to different Central America cities and then to Cuba.

The mission had gone too smooth. He knew in his heart that his friend Brady had been behind it all.

CHAPTER # 37

COLON, PANAMA, DECEMBER

Brady, along with his CIA contact Fred Anderson, watched from the roof of a warehouse down the street. Through the fading darkness, he could identify the form of his friend, Luis, overseeing the movement of the truck into the open space of the recently rented warehouse. This truck carried the sealed shipping container recently arrived from New Orleans via ocean freighter. Luis had no idea he was being watched. Although he suspected, he did not know Brady was in the area.

This was the building Luis had rented to be used for the exchange of the shipment to the Russians. It was now just past 6 p.m.; he was not to meet the Russian agent, Malko Lobren, until 2 a.m. Luis had never met the Russian, however, he knew him by reputation.

Malko Lobren, Brady referred to him as 'No Brain' rather than Lobren, was Russia's senior agent in Latin America; he controlled all KGB activity from Mexico through Central and South America. He had also developed a very efficient network of informants throughout Texas, New Mexico and Arizona that watches the activity around the U.S. military bases in those states. Although very fastidious and impeccably coiffured and ensemble, he was known to be brutal and heartless in his dealings. He controlled his agents and informants with fear. He had been in the Americas for almost 20 years and had developed a very tight and efficient network. In the newer Russia, his methods were in disfavor with some, however, his results were excellent. Having such a reputation did not really concern Luis. They would not be meeting as adversaries. This was simply an exchange of goods for both sides. Russia would get the computer and oil equipment, and Cuba would get the five and a half million dollars.

The meeting should take less than 30 minutes, and Luis would be done with the Russians. He just had to wait the eight hours until the meeting.

Luis (and Brady) watched as the truck driver pulled the door closed and placed a lock. Luis did not feel there was much threat to the container; this area was all warehouses with many such containers. He also felt the Russians could be watching the area. Luis and his driver left the area to enjoy some music and an evening meal.

Brady, too, suspected the Russians would watch the warehouse. This was his greatest concern. He had secured a warehouse down the alley from the one Luis was using. The only practical choice for the Russians to watch the warehouse was from one of the other warehouses on the street, as very few of the buildings had rear entrances, including this one. The Russians would only feel the need to watch the front of the Cuban's warehouse.

Brady waited a good ten minutes after Luis pulled away from the area. Using a small combat team radio, he gave the Navy CB Team Leader the signal to proceed.

In the warehouse Brady had rented was a team of 12 Navy Seabees from the Colon Naval Station. This was not a combat mission, nor in hostile territory, so the team was not burdened with weapons or other ordinance. Only the commander, Lt. Bond and the Senior Chief carried a sidearm. The CB's discipline, teamwork and ability to work with building materials was what Brady needed on this mission. This wasn't a destroy mission, no Seals needed. The buildings needed to be left exactly as they were found.

They had already loosened a large panel at the rear of their building. With the signal from Brady, they quietly removed the panel. The first two men out the opening sprinted down the alley to the back of the building housing the Cuban's shipping container. Each man with a noiseless drill, they set to work removing a panel from the rear of this building. The panel was removed and set aside. The rest of the team quickly entered the warehouse and proceeded with the task before them. One man vaulted onto the bed of the truck and, using a pair of metal snips, he removed the inspection seal on the door of the shipping container. Two of the other team members unlatched the container doors and swung them open. The team then went to work removing the crates of drill bits. They put the crates on the end of the truck bed; where another pair of CBs would carry one to the opening at the back of the building and pass it to waiting teammates. The crated instruments were then stacked two high on a waiting hand truck in the alley, to be taken down the alley to the warehouse they had just left. As soon as the last crate was out of the container, the doors were pushed closed but not latched. The squad of CBs was back out of the warehouse and the rear panel was replaced in less than ten minutes.

Brady had left his observation post to move this truck to another warehouse he had rented for his meeting with the Chinese buyer. Fred Anderson would remain atop the building to keep an eye on things.

While the panels were being secured, the other team

members had taxied the hand trucks down the alley and set about stacking the crated bits onto a pallet on the back of a truck waiting in this warehouse. Once the panels on the back of this warehouse had been replaced and the crates secured onto the pallet, most of the CB team went to the far corner into a small room that served as an office. Two of the men went to the front cargo door.

After about ten minutes, Brady entered the large space through the walk-in door near the cargo doors. He said few words to the CB team leader.

When Brady pulled the truck up, the two CBs pushed the two doors open. As soon as the truck cleared the door, they were quickly closed.

The CB Team would remain there for two to three hours until the truck returned. They would reverse the process of moving the crates back to the shipping container in the other warehouse. This all needed to be completed well before 2 a.m., when Luis was to meet the Russian to make their exchange.

Brady had not brought Luis into his confidence for this part of the night. He did not want to put Luis into the position of involvement. Therefore, the crates would need to be secured into the original shipping container long before 2 a.m. Brady's appointed time to meet the Chinese representative was 10 p.m. This gave him just one hour to make the exchange, then hijack the truck before it got to the wharf.

Brady waited, half seated on the step of the truck cab. This was not a normal experience for him, although he was in the business of gathering information from various sources, some reluctant and secretive. He really was not in the clandestine business. He did not normally operate in the world of undercover meetings or covert transactions. However, he had been well schooled in such things by both the CIA and FBI.

He was not particularly on edge as he was not meeting someone he would really consider an adversary. However secret, this was a business deal. He knew the customer in this, the Chinese, felt they were going to rip off the upstart naïve Cubans. The poor Cubans were way over their heads when dealing with the People's Republic of China. It was like taking candy from a baby for the Chinese when dealing with the third world Cubans. And that was exactly what Brady wanted them to think. The bigger the scam, the less noise they would make on the world scene. But Brady felt sure there would be some an uproar within the borders of the People's Republic of China.

Brady had arrived at this second warehouse near the wharf about 45 minutes early. Precisely at 10 p.m. there were three taps on the side door. Even though his driver was expecting it, the noise shattering the quiet startled him so that he nearly fell off of his stool near the door.

The man righted himself, then moved to open the door. With the door open, Brady could see two figures silhouetted by the partial moonlight outside.

The two men entered, and the door was secured. Once the door was shut, Brady turned on the tripod mounted spotlight to illuminate the back of the truck bed where the oil well drills were stacked on their pallet.

Without a word spoken, nor even any acknowledgement of Brady, the two men, each carrying a small satchel, went directly about their business at the truck bed. The man in charge surveyed the pallet of stacked crates. He randomly pointed to one of the crates. The other man leaped onto the truck bed and began unslacking the crates to gain access to the desired crate. He lifted it off the stack, set it on the bed, and slid it across to where the other man was standing. Then he pulled a small steel bar from his satchel and pried the crate open. With some effort, he hefted the bit from the packing in the crate and set it on a mat the other man had spread out on the truck bed. The man then began a very tedious and extensive inspection of the apparatus, using magnification, probes, punches and chemicals.

The only concern Brady had was about the time this was taking. He knew the bits were the genuine items the Cubans had taken from Morgan City a few weeks ago. His time was short to get these back into the shipping containers at the Cuban's warehouse.

After about an hour, it appeared the inspection was complete. Again, without a word spoken, the man on the truck replaced the bit back in its crate and reattached the lid. The other man replaced his equipment back in the large duffel bag.

Once the packing around the bit was restored to its original protective placement and the crate resealed, the man, with great effort, hefted it back onto the top of the other crates on the pallet.

Brady had brought steel banding material and the tool to tie the stacked crates together and secure them to the pallet. As Brady stepped onto the rear bumper to ascend onto the truck, the man handling the crates put his hand out to stop Brady. With his other hand, he took the banding tool.

While Brady watched, the man expertly banded the crates and pallet together. During this time, the man that had done the inspection had taken his bag and left the building. By the time the pallet was bound, a third man was standing next to the truck. It was the Mr. Wong that Brady had dealt with last summer in Vancouver.

Mr. Wong gave a questioning nod to the man standing on the truck. The man seemed to give a brief explanation, which was followed by a nod of approval from Mr. Wong. After which, the man hopped off the truck, took his satchel, and stood in the shadows.

"My associate tells me the items are exactly as we expected from such a noble trading partner as Cuba." Mr. Wong said as he turned to Brady. "My country hopes this may be only the beginning of future endeavors between our two freedom-loving countries."

Brady struggled to keep from laughing in the man's face. Especially knowing the man was about to hand him a bag of counterfeit money. He knew there was expected some similar verbiage in reply.

With as much sincerity as he could muster, Brady replied. "Our sentiments exactly, we are honored to deal with such a respected partner."

"I have the agreed sum in the requested various denominations of American currency."

Brady had requested the various denominations. He knew this amount of cash passing through the many levels of corrupt bureaucracy would result in many of the bills to become missing. The one hundred and five hundred dollar notes were small enough that the mid-level officials would readily pilfer a few from the cache. However, the bills were large enough they could not be easily passed anywhere but at a financial institution or a sophisticated resort or casino. Any of these institutions would readily spot them as fakes.

This would cause, if not great legal problems, then great embarrassment to the individual trying to pass them. It would be especially embarrassing to the higher level officials trying to use the thousand dollar notes.

The denominations were too large for common usage. The remaining bills would be quietly sealed and pushed to the back of the government vault in Caracas. No one would raise an alarm, as they would have to admit to the common but unspoken truth that they had taken some of the bills. They would also not want it known in an official capacity that they had let their country be duped to the tune of five million dollars. Brady was well aware of the problem counterfeit money caused the U.S., as well as the world economy. He was very confident none of these bills would ever get into circulation.

"Thank you, Sir." Brady replied as he went to the front of the truck and retrieved a large envelope from the front seat. He turned and handed it to the Chinese representative.

"And the computer discs with the promised information."

"I shall take these. We now need to get the truck to the ship."

"My driver will take it directly to the wharf." Brady replied.

"Very good. My man shall ride with him to the ship."

"I don't believe that will be possible. He will not be allowed through the cargo gate. He does not have the proper papers."

"He has a card identifying him as a member of the ship's crew. It is all very legal."

"That may be, but he will have to go through the gate for ship's company. Only local drivers and dock workers are allowed through that gate." Brady explained.

"I believe he will be able to manage that problem. He has a substantial roll of twenty-dollar bills."

Brady felt he should not push the issue much more to raise suspicion with the Chinese. The situation would be easier if the man didn't accompany the driver, but Brady knew he had this scenario covered.

"Very well, as you wish." Brady answered as he went to the large door and pushed it open for the truck to exit. The Chinese representative with the envelope went out the door as Brady was closing it.

At the entrance gate, the driver stopped. The guard recognized the driver but asked about the passenger. The driver explained he was a crewman from the ship they were delivering this load to. Turning, the guard shouted something into the small building that served as a guard shack. Another guard emerged from the building and went around the truck to the passenger side. The Chinese passenger handed some papers to the guard.

The guard studied the papers for a moment, then motioned for the man to get out of the truck. As the Chinese man descended from the truck, he handed the guard a few folded twenty-dollar bills. The guard smiled, put the money in his pocket, and motioned for the man to follow him.

The guard led the Chinese man into the small building, with the first guard closely behind. After a moment, the first guard returned and told the driver he needed to move the truck out of the gate. He pulled the truck up thirty yards and stopped. It was a good five minutes wait before a small pickup identified as the dockyard security stopped at the guard shack. A man seemingly in charge got out of the passenger side and went into the guard shack. After a couple of minutes, the first guard came to the truck and told the driver this was going to take some time and that he should proceed to the wharf area to unload his cargo.

The truck went a few yards forward, then turned between two rows of stacked ocean containers. As soon as he was around out of sight, the back of the truck was descended upon by three dock workers. However, they were only dressed as dock workers. They were a different team of CBs. Not any of which were involved with the warehouse movement of the crates earlier that evening.

Two of the men pulled the tarp covering the pallet and inspected the way they had put the banding on the crates at the warehouse. When satisfied, they jumped to the bed of an identical truck parked next to them. Both trucks were exactly the same model and color, had the same identifying numerals and insignias. On the bed of this second truck was a pallet stacked with crates matching those on the first truck. The CBs picked up a banding tool and banded these crates and pallet exactly as the ones on the other truck were banded.

The third CB had removed the license plate from the first truck and secured it to the rear of the second truck. When done with plate transfer, he jumped on the back of the first truck to pull the tarp over to the second truck. By the time he had moved the tarp, the banding job was complete. The three men secured the tarp over the pallet and crates.

This entire operation was completed in less than four minutes. The driver of the first truck was now in the second truck and drove down the row of stacked containers to the wharf near the waiting Chinese ship. All of this time, the guards had kept the Chinese man in the guard shack occupied. After probably exhausting his supply of twenty-dollar bills, they led him back out to the small security pickup and drove him to the waiting ship. He got there just as the pallet was being swung aboard and the truck was pulling away.

By the time the Chinese man and the cargo were on the ship, the three CBs had completed the rest of their task. They had changed some of the identifying numbers on the first truck, attached a license plate, and secured a new, different colored tarp over the crates. Another driver was at the truck waiting to return it to the Brady's warehouse where the original team of CBs would move it back to the Cuban's warehouse and container.

The Chinese had a pallet of used basic drill bits. There would be a lot of yelling and explaining to do in Peking someday. Brady figured they would not open the crates for at least a couple of years, as the Chinese were not yet doing deep drilling.

CHAPTER #38

Even though his meeting with the Russian was not for another two hours, Luis and his driver returned to their warehouse sooner than Brady expected. The CB team had not had time to move the crates back into the Cuban warehouse. Brady had just returned to the warehouse roof to join the CIA agent as Luis arrived at the warehouse.

Luis and his driver entered the warehouse and, using flashlights, began setting up a small array of low wattage lights. They had not yet noticed the unsecured container doors. It took them ten minutes or so to get the lighting set. When they turned the lights on, they immediately saw the problem with the container doors.

As Luis was climbing onto the back of the truck, there was a loud banging on the door at the front of the warehouse.

"Police, please open." Came a voice from outside the door.

Luis motioned for his driver to turn the lights off, then go to the door. Both Luis and the driver pulled out their service 9mm Berettas. Luis stood ten feet to one side of the door as the driver unlocked the door, then stepped away a few feet, both with their guns ready.

"It is unlocked." Luis yelled.

The door slowly opened. The man standing there held a flashlight. From the glow of the light, Luis could see he was in uniform and his gun was still in the holster. Both men in the warehouse quickly holstered their guns under their coats. They were not legal to be carrying weapons on foreign soil. The fit of their jackets well hid their guns.

"Good evening, officer. Is there a problem?" Luis asked as the police officer came through the door.

"Good evening, gentlemen. Yes, there is a problem, or was. I believe we have it taken care of now." The officer replied. "I am Sergeant Garcia of the Panamanian Police unit here in Colon. I am the watch commander tonight for the area. We had a report earlier this evening of a possible robbery here. Are you missing anything?"

Luis looked at his driver, then told him to turn the lights on. With the lights on, Luis led the Sergeant toward the truck. "Not sure Sergeant. We just noticed our container was open when you got here. Let us look." Luis knew there would be no use in trying to hide anything. No matter what, he wanted the Police to be gone by the time the Russian got here.

Once on the back of the truck, they opened the container doors to see if anything was missing. The computer cabinets were secure in their original place. However, the loose packing around where the drill bit crates had been made it obvious something was missing.

Stunned, Luis looked at the Police Officer. The Sgt. quickly explained. "I believe we may have what is missing. We got a call of something being removed from this building onto a truck in the side alley. When we got here, there was no one around."

"But our locks were still in place." Luis interjected.

"My officer noticed that all the buildings around seemed to be closed and locked. Things not seeming right, he called me. By the time I got here, he had noticed some bent metal and fresh scratches on the side door. It appears that they had pried the door open." Luis looked toward the door. The Police officer continued, "However, within the half hour one of our patrols stopped a truck from the dockyard. The truck had no taillights, as is the case with most of their trucks. They don't use the lights in the yard, so when one gets broken, it never gets fixed. When my office approached the truck, the driver scrambled out the opposite side door and ran off into the dark. Turned out the truck had been stolen from the dockyard two days ago."

Luis felt a surge of encouragement. "What was the truck hauling? Where is it now?"

"It is a dozen or so small crates. About what would fit in the empty spaces in your container. My officer is with the truck about five miles from here. Another officer went to the dockyard to get a driver to retrieve the truck."

A new feeling of dread fell over Luis. "Can I get my stuff back?" He knew the mountain of paperwork and red tape involved if this had happened in Cuba. Worst of all would be the explaining of the cargo. In Cuba, they would seize the rest of the cargo as well.

"I can have the driver bring it back here if you like. If you have the proper paperwork, manifest and shipping documents, it can be returned to you now."

Luis was almost without words. How could he be so fortunate? "That can be done now?" He asked in shock.

"We will never catch the men responsible for this, therefore no one to prosecute. Holding it as evidence will just be a burden to us both. If you will sign that it is all returned and undamaged. We already know it is not contraband or drugs. You can list it as anything you want. Getting it out of our system makes for much less work and much less paperwork. My pile of paperwork is already endless. This works to both our advantages. I am sure you want your merchandise back."

They had the warehouse doors opened by the time the truck returned with the drill bits. They had replaced the crates and closed the container a good forty-five minutes before the Russian was scheduled.

Brady and his CIA contact remained on the roof of the nearby warehouse the whole time. He had radioed the CB leader in his other warehouse to let him know the team would not be needed again that evening, but to remain there until he contacted them. Brady did not want any unusual activity in the area until the Russian had left with the container.

Brady spoke to the CIA agent. "Your friend in the police seemed to have done a very convincing job, as well as your friends at the dockyard."

"They do well for us. We help them from time to time and we pay well. Don't know if any of it ever gets home to the mamacita of the house, but these guys are happy. How much you think they fleeced off the Chinese?"

"Probably all he had. Chairman Egg Roll may not be able to buy a new porn movie this week."

Luis did not latch the container doors after replacing and securing the crates in the container. He sat on the back of the truck bed. His driver was seated against the wall near the door. Luis replayed the incident of the drills being stolen. How could it have happened? Why this particular warehouse on this particular night? He got up and walked over to the side door that had been forced open. On close inspection with his flashlight, he saw what he felt was the reason. There were other, older scratch marks around the latch. Also, he could see where the frame had been bent, then pounded back into shape. This warehouse had been broken into before, probably why it was not being used. Someone monitored the building, possibly the owner, until it was rented. Looking secure to a tenant, it was fairly easy to gain access for someone knowing how this latch was positioned.

Luis did not have long to wait, as there was a knock on the door at ten minutes before two. Luis turned off the lights as his driver went to the door. "What do you want?" the driver asked.

"I am here to meet a Comrade." was the reply from the outside.

The driver unlocked the door and pulled it open. Two men in dark suits entered, one man carrying a leather duffel bag and the other a small canvas bag.

"I am to meet Mr. Quiroz." The man in the lead exclaimed.

Luis turned on the array of lights. "I am Luis Quiroz. I believe you would be Mr. Lobren. Am I correct?" Luis knew this to be correct. From his reputation, it was obvious. The man was dressed impeccably. The cloth protruding from his breast pocket was set perfectly, and the knot of his tie did not have the hint of a ripple.

"Comrade Quiroz, it is a pleasure to meet you." Just as Luis had heard, the man had a very charming and disarming manner. One immediately felt comfortable in his presence, unless one knew the truth about the man.

"It is also a great pleasure to meet you." Luis forced himself to be congenial, but could not bring himself to use the comrade verbiage. Especially with someone as violent as this man. "I have opened the container for your inspection."

The Russian agent walked to the back of the truck and, using a flashlight looked around the container. "I know nothing about oil drilling or computers. If you say that is what they are, then I am satisfied. The fools in the military wanted them, so I make the exchange. They too would know nothing about what they are purchasing. They do not even have someone they can trust with this amount of money to make this exchange. Close the container, please. My man will apply a seal." The second man climbed onto the truck bed.

From his canvas bag, he removed an unused shipping seal and a crimping tool. While he was doing this, the Russian agent handed the leather duffel bag to Luis. "As the fools agreed, five and a half million in various denominations of American currency. If you want to count it, please do it quickly."

Luis could feel the disdain in the Russian agent's voice.

"That will not be necessary; we are trusted trading partners, not adversaries."

"Mr. Quiroz, you are much too refined for this type of work."

"I, as you, serve my country as best I can."

"If we can please open the doors, my driver will take the truck now."

Luis' driver had opened the doors. Luis walked to the opposite side until the truck had left, followed by the Russian. As the Russian reached his car, he turned to Luis. "Very nice meeting you, Senior Quiroz. Have a good evening."

Luis and his driver closed and locked the large doors. It took them another ten to fifteen minutes to take down the light array and gather up any other scraps left. Their business was done here, they went to their car for the trip to Panama City.

Brady and Anderson remained hidden on the roof until after 2:30, when they heard the truck, as well as both the Russian and Luis, leave. They quickly left the roof and went to their car. They did not want to be too far behind Luis.

Brady radioed Lt. Bond with the CBs at the warehouse to tell him they could finish tightening the sheet metal panels on the buildings and they were done for the night.

CARRIBEAN
SEA
COLON
PANAMA CITY
P A N A M A
PACIFIC
OCEAN

CHAPTER # 39

A few miles out of Colon on the road back to Panama City, Luis came over a rise to see what appeared to be an accident on the road ahead. The highway was deserted this time of the morning. As they came closer, they could see a van lying on it's side blocking the right lane. They could not see if there was another car on the other side of the van. His driver slowed the car. As the headlights of their car illuminated the van, they could see a woman next to the van. She was mostly standing but leaning heavily on the rear door of the van. The driver stopped their car some fifteen yards from the van. As Luis' driver got out of the car, the woman pushed herself to a standing position. She began to slowly stagger toward them, seemingly unsure of her steps. Her yellow blouse and long grey dress were spotted with large blotches of dirt. It looked as though the accident had thrown her onto the pavement.

The driver met her about two-thirds of the way to the overturned van. Just as they met, the woman regained her stance and produced a gun from the folds of her dress. She pointed it at the driver. Luis reacted instantly, reaching under his coat for his Beretta. Just as his hand reached the butt of the gun, both front doors of his car were pulled open and the muzzle of a rifle was pushed against his neck. Out of the corner of his eye, he could see the business end of another rifle aimed at him from next to the steering wheel.

"No move. Now slowly bring your hand out of your coat. A sudden move and I shoot. Not matter if the gun is in your hand or not."

Luis knew the odds were heavily against him. Two guns pointed at him and he being confined in a small space. Luis also saw his driver go to his knees with his hands in the air.

"Put your hands on dashboard and do not move them."

As Luis complied, he felt a hand go under his coat and remove his Beretta from the holster. At the same time, the man with the gun to his neck yanked the leather duffel bag from between his feet. He could see his driver was now face down on the ground with his hand splayed out past his head. The woman had raised his coat up and removed his service revolver. She was now moving back towards the van. The men next to Luis closed the doors to his car and began moving toward the van. They were not more than a few feet away when a car topped the rise behind them. Both men began to run, each stopping for a moment to fire a full clip at the oncoming car. The men disappeared behind the van as the approaching vehicle seemed to speedup. As it passed them, Luis' driver was running back to their car.

The car curved around the van, then came to a screeching stop as automatic weapon fire began. Luis could not see what was happening. But there were a lot of shots being fired and he could hear glass being shattered. Just as the firing began, he had seen the woman disappear into the darkness at the side of the road. After the first minute, the hail of gunfire subsided to sporadic firing. A few more minutes went like this until it stopped completely.

Luis and the driver waited. It was a long five minutes before they saw a man come around the front of the overturned van. He had a duffel bag in one hand and a gun held down at his side in the other hand. A few more steps and he placed the gun back under his coat. When the man got fully in the headlights of Luis' car, he could see it was his friend Brady. Luis jumped out of the car and ran to him.

"I am always glad to see you, my friend, but rarely as happy as now. What are you doing here?"

"Just happened to be in the area, keeping an eye on things down here. What was this about?"

"Not sure. We came upon this accident and when we stopped, the woman was a decoy and the two men got me in the car."

"Yeah, she took off when the shooting started. Are either of you hurt?"

"No, we are fine. How about you and your friend? I won't ask who he is."

"He took a bullet in the upper arm. Not too bad. I will take him to the infirmary at the naval base in Colon. Don't want to explain a gunshot wound at the local hospital."

"What happened back there?" Luis asked. "We could see nothing from here, heard lots of gunfire. Sounded like a lot of automatic weapons."

"Did you recognize the guys at your car?"

"Never got much of a look, but they had Eastern European accents and they had Eastern Block automatics."

"They were pretty well armed with Czech Skorpions. One is dead, and the other is severely wounded. Doubt he will make it more than a few hours even if he gets to hospital now. If he makes it, he will wish he was dead. The Panamanian Police do not take kindly to this sort of thing. The woman was probably a local they hired to help. That's why she took off."

"Do we need to call the Police?" Luis asked.

"Not yet. Here is your bag and both your Berettas. You need to get away from here now. I will take care of this. You don't want the police to show up and you have to explain a bag full of money and two guns."

"What will you do?"

"I am going to leave it just as it is. It will look like a drug deal gone bad. Highway chase until one turned over, then a shootout. They shot each other. If the one lives, let him explain it. If he tries the truth, they will never believe it. You need to get going before someone comes along and sees you."

"Gracias Brady, I can never repay you for this."

Brady smiled. "You know better. What are friends for? Mi amigo."

Luis and his driver returned to their car as Brady walked back toward the van. As the driver maneuvered around the van and Brady's car, Luis could see the sparkling reflection of shattered glass around the area. There was another car there besides the one Brady was driving. The robbers were using that as their getaway vehicle. Brady stood next to his car, watching until Luis' taillights disappeared in the distance.

"OK, Captain Lehan. We can clean this up." Brady said into the darkness.

Immediately, eight figures in civilian work clothes materialized out of the darkness from the side of the road. There was also a ninth figure wearing a yellow blouse and gray dress. The 'dead and severely wounded' assailants also got to their feet. These were all U.S. Army Rangers from the American Army base in the Canal Zone.

The Rangers set about up righting the van and picking up all the spent shells. The 'glass' on the road was not a problem. It was crushed ice that had been spread around to reflect the light as if I was glass. It would be small puddles of water in another hour. The sound of shattering glass had been made by breaking panes of glass over a cardboard box in the car's trunk.

"OK Mr. Kinin, we have it all cleaned up and are ready to go." The Ranger Captain in command of the unit reported to Brady.

"Excellent job here, Captain. Call in your chauffer." Brady was referring to the chopper that had brought them here from the base and was now waiting to return them. All would fly out except the two that were to return the van and the car back to the location where the CIA kept them stored.

Within less than a minute, they could hear the thumping of the rotors of the chopper approaching. "Captain Lehan." Brady called.

As the Ranger approached with his lead sergeant, Brady reached in the leather duffel bag the Rangers, posing as gunmen, had taken from Luis. It contained the genuine money the Russian had given Luis. Brady had returned to Luis an identical bag with the counterfeit money from the Chinese. From the bag in his hand, Brady produced a banded pack of five-hundred dollar bills.

He handed the pack to the Ranger Captain. "Captain, throw your men a little party with this. Don't forget to invite the entire unit that chauffeured you tonight. Also, I know how tough this will be for you, but there is a group of CBs at the Naval Base. Invite them too. Contact Lt. Bond. Have them over to the party; not to fight. You guys are on the same team. His group made this all possible as much as your team."

The Captain took the pack of money and handed it to his sergeant. "You heard the man. Do you think you can organize a little party with this, sergeant?"

"Yes Sir, however you know Rangers don't believe in little parties. Them swabbies will probably drink us out of ice tea. But excusing your kindness Mr. Kinin, I don't think even we can go through all this money doing legal stuff." The wrapping band on the pack showed it was $25,000.

"I won't tell Bond you said that. Remember, you all would be one of them or them part of your group except for the sweet talk some recruiter gave. Put the rest of the money to use on base and with your command. Don't y'all have a scholarship or benevolent fund? I'll clear it with your command so the source won't be questioned." Brady said as he turned to walk away.

"One more thing Mr. Kinin." The Captain had a question. "Are you really the Lt. that walked out of Vietnam to the air base in Thailand?"

"Not really the best three weeks of my life." Brady answered.

"I was at Kha Sanh a couple years before that, Sir." the sergeant interjected. "After that ordeal, I would think Ranger training was your next logical choice."

"Where does logic fit in the Army life?" Brady replied rhetorically. Then he continued, "You guys do that sort of thing because you want to. I am more of a fishing pole and six-pack guy." Brady replied with a laugh.

"I would still like to shake your hand, Sir. You are a Ranger, but just don't know it." The sergeant replied as he put out his hand to Brady.

"Your story is still a legend at Ranger training. It is the master plan that is used in escape and evasion training." The Lt. added as he too shook Brady's hand.

"Best of luck, gentleman. Don't you have a party to arrange?" Brady replied as he returned to his car.

Within the next three minutes, there was nothing left at the scene except some ice scattered on the road.

As he put the car in gear and moved off. "Well, Mr. Fred Anderson, your help was invaluable, and your people worked superbly."

"Your boys in uniform seemed to do a real bang-up job also, so to speak. What about the Cuban?"

"He will get the money turned over to his security people at the embassy immediately. I understand it will be given to Valenzuela tomorrow to pay off purchases of fuel."

"How many Frito Banditos you think will get caught with their hand in the cookie jar?"

"Not enough."

CHAPTER # 40

The next day Brady, dressed as a businessman in downtown Panama City, was sitting in the lobby of the Hilton. He knew that Lobren, the Russian agent, would leave for the airport soon. The Russian was scheduled on a 2 o'clock flight out of Panama. He had heard the bellman ordered up to Lobren's room for luggage transfer. Brady casually moved over near the bank of elevators. When he saw an elevator leave the eighth floor, he moved near the door but remained off to the side. When the door opened, Lobren stepped out and turned to the bellman that was maneuvering the luggage cart out of the elevator. He told the bellman to take his luggage to a taxi while he checked out.

As the bellman began to pull the cart away from the elevator, Brady stepped forward to enter the elevator. When he passed the end of the cart, he placed the leather duffel bag on the cart among the rest of Lobren's luggage.

The bellman was placing the last bag in the taxi when Lobren came out the door. Half way to the waiting taxi, three men approached him. One stopped in front of Lobren and the other two took a position on each side of the Russian agent.

Speaking in Russian, "Comrade Lobren, come with us, please." The man in front said.

"Who are you and what do you want?" Lobren demanded.

"We are from KGB, Special Security. Come with us, do not make a scene."

"My bags are in the cab. I have a plane to catch." Lobren was pleading now. He knew what Special Security was. They were the internal police force of the KGB. Being confronted by this unit held a very ominous meaning. He was in trouble, but he could not think of why.

"Where you are going, you will not need your luggage." The man said as a car pulled up next to the taxi.

The two men next to Lobren took his arms and escorted him into the back seat of the waiting car. The man that had spoken to him went to the back of the taxi and removed the leather duffel bag. Lobren knew immediately that was the bag he had given the Cuban with the five and a half million dollars. They transferred the rest of his luggage to the back of the waiting car.

EPILOGUE

Brady was on a routine information gathering trip through his usual territory of southern Europe. He had made arrangements to meet Hans Freling when he was in Italy. It was just a few hours' drive from Vienna to Venice, a town they both liked.

As Hans approached the table, Brady stood to shake hands.

"So nice to see you, Brady. How do I ever thank you and your country for what you did for my cousin and his family? He has written me three letters since he has moved to Omaha. They love it there. The family is learning English rapidly, the children will be conversant enough to enter school next year. The surgeon in Rome did a fantastic job on the boy's chest. I wish I would have known he was there. But I understand why I wasn't told. His daughter is a nurse, so she has been able to find a job as a nurse aide at a hospital. When her English is good enough, she will go to school to get enough hours to get her license as a full-time nurse. My cousin is thrilled with his job at the railroad there. Doing the same thing he has been doing for the last twenty years. Because of his experience, the language has not been much of a problem. I guess moving railcars is the same everywhere."

"I believe his information was worth the effort." Brady replied.

"But Brady, for you to do the job as you did. That is unbelievable. And you were hurt as well. How are you doing?"

"I am OK. My shoulder is still a little stiff. The doc says I should quit damaging the same place.I should choose a new spot. I told him I prefer no more anywhere."

"This meeting is so much better than our last meeting in Oslo. I was so upset about what was happening. I knew you would make it right if anyone could."

"How about if I make it a little more right?" Brady said as he removed an envelope from his coat pocket and pushed it across the table to Hans.

"That is a very thick envelope. I want nothing for my part. What you have done is more than enough." Hans replied.

"Yes, but a smile and a handshake does not pay the shopping bill your wife is running up right now." Brady said with a laugh.

"True, but this is so big. I will send this to my cousin in Omaha. He gave up his home, everything, even his wife. I did nothing. He is the one that has given the USSR a black eye."

"Well, let me tell you how it came to be." Brady began explaining the entire story. He left out the part of his friendship with Luis. He just said they had picked up intelligence about the planned taking of the computers and drill bits. They then had come up with the scheme to dovetail with the Cuban plan.

He also did not tell Hans about his cousin's family being kidnapped twice. Since the kidnapping, the CIA had taken responsibility for the family. Also not revealed to Hans was his relative's current status. The mailing address they kept was in Omaha. They were to let no one know where they were or by what names they were using. They had relocated to Oklahoma City. Dmitry, now Olav from Finland, was working for the U.S. Marshal Service. He scheduled and routed their planes, moving prisoners around the country.

As the story unfolded, Hans ask. "How did me passing the information of a 'new to the scene Russian' buying a villa in Morocco fit in the scheme?"

Brady continued the story. "The fake auto accident in Panama was the only way we could come up with to get the money switched with the Cuban." Again, this was where Brady had to be very careful so as not to reveal his friendship with Luis. He had to change some of the story.

"The Soviet's top agent in Central America was to make the cash exchange. While we had the bag with the genuine money, I liberated a few packs. Part of which makes that envelope so thick. So thank the Russians. We had to set it up as though Lobren was trying to disappear with the money. We had someone go to Morocco and place a down payment on a villa. With you passing the information to the Russians, they would investigate and determine it was Lobren. The man we had go to Morocco looked very much like Lobren. When the Russians looked into it, they were led to Lobren. They knew he was handling a five million plus cash transfer in December. The purchaser had told the bank in Morocco he would have the money around the end of the year."

"Why didn't they stop him then?" Hans asked.

"They were not certain. He was too good an agent to lose if it wasn't true. They had no real solid evidence. They needed to wait until they had proof. We had gotten three passports made with his picture in each. All three were from different countries using different names. We had them made by a forger in Paris. Not someone the KGB would have ever done business with. Once we knew when he was flying out of Panama, we made him a reservation using the name on one of the false passports. We had him going to Caracas, then to Columbia under a different name, then to Cairo with the third name. These three passports were in the bag with the money when I sat it on the luggage cart in Panama City. With the passports, the KGB could easily see where he was going."

"Yes, I can see that would be what someone would do if they were trying to disappear."

"What ever became of Comrade Lobren?" Hans ask.

"Don't really know. Probably went to their embassy first to sort things out. Having the bag of cash with him pretty much condemned him, but the air reservations would have sealed the deal. No way he could explain that away. We weren't that interested in following, however there has been no record of him ever leaving the country. Could have taken him out on a private jet. But KGB Security is pretty brutal and quick. It is possible he never left the country, they will never find his body in the jungle and swamps. His organization is in complete disarray in Latin America. It'll take them years to put it back together."

"Brady, that is one of the best stories you have ever brought me. Along with what you did for my family, I feel I should pay for your dinner."

Brady knew that wasn't going to happen.

ABOUT THE AUTHOR

R.T. grew up in Arizona. He served a tour as an Officer in the US Navy. After that, he followed many varied career paths allowing him to live in Europe, Japan and four time zones in the US.

Currently, he resides with his wife in Hilton Head, South Carolina.

You can reach him at ryewrites@hotmail.com

f

AFTERWORD

I hope you enjoyed this brief escape from reality.

Please take a moment to write a review on Amazon. This will be a much appreciated effort by your fellow readers and myself.

Reviews help readers like yourself select their choices and helps me get a better insight into what my readers like.

It cost you only a moment of time yet you will be rewarded with a smile from yourself, other readers and myself.

Thank you,
RTR

Made in the USA
Monee, IL
31 March 2023